Dear Readers,

This spring, we're willing to bet a *woman's* fancy will turn to love—with four brand-new Bouquet romances full of passion and laughter.

Award-winning author Vivian Leiber begins a three-book series titled "The Men of Sugar Mountain" with **One Touch,** as high school sweethearts confront the past—and dream of a shared future. Beloved Silhouette and Zebra author Suzanne McMinn offers **It Only Takes a Moment,** a charming present-day fairy tale in which a feisty woman proves that even a prince must remember he's a man.

Nothing stays the same forever. In **Charmed and Dangerous,** Silhouette author Lynda Simmons presents a woman who never thought her childhood buddy would ever offer more than a shoulder to lean on—until she discovers he's willing to give so much more. Last is Anne DeForest's **The Cowboy and the Heiress,** the passionate tale of a woman searching for independence and finding that true love is the greatest freedom of all.

With spring flowers ready to bloom, what could be more fitting than a Bouquet of four fabulous romances from us to you?

Kate Duffy
Editorial Director

NAKED PASSION

"You've never been skinny-dipping, have you?"

"Of course I have," she said, the soul of indignation. But the effect was lost since he wasn't looking. She heard the unmistakable sound of a zipper lowering.

"So," he said, as his jeans hit the ground, "do you need a hand with that dress?"

"Just keep your back turned," she said, laughing as she tugged the dress over her head and dropped it on the pile of clothes at their feet. She was going to swim in the moonlight, and damn anyone who tried to tell her it was wrong.

"You're not peeking, are you?" Sam asked.

"Of course not," she said, stepping out of her panties. "You're not peeking either, are you?"

"Yes."

She froze a moment, then checked over her shoulder. He stood half in darkness, half in pale and watery light, captured forever in her mind like a black-and-white photograph, a moment to be brought out years from now when she would remember him just this way. Strong. Hard. Male.

His arms hung at his sides as if there was nothing to hide, as his eyes met hers and began a slow, frank journey down the length of her, making her legs weak as her pulse grew stronger, more urgent.

"Do you have any idea how beautiful you are?" His voice was low, and a wicked smile curved his lips as he came toward her. . . .

CHARMED
AND
DANGEROUS

LYNDA SIMMONS

Zebra Books
Kensington Publishing Corp.
http://www.zebrabooks.com

ZEBRA BOOKS are published by

Kensington Publishing Corp.
850 Third Avenue
New York, NY 10022

First Printing: April, 2000
10 9 8 7 6 5 4 3 2 1

Printed in the United States of America

*For Shannon, who is both charming
and dangerous, with love.*

ACKNOWLEDGMENTS

I would like to thank the following people for their help in the development of this book:

Brian and Betty McGowan, for allowing me to pat the llama, and get up close and personal with wallabies, ostriches, emus and a potbellied pig. Your generosity and gracious hospitality will always be remembered.

Olga Truchan and David Scott, for taking me behind the scenes and into the world of the food stylist and photographer. Experiences like these allow an author to give a ring of truth to her writing.

Jackie Buckner of Food for Film, who shared her tricks of the trade and made me look at television commercials more closely than I ever had before.

Tom Decillis, who knows more about jukeboxes than anyone I have ever met.

Michael Hancock of Denison's Brewing Co. for showing me the ropes. And The Golden Horseshoe Group of Seven for getting Max out of the closet.

No book is the child of only one mind. Thank you for sharing your knowledge and experiences and helping this story to come to life.

ONE

"A night for magic," the giant on the barn roof hollered.

A group of passing elves burst into a barbershop version of "Bewitched, Bothered and Bewildered." And even before the dragon at the gate blew fire across her fender, Maxine Henley knew she'd picked the wrong weekend to come home.

"None shall pass," the dragon called, still breathing sparks as he lumbered over to her car.

Max sighed and rolled down the windows while her gaze moved past him to the snake charmers by the pond, the striped tents outside the paddock, the bandshell near the barn; knowing as sure as the sweet scent in the air was cotton candy that, on the other side of the ridge, the midway would be crowded, noisy and very profitable.

Longest day of the year and once again Summer Solstice Bizarre was in full swing at the Henley family farm. It had started fifteen years earlier as a simple promotion for her mother's bed-and-breakfast. But unlike the grape-stomping festivals and the Spam-carving contests, Summer Solstice Bizarre had caught on, blossoming into an annual event and earning itself a spot on the "must see" lists in the Blue Ridge travel guides. And the banner fluttering above the gatehouse confirmed what the giant had promised—A CAPELLA ELVES, FABULOUS FAERIES AND GNOMES AS YOU'VE NEVER SEEN THEM.

Max groaned and reached for her purse. How could she have forgotten the gnomes?

"What manner of beast—" the dragon started, then stopped dead and stared at her. "Maxine?" He doffed his head and thrust a claw through the open window. "By God, girl, it's good to see you again."

"You too, Ben," Max said and had to smile as she shook the scaly paw. While his hair was whiter than she remembered, and the lines around his eyes deeper, Ben Morgan's grin was as broad as ever and his flames even brighter. And if he was still playing gatekeeper, then it was a good bet that his brother Tim was the giant on the barn roof. Proving what Max had figured out years ago: Nothing ever changed in Schomberg, Virginia.

"Too bad you didn't get here earlier," he said, hanging on to her hand as he pulled a stamp from his pocket. "You've already missed the fire-eaters. Fairies too, most likely. But the midway's open till midnight." He raised a brow. "How's your pitching arm these days?"

"Rusty," Max admitted.

"That's what comes of living in the city." He stamped a blue faerie above her wrist, then dropped the hand-stamp back into his pocket. "Makes you soft."

It was on the tip of her tongue to mention the name of a gym in New York where her picture hung on the Hard Body Wall of Fame. But the chance was lost when he slapped his claws on the roof and grinned at her. "I hear congratulations are in order. When's the big day?"

Max shouldn't have been surprised. Her mother had no reason to keep the news from Ben. And Ben would naturally tell his brother, who would say something to his wife, who probably mentioned it in passing at Bingo one Friday night, until at last the whole town knew that Maxine Henley was tying the knot—because if there was one thing that moved with any speed in Schomberg, it was gossip. Especially when it concerned one of the Henleys.

She wasn't naive enough to think that any of the old stories had been laid to rest, but she'd promised herself that she wouldn't dwell on that this weekend. So she smiled at Ben and tilted up her left hand, absently watching the play of light through the diamond on her third finger.

"We haven't set a date yet," she said, already feeling a smile tug at her lips—the same one she'd been wearing since the night Peter popped the question.

Her lips pursed. Okay, so "popped" wasn't the right word. "Dropped" was probably better. He'd dropped the question while making a list of props for their next project—a recipe book for Valentine's Day. White tablecloth, red roses, the best strawberries she could find. Then he'd put down his pen. And a ring, he'd added. "Unless you're sure you wouldn't rather just live together."

His proposal hadn't gone the way she'd always imagined, but then, very little in life ever did. So why dwell on hearts and flowers, when the real issue was common goals and shared interests, something she and Peter had in abundance?

"We'll probably take that walk down the aisle some time next summer," she told Ben as she pulled her hand back inside the car. "But since we'll be working in Virginia Beach for the next two weeks, it just made sense to stop by the farm and let him meet my mother before the wedding."

Max didn't see any reason to mention that her mother had flat out refused to come to New York, insisting that the elusive Peter Ross had an obligation to come out and meet his future mother-in-law face-to-face on her own turf. To sit at her table and understand exactly who and what it was that he was marrying into.

As if it matters anymore, Max thought, her gaze drawn to the rambling old farmhouse in the distance. The one that had been in the Henley family for over a hundred years, and Max would gladly sell to strangers without a second thought.

She wondered for a moment if she should have taken Peter's advice after all. Simply refused to be bullied, and told her mother that they'd see her at the wedding. But for once, Max had agreed with Eva. Some traditions couldn't be trampled on, even if they were corny and antiquated. Like insisting on a wedding, she mused, when living together made perfectly good sense.

It was what came, she supposed, of living in Schomberg during those all-important early years—a sentence her own children would never serve.

She dragged her purse over from the passenger seat. "How much are Bizarre tickets these days?"

Ben waved away her money. "My treat. In honor of your upcoming wedding. Where is the lucky man anyway?"

Max looked up at him. "He isn't here yet? I'm surprised. He came down a few days early to make sure everything was set for Monday. He was supposed to come straight to the farm, and I'd find my own way in from the airport." She glanced at the clock on the dash. "I hope he's not lost."

Peter was one of those men who would not ask directions to save his soul, and consequently spent a great deal of time going in circles. But Max tossed the thought aside with her purse, sure that he would have called her by now if he was having trouble. "When he gets here . . ." she said to Ben, then jumped, startled, when a gnome stuck his head through the passenger window and grinned at her.

"Keep this safe," he whispered, and tossed an emerald

into her lap. "Something good will come of it." Then he winked and hobbled off, disappearing into the shadows.

Max blinked at the bit of glass in her lap. "Where does Eva find these people?"

"You think that's good?" Ben's smile broadened. "Go have a look at the fishpond. Your mother has outdone herself this year."

"I'll take your word for it," Max said and dropped the emerald onto the passenger seat.

Once Peter arrived, they could go to the fishpond or the Fairies Wheel or anything else he wanted to see. But there was no way she was going in alone. The farm would be crawling with high school buddies, Sunday school teachers and God only knew who else, all of them bursting with congratulations and questions.

How long have you known him? Planning any children? Are you going to let your hair grow?

She absently ran a hand over her cap of silky black hair, still not used to having it so short but liking it more each day. Professional, it said, and more importantly, all grown-up—an important consideration for a woman who had tired of being "cute" years ago.

She gave her hair a shake. Definitely not, she decided, and glanced into the rearview mirror as a black van pulled off the highway onto the driveway. She dropped the car into gear and smiled up at Ben. "When Peter gets here, tell him I'll be waiting at the house."

"How will I know him?"

"Blond hair. Silver Jag." She shrugged, suddenly awkward in front of this man who probably wouldn't know a Jag from a Saab, and wouldn't care to either. "He's hard to miss."

"I'll keep an eye out." Ben picked up the dragon's head and settled it on his shoulders. But instead of stepping back, he looked down at her again. "Maxine, you should know that Gwen's back."

She stared at him, taking in the news. There was no mistaking who he meant. Gwen Harper. Red hair, blue eyes, a sprinkling of freckles across a laughing face. Her brother's old girlfriend. The one who had killed him.

"She's renting a cabin from the Connors," Ben went on. "Up by—"

"I know where it is." Max consciously softened her tone. "How long has she been here?"

"Couple of weeks. She doesn't come down much. Only seen her once myself." He paused and looked along the driveway to where the van was bouncing toward the gate. "Eva didn't say anything because she was afraid you might not come."

Max couldn't fault her mother there. She probably wouldn't have made the trip if she'd known. But she was here now, and she'd made up her mind when the plane touched down that she wasn't going to let anyone or anything spoil her happiness. She was a bride-to-be, a woman on her way to a whole new future. And nothing could take that away.

She lifted her foot off the brake. "It's only a weekend, Ben. As long as she doesn't bother me, I won't bother her. And thanks for telling me."

He nodded and turned to the van. "None shall pass," he called and blew a long yellow flame into the air for emphasis.

Max laughed when the driver stopped about twenty feet back from the gate and everyone inside the van sat up very straight.

"First-timers," she said.

"My favorite flavor." Ben glanced back. "You want to help out? I've still got a sword in the gatehouse."

For just a moment, Max was tempted. Tempted to stand at the gatehouse the way she had years ago, watching the faces in the cars while Ben worked his fiery magic and she hustled back and forth with change. She tapped her fingers on the steering wheel, picturing Peter's face when the dragon's fire whistled across his bumper. Her mouth twitched into a smile. It would serve him right for being late.

But she was in shorts and a tanktop, hardly a suitable costume for a dragon's assistant, and she hadn't wielded a proper sword in more than a decade. Besides, she'd made up her mind to put Summer Solstice behind her the day she left home, and she didn't want anyone to think things were different now.

"Thanks, but I really can't." She poked her head out the window as Ben lumbered off. "One of these days you'll have to show me how that costume works."

He glanced back. "You get your mother to go to the movies with me and I'll show you how the giant's harp works as well."

"I'll never find out the secret, will I?"

"Not in this lifetime. Mind the peacocks as you go. The Bizarre's got them a little rattled." He turned back to the van. "What manner of beast is this?"

"They're not the only ones," Max said, laughing as she focused on the narrow lane ahead of her.

She followed the arrows to the fork, but instead of continuing on to the parking lot, she swerved around the pylons and headed up to the driveway to the house. The sun was almost gone as she turned off the engine and glanced into the rearview mirror. She half expected witch security to be hot on her trail but saw only fireflies winking at her from the bushes. She was alone, which suited her fine. But it was also the reason why she jumped again when someone reached through the window and tapped her on the shoulder.

God I hate gnomes, Max thought and jerked her head around.

But instead of a red cap and beard, she found herself looking into a pair of exotic green eyes. Too green, really, but they suited the woman behind them. She was blond and pale, almost ethereal in a gauzy white dress.

"My name is Iona," she whispered. "Do you have the emerald?"

Max laughed and reached for the jewel. "The gnome told me to expect something good, but I didn't believe him."

"Never doubt a gnome," the woman said solemnly, then held out a hand. "Quickly, give me the gem."

Max handed her the bit of glass. "My mother put you up to it, right?"

"No one put me up to anything." Iona closed her hand and opened it again. A small box now sat where the emerald had been.

"Nice," Max said, nodding her approval, but Iona said nothing as she opened the lid and withdrew something from the box. She mumbled a few words and then pressed whatever it was into Max's palm and closed her fingers around it.

"This is a love charm," she said at last. "Very old, very powerful. Wear it close to your heart, and when the moon smiles, the right man will find you, guaranteed."

"That's nice to know since I was afraid he was lost," Max said, trying not to laugh as she drew her hand back. Whatever Iona had put in there, it wasn't moving or pulsing or even warm, which offered some comfort.

She opened her fingers slowly. The charm was nothing more than a small pillow of red satin with a rose embroidered on top in gold thread. It looked suspiciously like a home-ec project. A failed one at that.

She looked up into those green eyes. "The act is very good, but they should have told you I don't need a love charm." She showed off the ring, wiggling her fingers for the best effect. "I'm getting married. But if you have something in a career charm, or maybe a weather charm, because we're going to the beach—"

Iona closed Max's fingers around the pillow again. "Be sure to wear it night and day. The charm must feel the beat of your heart and learn the rhythm of your breath. Once it knows you well, the magic will draw him to you—"

"When the moon smiles, yes, I got that part." She lowered her voice. "But when exactly does the moon smile?"

"You'll know when you see it," Iona whispered as she stepped back from the car.

Max smiled and held out the charm. "As much as I love your act, you really should give this to someone else—"

"The right man," she whispered as she disappeared into the shadows. "Guaranteed."

"Right," Max said, but she couldn't help laughing.

Wrong charm or not, Iona had definite star quality. And whatever was at the fishpond would have to go a long way to beat her.

Max tossed the charm onto the dashboard and stepped out of the car. She glanced up at the moon, wondering briefly if that was a smile she saw on that big round face. Then she closed the door and stood a moment, jingling her keys as she listened to the crickets, the music of the river as it wound past the house and the click of her cooling engine. The peacocks were quiet and the midway seemed a long way off. So she shoved her keys into her pocket and leaned back against the car, in no hurry to go inside just yet.

Again, everything was as she remembered. Same mountains hunching in the distance, same white picket fence, same sign on the wall: PEACOCK MANOR, NOT YOUR AVERAGE BED-AND-BREAKFAST. And as usual, the front door was wide open and every light in the house turned on, even though Max was sure that neither her mother nor the dog nor any weekend guests would be within a quarter mile of the place.

If her guess was right, Eva was sitting in a tent right now, telling fortunes to wide-eyed teenagers and gullible adults. Making up stories of tall dark strangers and trips over water, promising futures that were bright and full of hope. And nothing at all like the ones they would really have if they stayed in Schomberg.

She turned and reached into the car for her cell phone, suddenly anxious to talk to Peter, to know where he was, why he was so late and how much longer she was going to be there alone. On the third ring, his voice mail kicked in. "You've reached Peter Ross, food photography specialist—"

"Great," Max muttered and tossed the phone back into the car, catching sight of Iona's charm on the dashboard as she straightened, the gold threads sparkling almost too brightly.

Max picked up the tiny pillow and turned it over in her palm. "The right man will find you," she muttered, then looked back along the driveway. "So where is he?"

"Excuse me, miss," a male voice said, and she jumped for the third time that night. "I seem to have lost my phone number. Could I have yours?"

Max spun around. She'd know that voice anywhere. She'd just never expected to hear it in Schomberg. She smiled as she stuffed the charm into her back pocket. "Your lines don't get any better with age, O'Neal."

"I'm a little out of practice." He grinned as he stepped from the shadows. "How are you, Max?"

"Better now," she said, meaning it.

Sam O'Neal had been the boy next door, her older brother's best friend and the one voted most likely to get out of Schomberg. She'd had a crush on him once. The kind of heart-pounding, breath-stealing obsession that fifteen-year-old girls do so well. But as she watched him come toward her, she wondered if it was her imagination or perhaps some trick of the light that made him look even better than she remembered.

He'd always been tall, with strong features, dark eyes and a mouth that was given to laughter easily and often. But his shoulders were broader now, the muscles of his arms well defined beneath a shirt that looked soft and worn. While he'd usually dressed as he chose and done as he pleased, there was a more relaxed air of confidence about him now, a sensuous tilt to that mouth that she'd never noticed before. And an aura of masculinity that was so powerful it was almost palpable.

Max moistened her lips even as she felt the faint shift in her shoulders, the tiny flicker of awareness that was as unexpected as it was inappropriate. This was Sam, after all. The one who had taken all her baby-sitting money in a poker game, dared her to steal peaches from the Jenkinses' orchard. And turned out to be the best friend she'd ever known.

"I can't believe you're here," she said, rising up on her toes as she wrapped her arms around his neck. "And without even a hint of elf anywhere."

"I hid until they ran out of size eleven curly toes."

She looked up into his eyes and for the first time was glad that she'd made the trip. "I have missed you," she said softly.

"Me too," he said, kissing her lightly, the way any friend might, and pulling her close for a hug.

She held on tight, feeling the strength of his hands on her back, the hard wall of his chest against her breasts and a warmth from both that reached through her fine cotton tanktop, making her shiver.

Confused, she let her arms slip from around his shoulders and took a step back, wondering for one brief moment if he would stop her, maybe hold on a moment longer. And what she would do if he did.

Of course he let her go without the slightest hesitation. Exactly as a friend would do.

"We have a lot of catching up to do," she said, dipping her head as she fumbled with her keys, hoping her voice didn't sound as breathless as she imagined. "Come on inside. There's bound to be coffee on, and you can tell me everything you've been up to."

"Everything?"

She laughed, as much at herself as the look on his face. "What's the matter, O'Neal? You have something to hide?"

"Absolutely," he said softly as he watched her spin away, taking herself safely out of reach.

"I'll want details, of course," she called over her shoulder.

"Such as?" he asked, trying not to notice the curve of her thighs or the sway of her hips as she walked back to the car, when all he could think about was holding her again, feeling that tight little body pressed against his and kissing that perfect bow mouth.

". . . such as where you've been, what you've been doing . . ."

He gave his head a sharp shake and followed her. What was wrong with him anyway? This was Max. They'd grown up together. Seen each other in braces. She was like his sister, for God's sake. Even if she didn't look much like the girl he remembered. Or smell like her either.

". . . who you're with . . ."

Sam wasn't aware of the smile that curved his lips as the memory of grape lip-gloss and coconut sunscreen drifted through his mind. It was the summer before he went away to college. The same summer she turned fifteen. She bought a bikini she never wore, cigarettes she never smoked and that damned purple lip gloss. And he'd watched her hover on the edge of adulthood, realizing for the first time just how beautiful she was going to be.

Sam drew in a long breath, let it out slowly and congratulated himself on how right he'd been. She was not only beautiful, but sexy as hell. And more importantly, another man's fiancée—Peter Ross, Food Photographer, Eva had told him. And Sam couldn't help wondering what Peter thought of his intended wearing the kind of shorts that could make a man weep.

". . . and why on earth you're here," she continued.

The mermaid, Sam reminded himself, as the reason he'd come up to the house in the first place finally came back to him. A striking blond mermaid named Ruby had run out of prizes at the fishpond. Naturally, he'd offered to make the trip, and as soon as he got back, he and Ruby were headed for the bar. He frowned and glanced over at the stack of boxes he'd set by the driveway. Or was her name Pearl?

Jade, he decided, and hoped she was still wearing a name tag when he got back.

"How long are you staying?" Max asked as he walked toward her.

He hesitated, caught off guard and without an answer. Not one that he could give quickly, at any rate. He needed time to explain, to make her understand the choices he'd made, the things that had happened and why he'd be around for a while yet.

But she misunderstood his silence, and he watched her smile fade.

"Tell me you'll be around for the weekend at least."

"Count on it," he said, taking the out. There would be time enough to tell her exactly how long he'd be in Schomberg. And why.

"Wonderful," she said, but she wasn't looking at him anymore. She was staring out across the fields, to where the lights of the midway were just visible over the ridge.

"Gwen's renting a cabin from the Connors. Did you know?"

"I heard, yes."

She nodded and bent her head, staring down at her shoes. "Do you think she'll stay?"

"She might," he said, because it was true, and he was holding back enough already.

She gave a short laugh. "I can't believe she had the nerve to show her face again."

He hesitated, choosing his words carefully. "It's been a long time, Max. Things change. People change."

"I suppose." She looked over at him. "But it doesn't undo what they've done." She waved a hand, as if pushing Gwen, the past, everything behind her. "Enough of that," she said, her smile so sudden and bright, it took him a moment to catch up. "I'm just glad you're here. And I have to know, did you ever take Wall Street by storm?"

He smiled. "They still haven't figured out what hit them."

"I knew it," she yelled and popped the trunk open.

Sam laughed, glad to be on easy ground with her again. "I hear you're doing well too. Your own business. Matching luggage. I'm impressed."

"Don't forget the condo on the lake."

He gave a low whistle. "All that and a wedding too."

"Life is good," she said, showing off the ring. "How about you? You married with a million kids yet?"

"Not yet on either count."

"Then I have just the thing." She pulled a little red pillow from her back pocket and dangled it in front of him.

"What is that thing?"

She leaned closer and lowered her voice. "A love charm. Very old, very powerful." Her mouth twitched, trying to hold back a smile. "Guaranteed to bring the perfect man, but I'm sure we could fix that."

"I'll pass, thanks."

"Suit yourself," she said, tucking it back into her pocket. "But just remember, it was you who doubted the gnome."

Sam swung her bags out of the trunk and slammed the lid. "I'll take my chances."

She laughed and dashed ahead to open the gate. "It's so nice to know I'm not the only sane person in Schomberg. Speaking of which, you still haven't told me why you're here."

He followed her up the porch stairs. "They ran out of prizes at the fishpond."

"And my mother corralled you into coming up to get more." She shook her head and held the front door for him. "I'll help you with them if you like, but I was wondering more about why you're in Schomberg in general, not at the house."

He moved past her into the hall and set the suitcases at the bottom of the staircase. The time to be straight with her was now, while it was still quiet. While she was still smiling.

"Max," he said, but her cell phone chirped and she was off again, dashing down the porch stairs to her car.

"Hold that thought," she said as she reached into the front seat. "It has to be Peter."

Sam stepped back out to the porch and crossed to the railing.

"Maybe the three of us could have dinner while we're here," she said as she punched the button. "Is there a decent place to eat in town these days?"

"There's one," he said, knowing she wouldn't hear. And maybe just as well.

"Henley Food Stylists," she said into the phone. And Sam knew by the way she smiled that it had to be Peter.

"I hope you're close," she was saying, "because I am about to play catch up with a very handsome old friend."

Sam shook his head as he turned and heard her laugh—a low, husky sound that had him looking back. And smiling when she blew him a kiss.

"I'm sorry, Peter," she said, laughter still in her voice as she turned and walked the length of the car. "Where did you say you were?" Her steps faltered. "New York? What on earth are you doing there?" Her shoulders squared and her tone was suddenly all business. "It's the Webster account, isn't it? I knew I shouldn't have left until I spoke to them." She checked her watch. "I'm already on my way—" She paused, listening, her arm slowly dropping to her side. "Then what's wrong?"

Sam went down the stairs. Whatever was happening between them was none of his business, and the mermaid was waiting. But when he reached the driveway, he caught the change in her tone and glanced back.

She was standing perfectly still now, chin lifted, eyes squeezed tightly together. "And when exactly did you realize that you don't want to get married?"

And Sam knew he wasn't going anywhere just yet.

TWO

Peter sighed. "Max, be reasonable. I didn't plan this."

Be reasonable. She let the concept sit between them a moment, thinking more about the tone in which he'd said it than the idiocy of the words themselves. She'd heard no anger, no reproach. Just confusion, which was worse.

Her legs went suddenly numb and she sank down on the steps, cradling her head in her hand. "I don't understand. When did this happen? When you were having coffee? In the shower perhaps—"

"Don't do this."

"Do what? Try and make sense of something so ludicrous it's hard to believe it's not a joke?" She paused, hoping for a laugh, a gotcha, maybe even an apology, and resigning herself to the silence. "Except it's not, is it?"

"Max, please. Try to understand. I was halfway to the farm when it struck me that I was on my way to meet my future mother-in-law. My *mother-in-law,* Max." He paused, and she knew he would be pacing now, doing his usual telephone circuit—living room, dining room, kitchen, hall. And again. Living room, dining room, kitchen—

"The idea of meeting your mother made the whole thing real," he said, forcing her to come back, to listen. "I need to adjust, be sure we're doing the right thing.

That's why I'm not coming out. And it's why I don't want you in Virginia Beach next week either."

Max got to her feet. "But we have a job—"

"*I* have a job."

She gripped the phone tighter. "What are you trying to say?"

"I'm saying I'll pay you as agreed, but I've hired another stylist."

She wandered from the porch to the gate, needing to move, to make a circuit of her own. Stairs, fence, bird feeder, anywhere at all as long as she didn't have to stand still and listen to her world fall apart. "What about our vacation? Two weeks of sun and sand—" She stopped, aware that she was on the verge of begging.

"Take the two weeks off," he said. "Go somewhere nice. On me . . ."

But the rest was lost when she turned and spotted Sam by the edge of the driveway, watching her.

Her feet froze while heat crept into her face. She thought he'd left, had assumed herself alone, yet there he was, walking toward her now. How much had he heard? How much did he know? But as he came closer, the compassion in his eyes left no doubt in her mind. He'd heard everything.

"Max?" Peter's voice seemed far away, oddly distant. "Max, are you still there?"

She looked down at the phone in her hand and quickly pressed it to her ear again. "Of course I'm here," she said, turning away from Sam only to see a golf cart rumbling up the driveway.

Her mother yoo-hooed from the front seat, the dog beside her barked and the couple in the back waved. Max's heart sank.

"Why now?" she said on a sigh, and Peter was off again.

"Because we need to be sure. To take a bit of time and figure out what we really want."

Figure it out? She wanted to get married, have kids, a mortgage. Life insurance even. Her gaze was drawn to the porch, the window boxes, the sign by the door. It was so simple when she thought about it. All she really wanted was to be part of a family again. Just not here.

The golf cart came to a stop behind her car. The dog, a black lab sporting a red neck scarf, bolted out ahead of everyone, leapt over the picket fence and dashed headlong at Max.

"Miss Marple," Max whispered, and found herself smiling in spite of everything as she bent over to greet her dog; realizing too late that the charging puppy was not Miss Marple—just another thing her mother had never mentioned.

"Columbo, come back here," Eva Henley called, then swung her legs around and jumped out of the cart. "Whatever you do, don't let him . . ."

"Jump?" Max grunted as the dog's paws landed on her chest.

"Columbo, get down," Sam said.

The dog dropped and rolled over for a belly rub, just as Miss Marple had always done.

"Marple is gone," Sam said softly. "Columbo is her grandson."

Max swallowed a sudden lump in her throat and reached out to pat the dog. "Nice to meet you, Columbo," she said, realizing that some things had indeed changed.

"Max, what's going on there?" Peter demanded. "Who's with you?"

"Just the welcoming committee," Max told him.

But there was no time to explain further as her mother hurried across the lawn, her long skirts swirling around her ankles. She was tiny and slim and looking every bit the gypsy in her gold head scarf and hoop earrings.

"There she is," Eva all but sang to her guests. "The beautiful bride-to-be."

Sam stepped up behind Max. "Do you want me to head them off? Give you some time?"

"No," she whispered, then slapped a hand over the mouthpiece and twisted her head around to look at him. "Why are you still here anyway?"

"Who's there with you?" Peter asked again.

Sam shrugged. "I thought you could use a friend."

"A friend would have gone for a walk." She turned away and lifted the phone again. "It's just Sam. Someone I used to know."

"Is that my future son-in-law on the phone?" Eva called. "Tell him I'm keeping my crystal ball warm for him."

"I will," Max called, forcing a smile.

Sam leaned down to whisper in her ear. "What are you going to tell her?"

"Nothing. And neither are you."

Peter's voice rose. "Max, what is going on there?"

She smiled into the phone as her mother drew nearer, but her eyes were still on Sam. "Okay, honey. I'll see you later." Peter fell blessedly silent and she pushed ahead. "I miss you too, babe." Then on a sudden burst of inspiration, she blew a kiss into the phone, said a quick good-bye and pressed END.

Sam pursed his lips. "A bit overdone if you ask me."

"Well, no one did," she said, and stepped forward to meet her mother.

Eva Henley's hugs were never subtle or restrained. And she never, ever, kissed the air beside anyone's cheeks. *Full contact affection,* Max mused as she was swept into her mother's arms. No wonder all her dogs were jumpers.

Eva stepped back and drew her guests forward. "Bob,

Sylvia, this is my daughter, Max. And you already met Sam down at the fishpond."

Sylvia nodded. "The man with the mermaid."

"And more importantly, the man who owns the Schomberg Tap Room," Eva put in.

Max looked up at him. "Schomberg Tap Room?"

He closed his eyes. "Max, I—"

"Didn't he tell you?" Eva waved a hand. "Well, he's never been one to brag, but he's built the most interesting little brewery right in the middle of the old tavern. Copper kettles, wooden barrels, looks like something right out of the past."

He sighed and looked down at Max. "I was going to tell you," he said, but she turned away and made it a point not to wonder about mermaids or tap rooms, or anything else that he'd been doing. Like he'd said, things change, people change. But it hurt all the same.

So she shifted her attention to her mother's guests instead. They were both tall and robust, with matching baby carriers strapped to their chests. Max held out a hand. "Nice to meet you," she said and smiled at the carriers. "New arrivals?"

Sylvia nodded. "Just two months old."

"Twins," Bob added, and folded back the edge of the carrier so Max could peek inside.

But as she leaned closer, a furry head poked out and sniffed the air.

"What *is* that?" she yelped and jumped back, banging smack into Sam.

"That's Kanga," Sylvia said, then patted the lump in her carrier. "And this is Roo."

"Wallabies," Sam whispered, his arms closing around her, steadying her.

"For the petting zoo," Eva added, then frowned at Max. "Did I forget to mention that in my last letter?" Eva flicked a wrist. "No matter. You and Peter can see all the new babies tomorrow. The llamas too, of course. And speaking of new babies, let me see that ring of yours. I've been so curious ever since you told me you were engaged."

"Go on, Max," Sam said. "Show her the ring."

Max tipped her head back, and it was then that she realized she was still in his arms. Just leaning in, warm and comfy, as though that was where she belonged, when the arms that should be holding her were hundreds of miles away. And slowly slipping farther from her reach.

"The ring, yes." She pulled away to stand on her own again, and thrust out her hand. "I designed it myself."

Eva held Max's hand up to the moonlight. "It's beautiful. Simple yet elegant. Just like you." She twisted Max's hand so Sylvia could see. "Isn't this lovely?"

While the two of them fussed, Max looked down at her feet, over at the car, anywhere but at the ring, which now seemed huge and garish. Three full carats of clear, sparkling lies.

"Where is your fiancé?" Sylvia asked.

"Delayed," Max said and gave a sharp nod as she pulled her hand back. "He's been delayed."

"Nothing serious, I hope." Real concern replaced Eva's smile. "He's not hurt or anything, is he?"

Guilt held on to Max's tongue a moment, making sure she took a good long look into her mother's eyes before letting her speak.

But how could she tell her the truth? What was the truth anyway? She didn't even understand it herself. But to admit that Peter wasn't coming tonight would mean wagging tongues all over town tomorrow. And she'd already supplied the Schomberg gossip mill with enough grist to last a lifetime.

So she shoved guilt aside and put on what she hoped was a reassuring smile. "No, he's fine. Just a minor problem with a job. He'll be here soon."

She glanced back at Sam. Everything from the set of her shoulders to the tilt of her chin dared him to say something, to call her on the lie. But he knew that this was neither the time nor the place to challenge her. So he turned and headed for the porch instead. "I'll finish taking those bags upstairs. That way you can get settled in properly."

Max hurried to catch up. "Don't trouble yourself."

"For you and Pete . . ." He smiled and swung open the screen door. "Nothing is too much trouble."

"You're in your old room," Eva called after them. "I hope Peter doesn't mind pink." Sam could still hear her talking as the door slammed shut behind them. "You never know about men and pink."

Sam slowed at the top of the stairs. "Third door on the right, if I remember correctly."

Max pushed past him and reached for the suitcases. "I can take it from here."

He held on, waiting until she raised her head and looked at him. "How long do you think you can keep this a secret?"

"I'm not sure. How long did you think you could keep the Tap Room a secret?" She tugged at the bags. "I suppose you're partners with Gwen too. That would make everything perfect."

He jerked the suitcases to the side. "Ben Morgan is my partner."

"Ben?" Her laughter was harsh and forced. "This just gets better and better."

"Max, I'm sorry. There just wasn't a right time to tell you."

She leaned closer, her voice low, cold. "Then you'll understand why there isn't going to be a right time for me to tell Eva my little secret either."

"It's not the same thing and you know it."

"Just how is it different?"

"I wasn't trying to make you believe a lie."

The front door swung open again and footsteps could be heard in the hall below.

"Head on into the kitchen with those little ones," Eva said to her guests. "I'll put on some tea, and there's a cake in the pantry with your name on it." She paused and called up the stairs, "Max, honey, what does Peter like for breakfast?"

"Anything," Max shouted, then leaned over the banister and added a smile. "He's easy to please."

"I can't watch this," Sam muttered and continued along the hall. He hesitated a moment outside the second door—Brian's old room—and wondered if Eva used it at all.

"She works too hard," Max muttered as she pounded along the hall. "The people, the animals. This place is nothing but a drain on her."

"This place is her life," Sam said, pushing open the third door on the right. "And you're going to have to tell her about Peter soon."

"Maybe," she said, staying just outside the room, making no move to enter.

Sam dropped the bags beside the bed and followed her gaze to the braided rug, the bookcase, the sliding door that led out to a deck above the sunroom. The room was a tiny gem of white, rose and green, exactly as it had been the day she left, and his heart squeezed when she finally took a few steps forward.

She moved slowly, pausing to touch a lace-edged pillow, inspect a shelf of books, finally stopping in front of the dresser, a half-smile on her lips as her eyes moved over the mirror framed in shells. "I can't believe they stayed on," she said, more to herself than to him, and reached out, running a finger gently along a row of tiny purple shells. "I made this the winter we went to Fort

Myers." She looked over at him, the smile still on her lips. "I was ten years old."

"Your mother never could throw anything away."

"Too bad," she said, her voice suddenly flat, the smile gone as she picked up a suitcase and tossed it on the bed. "I'm sure her guests would appreciate something a little newer." She yanked back the zipper and flipped open the case. "And as far as telling her about Peter is concerned, I'm going to wait a while yet. Why let the gossips get started on something that may be only temporary anyway?"

"Temporary?"

"Peter just wants time to think. To be sure." She lifted a cosmetic bag from the suitcase and tossed it on the dresser. "Chances are he'll show up here tomorrow morning with flowers and champagne. And there I'll be with egg on my face and a fiancé on my arm, all because I jumped the gun."

"Max, I know how hard this is—"

"How can you possibly know anything?"

"Because I've been there." She looked over and he nodded. "This time last year, I was planning a wedding too. The hotel was booked, the invitations ordered. But when I started talking about the pub, my fiancée decided we weren't traveling the same road anymore, handed me back the ring and walked out."

Her expression softened. "Are you all right?"

"I am now," he said, realizing for the first time in months that he really was. "We just expected different things from the relationship."

"Which makes your situation completely different from mine."

He watched her lower her head and busy herself with the cosmetics bag, making a careful line of bottles, tubes and brushes across the top of the dresser. Shampoo, toothpaste, hairbrush, deodorant. "Peter and I are traveling exactly the same road and want the same things from life." Hair spray, lipstick, eyeliner. "We work together, we like the same restaurants and we never, ever fight. In fact, I can't remember—"

"Max, he dumped you."

She banged a mascara wand into the lineup. "He did not dump me."

"What would you call it, then?"

"Cold feet. Or maybe just cool feet. And cool feet can always be remedied with the right kind of heat."

"That's right, I almost forgot. You've got a love charm." Sam shoved her suitcase to one side and stretched out on the bed. "Poor old Pete doesn't stand a chance."

She pulled the little red pillow from her pocket and dropped it on his chest. "You're the one who needs this. I have other kinds of heat in mind." Reaching into the suitcase, she lifted out a delicate white nightgown, still new, with all the tags attached, and held it in front of her. "How's this for hot?"

The silk shimmered across her breasts and belly, molded itself to her thighs and fluttered around her ankles. It was the sort of gown that begged to be touched, and would slide easily to the floor. And Sam knew exactly what kind of heat it would generate when there were no shorts between the silk and her flesh. Which made Mr. Peter Ross even more of a fool.

"It's pretty good," he said, sitting up. "Only trouble is, Pete can't see it if he's not here."

She smoothed a hand over her hip. "Memory will serve him well."

He stared at the tags a minute, then reached out and grabbed them. "If things are so hot between you and Pete, how come these are Christmas sale tags?"

She snapped them out of his fingers. "Because I've been saving it. Waiting for the right moment."

"That's a switch." He folded his arms behind his head, watching her closely. "So I suppose you don't wear your new shoes home from the store these days. Or read your magazines in the parking lot."

"I still do that," she admitted. "But I don't eat chocolate bars in the checkout line anymore." She shook the nightgown at him. "And this is a completely different matter."

She ripped the tags off and tossed them into the wastebasket before shoving the gown back in the suitcase. "Enough about me; tell me about this Tap Room you have now. And your triumphant return to Schomberg."

"Not triumphant. Just necessary." But he was more interested in the way she was putting her cosmetics back into the bag again than in explaining himself.

Something wasn't ringing true here. She wasn't being honest with him, and while he couldn't put a finger on what it was, neither could he let it go.

He rose from the bed and walked toward her. "The pub is open now. Just a small place, but it's fun. I think you'd like it."

She picked up the shampoo. "When Peter comes, we'll be sure to drop by."

"I'll look forward to it." He laid a hand over hers, holding her still. "I just wish I could figure out why you're so determined to marry this guy."

She didn't answer right away. Just stared at their hands, as though needing time to compose the right answer. Then she turned her head slightly to look at him, her voice softening. "Because it's what I need. It's what we both need."

Her hand was small beneath his, and delicately boned. Her bluster had always made it easy to think of her as strong and sturdy. But as he stroked a thumb across her fingers and watched her moisten her lips, Sam knew she was as soft, as vulnerable as any woman. And if Peter hurt her, he was going to have a lot to answer for.

"Are you sure?"

"Of course I am. This isn't something I leapt into blindly." She pulled her hand away, brisk again as she toyed with the shampoo bottle. "Peter and I are good together. Why, we went looking for studios just last week, and we both loved the same one immediately."

"Very romantic. But what do you crazy kids do for fun?"

She sent him a bland look. "We travel. Exhibitions, trade shows . . ." She held up a hand. "I know, I know. That's work too, but we enjoy it. It's what we do, who we are. As hard as this may be for you to accept, Peter and I are a real team. And I cannot believe that it's over. We have plans, jobs that need to be done. Office furniture, for God's sake." She dropped the shampoo into the bag, closed the snap and carried it to the bathroom. "And Peter's far too practical to throw it all away."

"Practical?"

She tossed the bag onto the bathroom counter. "You know. Steady, dependable—"

"Safe?" he finished for her.

She walked back to the suitcase but wouldn't look at him as she passed. "What's wrong with safe?"

"Nothing, I suppose, if you love each other." He drew up behind her and she stiffened. "Tell me, Max, do you love him?"

"What kind of question is that?"

"An honest one. And I expect an honest answer." He took hold of her shoulders, made her face him. "Do you love him?"

"In my way," she said quickly, and he made no attempt to hold her as she turned away.

"What does that mean?"

"It means that my way probably isn't your way, but

it's right for me." She hauled a terry cloth robe from the suitcase and closed the lid. "You always were the romantic, Sam, you and Brian both. And while it may be charming to some, if you start talking about grand passion and soul mates, I may just throw you out."

"When did you get so cynical?"

"I'm not cynical. Just sensible." He raised a brow and she let out an exasperated breath. "Sam, trust me. Peter and I have what matters, common goals and shared interests. Everything else is just song lyrics, fluff. And I won't get caught up in that again. Brian was romantic enough for both of us. For all the good it did him." She shook her head as she zipped the suitcase. "Who dies at eighteen, anyway?"

"Max, it was a long time ago—"

"A lifetime. Brian's lifetime." She looked over her shoulder at him. "I wish I could be more like you. Just forget everything that happened and move on—"

"You can't really think that I've forgotten."

She held his gaze. "I don't know what to think anymore. All I know is that you're here in Schomberg, opening a pub, kidding yourself that this is just some happy little Mayberry—"

"I'm not kidding myself about anything," Sam said, and reached for her. But she was too fast, spinning away to pace the room, her eyes moving from the bed to the mirror to the rug on the floor. As though she suddenly had no idea where she was or how she'd come to be there.

"Do you remember the pact we made the night Brian died?" she asked. "How we swore that if we ever got out of Schomberg, we'd never look back? Yet here we are. You and me, even Gwen. The only one missing is my brother. Poor Brian, who bet his life on love and happily ever after and lost. He'll never get married or have children or rock on the porch of this godforsaken farm in his old age. And all because of her." She stopped abruptly and stared out the window, all of her bravado draining away on a sigh. "If that's love, I'll take trade shows and office furniture any day."

"Marriage isn't a trade show, Max, it's a vow. A promise to stay together, no matter what happens. It's exciting and terrifying, and impossible to hold on to without love."

She shook her head. "No, Sam. Love is what's impossible to hold on to. Love, with all of its expectations and broken promises." She came closer, her eyes begging him to see, to understand. "I don't need to marry Peter, but I want to. When I'm with him, none of this exists. Not the town, or Brian, nothing beyond what we have in New York. What we have is safe, secure, and believe it or not, I like it that way."

"But it won't be enough," he said softly. "Not in the long run. Not for you."

She gave him a sad little smile. "If that's what you think, then you really don't know me at all anymore." She crossed to the door and opened it. "You may not like the choices I make, Sam, but if you're really my friend, you'll support me. And if you can't do that, then the least you can do is leave me alone."

Her spine was rigid, her head high. Proud, stubborn and alone. He went to her, needing to hold her, to protect her from her memories, her demons, herself. But she flinched when he touched her, pulled away when he took her hand. And it occurred to him that she was right. They really didn't know each other anymore.

She opened the door and he went through to the hall.

"Thanks for coming by," she said, already closing the door, shutting him out. "It was good to see you again."

He put a hand on the door, holding it open, surprising himself as much as her. "Max, please," he whispered, and the air was suddenly charged, expectant. As though everything could change in the next moment, if only one of them would close the gap.

Her eyes were wide now, luminous and soft. If she'd been another woman, he might have touched her cheek. Might have drawn her close and kissed her softly, taking the lead and discovering where the moment might take them.

But the ring was there, just a sparkle of light on her finger, but enough to hold him back, make him reach into his pocket instead. "Good luck," he said, taking out the little red charm and tucking it into the front of her shirt. "You're going to need it."

THREE

As lifestyle magazines went, *Mountain Living* was neither the glossiest nor the thickest. But it was the most trusted, delivering honest evaluations of shopping, arts and entertainment throughout the area four times a year. The summer edition featured mountain dream homes, a guide to biking in the Highlands and, on page twenty-four, a one-thousand-word article on Schomberg's newest addition, the Tap Room.

". . . if you go nowhere else this summer," Sam said, reading aloud as he scanned the piece, "make sure you hit the Schomberg Tap Room, where good food and a great time go hand in hand."

He slapped the magazine down on the bar. "Gentlemen, I believe we have arrived."

Ben Morgan grinned and saluted with his coffee, it being too early for anything stronger. "Was there ever any doubt?"

Michael Schmidt, the chef they had stolen from Collette's down in Charlottesville, came around from the kitchen and handed Sam a plate. "Yes, yes, we're marvelous. Now taste."

"It's got peanuts," Ben warned.

Michael's nostrils flared. "Pine nuts," he said, enunciating carefully and smoothing a hand over his buzzed hair. "This is pasta primavera and those are pine nuts."

Ben shrugged and went back to polishing glasses. "Just so he knows."

Sam smiled and rolled a strand of pasta around his fork.

Michael stood, barely breathing now, while Sam sampled. "Well? Well?"

"It's good," Sam said, taking another bite. "Light, creamy—"

Michael leaned closer. "Perfect for a light beer, wouldn't you say?"

Sam glanced over at Ben, who didn't so much as blink. "Michael, you know we don't make light beer—"

"And we never will," Ben muttered. "Not as long as I'm brewmaster."

Michael drew himself up and Sam took another forkful to ease the blow. "This is really very good. Are you going to put it on as today's special?"

"In the pub?" Michael whipped the plate out from under Sam's fork. "I don't think so." With a toss of his head, he reached into the pocket of his white jacket and produced a slip of paper. "Burger and fries is special enough," he said with a sniff, and stomped off to the kitchen.

"Pompous ass," Ben muttered, finally looking up as Michael disappeared. "Who puts peanuts in spaghetti, anyway?"

"Pine nuts," Sam whispered, and got out of the way fast, narrowly avoiding the snap of the polishing cloth.

It was an ongoing argument. Michael envisioned a tiramisu and swordfish menu for the future dining room, while Ben favored thick Virginia ham and generous slices of buttermilk pie. Sam didn't much care, as long as the customers came.

Stopping to pour himself another cup of coffee, he took a piece of chalk from the shelf under the bar and headed over to the specials board, grateful that there had been no bloodshed over the pub menu at least. The Tap Room featured standard pub fare—wings, nachos—and the best home brew this side of the Blue Ridge Mountains.

Ben's skill with a kettle had been widely known in Schomberg long before Sam opened the pub. Ben had been making home brew for most of his fifty-nine years, a craft he learned from his grandfather, a moonshiner from way back. But the Morgans had followed a different drummer. While everyone else on the mountain was still making corn whiskey, the Morgans were brewing up ale to be proud of—strong, dark and pure as a mountain stream.

Ben had carried on the tradition on his kitchen stove, using his wife's canning pots and measuring cups to produce award-winning recipes and arguments in equal numbers. By the time his wife left, Ben's stout had become a staple at the Schomberg Fall Fair, and his bitter the stuff of legend.

Which was why Sam had found himself standing outside Ben's door when the idea of restoring the old Schomberg Tavern to its former glory just wouldn't go away.

He'd had no business plan, no demographics study, none of the things he would have demanded of anyone looking for his backing in New York. Just a real estate listing, a gut feeling and a sudden, inexplicable need to stay.

Nearly a year later, the pub was up and running and the name Schomberg Tap Room was beginning to spread outside the county. With a little luck and a ripple effect from the *Mountain Living* article, they might start to break even by Christmas. And then he could finally relax.

Sam scribbled the hamburger special on the board, then carried his coffee through the front door and sat down on the step. He sent a nod across the road as the lights flicked on at Tracy's beauty parlor, raised his mug when Howard came out to change the pictures in the window of his real estate office and lifted a hand in salute as Jeff wheeled a barbeque out to the front of his hardware store.

Over at Cy's Deli, rumor was that Howard had his hair colored in Tracy's back room. Some folks wondered what else went on back there, but Jeff swore everything was aboveboard, since Tracy was still carrying a torch for Stan over at the Kwik Way.

Sam smiled at a passing pickup, and the driver honked back. Just a typical Saturday morning in Schomberg. Every face familiar, every name known. While it made privacy difficult and gossip a way of life, it also made it impossible to ignore the woman talking to herself in front of the post office.

She wasn't just a crazy person, she was Molly, who had wandered off again to sit under the statue honoring Schomberg's war heroes and read the names of her two sons, Albert and Walter. And no one was surprised when Cy took her into the Deli for a coffee. Molly's family would come to collect her soon enough, and she wasn't hurting a soul.

Sam shook his head as he rose, still finding it odd that the very things that had driven him away years ago were the same things that had drawn him right back.

He'd taken a risk in moving back to Schomberg, gambling everything he had on a town that was still small and unsophisticated, and had only recently recognized its own charm.

Subdivisions had sprouted in areas he'd last seen as farms and orchards, while outlet malls and shopping centers drew even the old-timers away from Schomberg's main street.

Yet there were people trying to breathe new life into the town with shops like the Looking Glass down the road and the Peanut Gallery near the highway. And of course there was the Tap Room, the most ambitious of all, with the most potential for disaster. Still, as he turned back to the pub, he couldn't name a single regret. Or find any way to make Maxine Henley understand why.

He sighed and set the cup in the tub under the bar, wondering what difference it would make anyway. She was only there for the weekend. Then she'd be off, chasing down that fool of a fiancé, hoping he'd marry her just so she'd be safe. From Gwen, from Schomberg. From Sam himself.

"Excuse me," a voice called. A woman of about sixty smiled at him from the front door. "I've got a delivery for Ben Morgan."

"That's me," Ben said, hurrying around the bar.

"More equipment?" Sam asked as Ben took the clipboard from the woman.

"An ostrich," she said.

Sam watched Ben sign the bill. "We ordered an ostrich?"

"It's not for us." He handed her back the pen and grabbed his Hillcats baseball cap from the hat tree. "It's for Eva Henley. She's got those other two, so I thought she might be willing to take a stray."

"A stray ostrich?" Sam asked, following them out the door and down the stairs to where a pickup truck with a horse trailer waited by the curb.

"It's a national tragedy," Ben said, slapping his cap against his leg while they waited for the woman to open the top half of the trailer door. "Once the bottom fell out of the market, people just started taking them up in the woods and letting them go."

Sam stood back as the door swung open. The bird was tall, a good six feet, with huge blue eyes and a neck that stretched it up to seven feet as it inspected them.

"So you're telling me the woods are full of ostriches."

"Cruelest thing you ever saw," Ben said, walking from

one side of the trailer to the other while the bird's head followed his every move. "You have to know where to look, of course."

Sam laughed. The bird blinked. And Ben's shoulders slumped. "You're not buying it, are you?"

"And neither will Eva."

Ben rubbed a hand over his mouth. "Okay, how about this: The owner couldn't afford to feed him, so I took him off his hands."

"Better. But where did you really get him?"

"Fellow over in Roanoke. The bottom did fall out of the market, so I got a good price. But don't tell Eva. She'll feel obligated to pay me, and I don't want anything for it. She just needs a male over there."

Sam raised a brow and Ben smacked him with his cap. "A male *ostrich*. She ended up with two females, and of course she didn't have the heart to send one back because it might feel unloved. But she still needed a male." He sighed and looked over at Sam. "Give me your word that you won't say anything."

"You've got it," he said. "But tell me something: When are you going to give up on Eva?"

Ben looked thoughtful for a moment, then reached up to pat the bird's neck. "Never, I suppose. It'd break her heart." Sam laughed, but Ben merely shrugged and fished his keys from his pocket. "It's true. Somewhere in that ornery heart of hers, she loves me. I can feel it."

The driver returned to the trailer and Ben scratched the address for delivery on the card for her. "Don't get far behind," she said, shooing the ostrich back and closing the trailer. "I don't have time to wait."

"I'll be right behind you." Ben jingled his keys as the pickup pulled away. "You want to come along? Give me a hand with this bird?"

Sam shook his head. "I don't think Max would like that very much."

"Why not?" Ben stopped jingling as his eyes narrowed. "What did you do to her?"

"Nothing. We just didn't see eye-to-eye on a few things, that's all."

"Because her fiancé didn't show up?"

"Word certainly gets around."

Ben glanced over at Cy's. "Not yet, but it will." He slapped his cap against his leg as he turned back to Sam. "She's an odd one, that Maxine. Comes across all feisty and independent, but inside she's fragile as glass, and like to break just as easy."

Sam couldn't help seeing her as she'd been the night before, proud and alone, running from a past that made no sense to a future that held no love. But as she'd said herself, her decisions were her own, and it didn't matter what he thought.

"Well, she's somebody else's problem now." He slapped Ben on the shoulder and headed back to the pub. "And you better hurry or your bird will get there before you do."

"Is that what you told yourself the last time?"

Sam stopped halfway up the stairs and looked back. Ben stood at the curb, his expression unreadable. "When you went away after Brian died," he continued. "Is that what you told yourself? That she wasn't your problem anymore?"

Sam felt the tiny hairs on the back of his neck rise as he came back down the stairs. "What are you talking about?"

"It's just strange, that's all, the way you've never once asked what happened around here after you left."

"It was such a long time ago. I didn't see a point—"

Ben cut him off with a wave of his hand. "The point is that the girl needed a friend, Sam. And you weren't here for her then either."

Sam was aware of a door opening and faces in the

window at Cy's, but he was in no mood to take this discussion elsewhere. "I was in college, for God's sake. Halfway across the country. How was I supposed to know what was happening back here?"

"She ran away," Ben said, and started walking toward his pickup truck on the other side of the street; setting a brisk pace, forcing Sam to hustle after him if he wanted to hear the rest. "More than once," he went on. "Seems she was looking for Gwen."

"Come on, Ben. Gwen lived in Washington. Why would she go that far on her own?"

Ben stopped when he reached his truck and glanced over his shoulder at Sam. "She went all the way to Boston once. Looking for you. Heard she hitchhiked most of the way."

Sam could almost see her standing out there on the highway with her thumb out, heading to Boston to find a boy who wasn't thinking about her at all. A boy who had consciously turned his back on Schomberg and everyone in it. Including the girl on the highway. He shoved a hand through his hair. He'd done exactly what they'd said they would do—get away and never look back. How could he ever have believed it would be just that easy? "Of all the stupid . . . She could have been picked up by anyone—"

"Police were the ones brought her back," Ben cut in. "She stayed put after that, but she made life hell for Eva. Fighting all the time, wanting her to sell the farm, move away." Ben sighed and settled his cap on his head. "Might have been easier if she had."

Sam slumped against the truck. "I didn't even write to her."

Ben put a hand on his shoulder, his tone softening. "She never held that against you. In fact, that was what snapped her out of it. You got away by going to college; she figured that was her out too. By Christmas, she'd turned right around. Went real quiet and got straight *A*s. But she didn't date or go to parties anymore. After a while she even stopped playing ball. It was like she'd already left."

Sam tipped his head back and stared up at the sky. "I didn't even come home in the summer," he said softly. "I told my father I had to stay because there was this fabulous job I had to take." He smiled over at Ben. "Do you know what it was? Telephone solicitation for magazines. I spent the summer on the phone to strangers so I wouldn't have to talk to anyone in Schomberg. Not even Max." He gave a short laugh. "Hell of a friend, huh?"

"You were young, Sam."

"Well, I'm not so young now." He sighed and pushed away from the truck. "But she doesn't even want my friendship anymore."

"She'd say that." Ben snapped around, looking straight at Cy's front window. And Sam had to smile as three faces turned away.

"Just like old times, isn't it?" Ben said. "You and Max at the center of all the best rumors." He gave his head a disgusted shake. "They'll start descending on the farm soon. All the old friends who didn't get to see her last night. They'll mean well, but it'll be hard for Max without that fiancé around."

Sam nodded. "She could probably use a little backup."

"Someone she trusts."

"Someone who cares."

"Someone who knows what's going on with that fool Peter."

Sam held out a hand. "Give me the keys. I hate the way you drive." He opened the truck and climbed into the driver's seat. "And call Michael. Tell him he's in charge for a while. That ought to make up for the pine nuts."

* * *

Max turned off the water, threw open the shower door and snatched up the cell phone from the tile floor. Shoving her dripping bangs out of her eyes, she quickly scanned the tiny screen, making sure the power was still on, the signal strong, hoping that perhaps a call had gone to voice mail while she'd been under the spray.

But there was no flashing envelope, no message telling her she'd missed a call. Nothing but the date and the time—only slightly different than it had been ten minutes ago.

Her fingers hovered over the buttons, as tempted now as she had been last night. How many times had she punched in Peter's number, only to press END before the connection was made, the humiliation complete? A dozen? Two? She set it down and grabbed a towel. More, if she was honest, but why start that now?

She went into the bedroom and snapped up the blind. The important thing was that the night had given way to a brilliant sun, a sky so blue it hurt and half a dozen llamas where the tents had been. Not a gnome or a fairy in sight. And Iona's love charm was safely stowed in the bottom of the wastebasket, right where it belonged.

Sanity had returned and life would get back to normal. She dressed quickly, smiling as a light cotton dress settled on her shoulders, positive that Peter would call today.

She glanced over at the cell phone in the bathroom. For all she knew, he was on a plane right now, rumpled and unshaven, desperate to see her, to explain.

Granted, she'd never seen Peter rumpled or unshaven, or desperate for anything, so she had a little trouble with the exact picture. But as she heard her mother's footsteps on the stairs, Max had every confidence that one would come to her.

But do you love him?

"Not now," she muttered, shoving Sam and his questions into the hamper with the towel, hoping to be rid of him once and for all and knowing the chances were slim. All night he'd been there. Every time she picked up the phone. Every time she closed her eyes—making her wonder, making her doubt herself for the first time in years.

"But not anymore," she said, and let the lid fall with a satisfying thump before answering the knock at the door.

Her mother stood on the other side with a wicker tray bearing a teapot filled with pink roses, a mug of steaming coffee and something on a plate.

"I figured you could use this." She pecked Max on the cheek, handed her the mug, then bustled past to set the flowers on the nightstand—doing three things at once, as usual. "I meant to have these here last night, but with Summer Solstice, I completely forgot."

Gone was the gypsy of the night before, the long skirts replaced by shorts and a sleeveless blouse, and her hair knotted on top of her head. As she watched her mother arrange the flowers on the nightstand, Max saw how she would look at fifty-three and wasn't at all traumatized.

"Bob and Sylvia left early this morning, but they said to give you their best wishes for your wedding," Eva told her, already pulling the comforter off the bed and starting in on the sheets.

"Bob and Sylvia?" Max asked, then nodded, remembering as she sipped. "The wallaby couple. Where are the little bundles of joy, anyway?"

"In the playpen out back, getting some fresh air." Eva gave the sheet a brisk shake and let it float down across the bed. "Breakfast is still on the buffet, by the way."

Max could smell it. Eggs, pancakes, real maple syrup and bacon. Knowing her mother, there would be pots of homemade jam and a basket of fresh rolls or muffins.

And it all would have been prepared after she came in from seeing to the animals.

"I tried a new banana bread," Eva was saying. "Wheat germ, oat bran. Very healthy."

Max strolled over to the bed. "And probably tasteless."

"Which is why I want you to try it." She nodded at the tray. "Have a bite and tell me what's missing."

Max peered at the slice of banana bread, instantly wary. "I told you before, nobody eats what I cook. How would I know what it needs?"

Eva rolled her eyes. "Just taste."

Max broke off a corner and sampled. Dry, flat—

Eva stepped closer. "So? What does it need?"

"Hair spray," Max said, refusing to be drawn into her mother's kitchen. "It'll give it a nice gloss."

Her mother turned back to the bed. "You're impossible."

"And you work too hard," Max said, deftly changing the subject as she brushed crumbs from her fingers. "This place is too much for one person. You need help."

"I've got help. Grab the other end of this sheet."

Max groaned and grabbed. "I mean permanent help. Someone to take some of the load."

"I have that. The Jenkins boys, remember them? Well, they're not holy terrors anymore and they come every day to help with the animals. And Ben has been marvelous about the petting zoo." Eva smiled and tossed Max a pillow. "Don't you worry about me. I'm fine."

Together they smoothed the comforter and fluffed the pillows. If Max closed her eyes, she could almost believe she was ten years old again, making beds with her mother while Brian and her father practiced setting a table downstairs—all of them learning how to run a bed-and-breakfast, needing to find more and more ways to make the farm pay for itself. She gave the last pillow a punch, amazed at how damn successful they'd been.

"It's too bad you went to bed so early last night," Eva said, taking a towel from the hamper and wiping it over the dust-free dresser. "The Bizarre had some great acts."

"I'm sure it did." Max smiled, wondering if Eva would own up to her part in Iona's act.

"I think you'd have really enjoyed the mermaids," Eva continued. "I know Sam did. Did he tell you about them?"

"No," Max said, making it a point not to wonder if Sam had gone back to the mermaid. Or if he'd taken her to the Tap Room, or what it looked like, or anything else, for that matter. She didn't care what he did, or with whom, as long as he stayed far away from her. "I did catch one of the acts," she said, and smiled. "Do you remember a gnome handing out emeralds?"

Eva nodded as she moved on to the nightstand. "It was a promotion for a shop on Center Street called the Looking Glass."

The Looking Glass, Max thought, how fitting in a town where a gnome was the White Rabbit and Iona was the Mad Hatter.

"The emerald is good for ten percent off on anything in the store," Eva continued. "Do you still have it?"

"I lost it somewhere." Eva didn't pursue it, so Max decided to push a little. "Do you remember a woman named Iona? Blond, wispy-looking."

"Iona?" Eva laughed and flicked the cloth over the shells on the mirror. "She's only the best fortune-teller this side of the Blue Ridge. Makes me look like the old phony that I am. Why? did you see her?"

Max couldn't help smiling. Eva knew perfectly well she'd seen Iona. Who else would have set her up that way? But if she wanted to play the game . . . Max wandered over to the window. "I saw her, but only for a moment."

"Really?" Eva asked, and from the corner of her eye, Max saw her stop dusting. "What did she tell you?"

"Something about a trip over water," she said and glanced back, sure that Eva would give herself away now.

But her mother only frowned. "That doesn't sound like Iona. Are you sure?"

"I didn't pay much attention," Max said, and waited a beat, certain her mother would find a way to lead the conversation around to charms and magic spells. But she simply said, "Too bad," and moved on with her dust cloth, making Max wonder if someone else might have set her up with Iona. But who?

"So where is this Iona now?" she asked.

"No idea. She only comes here once a year." Eva turned to look at her. "But believe me, if Iona ever stops me and has something to say, I will definitely listen."

Max could only stare as her mother went back to work. Eva might be the official host of the Bizarre, but she'd never been one to fall for it. She knew exactly how the giant got to be so big and where the OFF switch was for the singing harp. So why was she so taken with Iona?

Eva picked up the white nightgown from the chair and held it out to her. "This is lovely. Too bad Peter didn't get to see it."

"Yes," Max said, still wondering about Iona's charm and her promise of "the right man, guaranteed." But as she ran a hand over the silk, it wasn't Peter she saw—it was Sam; and she remembered the way his eyes darkened when she'd held the gown against her. The way his fingers tightened as she smoothed it over her hips. And her own inexplicable delight when he'd had to turn away.

She tossed the gown aside. Okay, so she'd enjoyed knowing that she got to him. That for once it was Sam O'Neal who had to look away and not her. What did that prove? Only that a teenage crush had a very long shelf life, and hers was obviously still fresh. For all the good it did her.

"He'll see it tonight, though," Eva was saying.

"Oh no he won't," Max said.

Eva gave her an odd smile. "But you said he was coming today."

"Today?" Max shook her head then, realizing who her mother was talking about. "Peter, yes. Well, actually, no. He's been delayed again."

"When did you find this out?"

"This morning," Max said, scrambling for an excuse. "I spoke to him on the cell phone earlier, and he's been called to an emergency shoot in New Orleans."

Eva screwed up her nose. "An emergency food shoot?"

"Happens all the time. The shoot is scheduled, the product is there and bang, the photographer gets killed or . . ."

Her mother looked horrified. "The photographer's dead?"

Max waved her hands, as if treading water. "No, just very sick and can't make it to the set, so Peter's filling in."

"What about the job in Virginia Beach?"

"On hold," Max said quickly. "It's a Christmas cookbook so there's some leeway there." About two weeks, if she was honest.

"Peter and you aren't taking a vacation then?" Her mother moved closer, giving Max the oddest feeling that she was being stalked. "So you've got two weeks free. Nowhere to go." Eva smiled and held out her hands. "Then why don't you just stay on here?"

Max backed up a step. She should have worked harder on that excuse. "I couldn't possibly."

Eva followed. "But I'd love to shop for a trousseau with you, help you plan your wedding. I've wanted this for you for so long, Max. Someone to love you, care about you. And now you have Peter."

Max ran damp palms over her dress. "Yes, yes, I do. But I really can't—"

"I didn't think I'd have the chance to share much of the preparations," Eva went on. "What with you in New York and me out here. But now here we are, you with vacation time and me without a guest for another two weeks."

She hesitated, as though needing to choose her words carefully. And they both knew, she was right.

"Max, I know things haven't always gone well in the past, but it could be different this time. We could have fun. You might even get to like the wallabies." She took a breath, moved another step closer. "We don't have to talk about Brian or Gwen. And I promise I won't try to get you to cook." She smiled. "What do you say? Can we give it a try?"

All of Max's resolve melted in the face of her mother's hopeful smile. How could she say no? It was only two weeks. Anybody could stand two weeks. And who could tell—maybe they *would* have a good time.

"Sure," she said, and found she didn't have to force a smile after all. "Why not?"

"It'll be great. We'll go shopping, have lunch at Sam's—"

"I'm not going to Sam's." Max flashed a quick smile to make her mother's eyebrows lower. "Not until Peter gets here. I want to have somewhere nice in town to show him."

Eva nodded. "That's a good idea."

"In fact, I don't want to set foot in the village until Peter arrives."

"Fine by me. We'll go down to one of the malls, or maybe out to DC. As long as you're here, that's all that matters."

Her mother was about to wrap her in another famous hug when a low rumbling caught their attention. Outside, Columbo was on the job, racing back and forth, sounding the alarm as a pickup rolled across the driveway to the barn.

"Oh, Columbo, it's only Ben." Eva leaned closer to the window. "And he's got one of my goats in the back. Silly thing must have got out again. I keep telling him he's going to get hit one of these days, but does he listen?" She looked over at Max. "You can't tell a goat anything."

"I'll take your word for it."

"There's someone with him too." Eva tilted her head to the side. "Looks like Sam."

"Sam?" Max asked, annoyed as much by the flutter around her heart as the fact that he had the nerve to come at all. She crossed to the window. "What does he want?"

"To visit with you, most likely." Eva turned away from the window and picked up the laundry hamper. "You and I are going to have such a good time. Just wait and see."

"I'm already excited," Max said, still at the window, unable to stop herself from watching Sam get out of the truck.

Oh yes, it would be a wonderful two weeks. Iced tea on the porch. Hiding from Sam in the barn. She laid her forehead against the glass. Why did he have to come back? To grill her, no doubt. He probably had divorce statistics with him, proof positive that love is essential to marriage.

She tipped her head to the side. And why did he have to look so good? Worn jeans, a shirt with the sleeves rolled up and boots. Standard issue country uniform, and yet the way those jeans fit—

She started when he turned and looked up at her, as if he'd known she was there. Then he smiled and waved, just like a friend would do. Only she didn't feel friendly at all.

She reached for the blind, drew her hand back, then reached again. She turned away, her face growing warm as her heart beat too fast.

"Max?"

She jerked around and saw Eva watching her from the door. "Is something wrong?"

Max pulled the blind down with a snap. "Of course not." She smoothed a hand over her hair, another over her dress, then held both hands at her sides, being careful not to fidget. "You go ahead, I'll just be a minute. Maybe put on something cooler. Shorts maybe. Of course a dress is usually best in this heat . . ." Max forced her mouth to close, to say nothing, to be silent for God's sake so her mother would leave and she could figure out what she was going to do next.

Eva shrugged. "Suit yourself," she said, and bent down to pick up the wastebasket too.

Max saw it all in a flash. Iona, the gnome, the damned smiling moon. It was a sign. Either that or an anxiety attack, but she didn't have time to ponder.

Eva hadn't set her up at all. Somehow Iona had found her on her own. And the pillow in that wastebasket wasn't strictly a love charm, it was a beacon. A way for Peter to find her, to come and take her home. Back to a place where pickups were people you met in bars and wildlife came with a leash. And Sam O'Neal with his questions and his damn sexy jeans would be no more than a distant memory.

"Don't touch that," she hollered, then gave a quick little laugh when Eva's eyes widened. "I mean, don't you dare carry another thing down those stairs." Max waltzed over and picked up the wastebasket. "I'll bring this with me when I come."

Eva backed out the door, still watching her. "That's fine, dear. And thanks."

"My pleasure," Max said, still smiling as she closed the door.

Her shoulders relaxed when she heard Eva's footsteps on the stairs. She wandered back to the window, pulled back the corner of the blind and peeked out. Sam was still there, and so was another truck with a horse trailer attached. Probably a giraffe, for all Max knew. But she had no time to think about livestock. Right now, she had to think about her future. A future far away from Schomberg.

She grabbed the charm from the wastebasket. It was warm and soft and she stroked a fingertip over the gold threads. The pillow was small, pliable, not really all that thick. Probably wouldn't be noticeable at all. No one would ever have to know, not even her mother.

She closed her eyes, gripped the charm. A beacon, she told herself. Not a love charm. It was all a question of semantics.

"Max, you coming?" her mother called.

"Be right there."

She positioned her feet, drew in a deep breath, stuffed the charm in next to her heart and waited. Warmth, as unmistakable as it was illogical, flooded through her, making her skin tingle and her heart beat faster.

She opened her eyes and went to the mirror, checking closely for telltale signs of the charm. But all she saw was a woman with wide blue eyes, hair that hadn't been blown dry properly and very pink cheeks.

She laid her palms against her cheeks and faced the door. "The right man will find me," she whispered as she walked. "Guaranteed."

FOUR

Max stood back from the trailer, well back. She'd seen pictures of ostriches, of course. Huge awkward birds with their heads in the sand, blocking out everything around them. But this one wasn't blocking out a thing, except perhaps the sun.

He was stretching that neck of his up as far as it would go and watching Eva closely as she approached; slowly, steadily, hand out and palm up, showing him she meant no harm—and making Max wonder if there were teeth inside that long beak.

"An orphan, you say." Eva smiled and glanced over at Ben. "Just how did this happen?"

The ostrich blinked at her, then turned to Ben to fill in the blanks.

Ben bent his head, watching his shoes as he strolled over to where she stood. "As I was telling Sam on the way over, a fellow in Roanoke couldn't afford to feed him anymore. Why, just look at him. Poor thing not yet a year old and like to starve soon." He lifted his head and looked at her. "So naturally I thought of you."

Max couldn't remember the last time she'd seen her mother blush so prettily or lower her lashes in quite that way. Probably not since before her father died, the year Max turned ten.

Such a long time to carry a torch, she thought. And

while she knew poor Ben was never going to get Eva to go to a movie, she couldn't help rooting for him all the same.

"We'll put him in with the others," Eva said.

"Others?" Max asked, instantly alert again. "How many are there?"

"Just Laverne and Shirley," Eva said. "I haven't decided on a name for this one yet."

Max stared as Ben opened the trailer and the huge creature put a knobby foot on the ramp. She backed up another step. "You can't put that thing in a petting zoo."

"Of course not," Eva said, and went back to cooing soft words to the ostrich as Ben guided him to the barn. The bird suddenly stopped, craned his neck around to look Eva right in the eye and snapped at a shiny pin in her hair.

Max gasped, wondering why in the world Eva wanted ostriches, and saying as much when the bird's knobby foot came down only inches from her mother's toes.

Eva looked back at her as the trailer pulled away. "Oh, Max, just think of the hats."

"Hats?" Max repeated, an image of musketeers and Monet paintings floating through her mind as the three went through the barn door and were swallowed into the gloom. She raised a hand, let it fall. "But who'll wear them?"

"You'd look good in one," Sam said.

She turned in time to see him rounding the side of the trailer, his hair swept back and almost blue-black in the sunlight, his eyes full of humor and a half-smile on his face. "One with a big wide brim."

She felt her pulse quicken and steeled herself against it, telling herself that it was only residual anger.

"And a bow," he added, still strolling, arms loose and easy at his sides. As though he had every right in the world to be there, with a goat trailing along behind him.

A smile tugged at her lips. It was hard to stay mad at a man with a goat on his tail. Still, she folded her arms and lifted her chin. "A bow?"

He nodded and ran a finger down her cheek. "With a great big feather that curls round and tickles you right there." Then he leaned in close to whisper in her ear, "And nothing else."

Max slapped his hand. "In your dreams."

"Yours now too," he said, laughing and easily dodging the next blow.

"Don't count on it," she said, irritated that he was probably right, and that Peter still hadn't called, and that the goat was nibbling the flowers on her dress.

Sam reached down, turning the animal toward the barn. "Get going," he said, and the goat wandered off, putting to rest the theory that you can't tell a goat anything. Max gave her head a disgusted shake. Another bit of farm trivia she'd be sure to put to good use in New York.

Sam turned back to her, still grinning. "Come on, Max. Don't tell me you've never dressed like that for Peter. Just a hat or a pair of high heels and nothing but a smile."

She looked away. "Are we still on this?"

His own smile faded as he came a step closer. "I don't believe it." He tipped her head up to look at him. "You haven't ever done that, have you?"

"Plenty of times," she said evenly, knowing how red her face must be by the heat creeping up her throat. The truth was that high heels and a smile had never occurred to her. And Peter had never once suggested it. Which meant what? That he was a gentleman. Sam, on the other hand, was anything but.

She put a hand on his chest and gave him a shove, needing room, air, a chance to see clearly. "Why are you here, anyway? A few more questions? A little something to show me the error of my ways? Because if that's it—"

"I came to apologize for last night." He took himself back a few steps. "I had no business judging you or Peter. And while I don't agree with what you're doing, I'll support you as long as you need me to. I just wanted you to know that before you leave."

Max stared down at her hands, confused. She hadn't expected an apology. And while it pleased her more than she would ever admit to know that he was on her side again, she wasn't sure she really wanted him around.

"I'm sorry about the hat too. I don't know what I was thinking."

It was a lie, of course. He'd been thinking about her in that hat from the moment he came around the corner and saw her standing there. The sun shone through that dress, showing only shadows, so his mind was forced to fill in the rest—something it had done only too well.

But it seemed to be a weekend for lies and secrets, so he stayed with his story, certain she wouldn't want to hear the truth anyway. Not when her own mind was still stuck on Peter. And a friend was all she needed.

"Thanks," she said and was standing beside him, forgiving and forgetting faster than he'd have been able to, but that was Max. And he was damn lucky to know her.

"But I'm not leaving right away," she added.

Sam shook his head. "I thought you were in a hurry to get back to New York."

"Things change," she said and headed over to the paddock, filling him in on what had happened as they walked.

She hoisted herself up and straddled the fence. "Which means I'm here for two weeks of trousseau shopping and wedding planning. And if you don't think you can keep up the front that long, I'll understand."

"You're determined not to tell her, then."

She met and held his gaze. "There's nothing to tell."

Sam nodded and leaned back against the fence. "Then

as far as I know, Peter was held up by an emergency job, and he'll be here as soon as he can. How's that?"

"Perfect," she said softly.

"Hey, what are friends for?"

She smiled then, the simple, easy smile of friendship, just before she turned to gaze out at the field. "I should go back up to the house. Peter might call."

"You wouldn't want to miss it."

She didn't answer, and he wondered what she was thinking. What it was that he saw in her eyes. And what she would do if he said to hell with everything and picked her up. Just swept her off that fence and carried her, laughing and kicking, all the way to the truck. They could drive for hours, finding someplace where they could be alone. Getting to know the people they'd become while shaking off the ones they had been. And finding out if there was any way to bridge the gap in between.

"Maxine Henley? Is that you?"

The voice echoed across the paddock, as familiar as it was shrill, shattering the peace and the fantasy.

They shuddered and turned. Sure enough, the woman waving from Eva's back door was Judith Anderson, homecoming queen of another era, holding a gift in one hand while she took a bite of something in the other.

Sam glanced over as Eva and Ben came out of the barn. The old man had been right about visitors, but even he looked surprised that it had started already.

"I knocked at the front," Judith was saying, "but when no one answered, I figured you were probably back here."

"Of course she had to walk through the house to find out." Max's eyes narrowed. "How long do you figure she was in there?"

Ben leaned an elbow on the fence beside her. "Just long enough to find out how many guests your mother has booked and what she's serving for breakfast these days."

Everyone knew that Judith ran a bed-and-breakfast in the new subdivision, a monster house of magazine charm and imported antiques that she passed off as family heirlooms to guests. She sent flyers to tourist bureaus, bought space in every tour book and travel magazine and never missed an opportunity to check out what the competition was doing.

"This banana bread needs a little something," she called, licking her fingers nonetheless. "But now that Max is here, I'm sure you'll discover what it is."

"And then she'll want the recipe." Max frowned at Sam. "I can't believe you used to date her."

"She was blond, I was young." He hung his head. "I'm so ashamed."

Ben laughed out loud, Max jabbed him with an elbow and Eva gave all three of them a long, hard stare as she swept past.

"Be nice," she warned, then turned her attention to her guest, her hostess smile slipping effortlessly into place as she raised a hand to wave. "Judith, what a lovely surprise."

"Southern hospitality at its finest," Ben said.

"Which is why I live in the north," Max muttered as she slid off the fence.

Sam figured Max hadn't used her hostess smile in some time, the way it was slow in coming. But then, all of a sudden, there it was, a trifle bright but holding bravely. And as he drew up beside her, he wondered briefly if she'd like a blindfold. "Where was that emergency Peter went to again?"

"New Orleans," she said, barely disturbing the smile. "We tell her the Christmas cookbook was postponed, the new client hired their own stylist and I'm having a lovely vacation."

"I can tell."

He watched her mouth twitch as she tipped her head back to look up at him. "What would I do without you?"

And as they stepped forward together, Sam found himself wondering exactly the same thing.

"Congratulations," Judith said, handing off the gift to Eva and holding out her arms to Max in one smooth move. "I wanted to be the first to say it, but I see someone beat me to it. How are you, Sam?"

"Just fine," he said, wincing as Judith kissed the air beside Max's cheeks before stepping back.

"Why, let me look at you," Judith said. "You haven't changed a bit. Well, the hair is new, but it'll probably fill in just fine before your wedding."

Max held that smile. "That's the dream, of course."

Judith looked at her blankly for a moment, then smiled again. "Well, it is just so good to see you again. And we've got so much catching up to do."

Max tilted her head to the side. "We do?"

"I should say so. I mean, I haven't seen you since that night Sam took me to the dance in Kleinburg." Judith laughed and turned to Sam. "Do you remember that? We stopped off here to pick up Brian and Gwen." She switched back to Max. "Of course, she's back now, you know. Looks good too from all accounts. But I don't know how she can stay up there all by herself."

From the way Judith kept talking, Sam figured she didn't notice that Max's chin had lifted ever so slightly, or that her fingers were drumming on her thigh. But he hadn't missed a thing.

"You were saying about the dance," he said to Judith and edged closer to Max. "What were you wearing again?"

"Blue, of course," and while she pouted and complained about men to Eva, he took Max's hand in his, holding it still behind them.

She didn't look over, but her eyes widened just a moment before he felt her fingers relax and lace themselves with his.

Judith was still talking, no one else noticed a thing and Sam couldn't help but smile. This, he realized, was exactly what friends were for.

"And Sam," Judith rattled on, "you never knew this, but I almost couldn't go that night." She laughed alone, one hand to her chest. "I lost a shoe. Felt like Cinderella, only before the ball, you know." She turned to Max. "And you were looking everywhere, remember?"

"Like it was yesterday."

Judith's laughter slowly subsided. "Well, I can't wait to meet your fiancé." She looked around. "Where is the lucky man?"

"He was delayed," Max said too quickly.

"That's what I heard." Judith dipped her chin. "Everything okay, hon?"

"Perfectly," Sam said, holding her hand tighter, not sure if he was keeping Max or Judith safe. "You've heard how well-respected Peter is, of course . . ." He paused, knowing Judith would nod whether she knew or not. "Well, a job came up suddenly on the coast. Very high level. Very hush-hush."

Judith looked confused. "I thought he took pictures of food."

Sam lowered his voice. "Haven't you ever heard of celebrity cookbooks?" Judith's eyes widened appropriately and he went on. "This particular celebrity is very selective. Would only work with the best. And that, of course, meant Peter."

Judith looked at Max with new respect. "You must be so proud."

"We all are," Eva said, handing off Judith's gift to Ben. "And since I'm sure Max would rather wait until Peter's here to open that, why don't we let Ben run the gift up to the house for now?"

Ben was already on the way while Eva took hold of Judith's arm and deftly turned her around. "While I know you girls would love to talk more, there's something I desperately need your opinion on. I have some giveaway ideas I've been thinking about for guests."

If Judith had been a dog, Sam figured her ears would have pricked right up. "Giveaways?"

"Little mementos of their stay." Eva gave her a sly smile. "With the B&B logo on it, of course."

Judith stared in awe. "I never thought of that." Then she twisted her head around and smiled at Max. "You don't mind if I talk to your mom for a little bit, do you? Maybe you can figure out what that bread needs while we're gone."

Eva glanced back. "I'm sure she'll try."

"Two eggs and a half cup of cream," Max muttered as the two walked away arm-in-arm. "And if she ever gives Judith the recipe, I'll kill her." She looked up at him. "My compliments on the celebrity cookbook. It was truly inspired."

Sam bowed his head. "My pleasure."

"By this time tomorrow, rumor will be that Peter is taking pictures of Elvis."

"Everyone knows how he loved to cook."

She smiled, but it wouldn't stay, and when she pulled her hand away, he let it go, unable to justify holding on any longer.

"Eva's giveaways were good too," he said and she nodded, but he knew she was already lost to him, her eyes still on the two figures on their way to the house, her mind much farther.

"I should have gone home when I had the chance. She's not the only one who'll want to talk about Brian and the old days, or bring me up to date on what Gwen's doing. And then they'll want to know about Peter, and where he is and when he's coming. And what will I do if he doesn't call?" She turned back to Sam. "Do you think anyone would notice if we got in your truck and just drove away?"

He shoved the fantasy down and crossed to where she stood. "Max," he said gently, "he'll come."

"How can you be so sure?"

"Because you were right. He'd be a fool to let you go."

She moistened her lips, glanced up at the house. "I should go get the cell phone, just in case. But then I might run into Judith—" She snapped around. "Do you think she'd look for me in the barn?"

"If she does, we hide."

The barn was cool and dark, and it took a moment for her eyes to adjust. Slowly everything came into sight, bringing the memories with it: concrete floor, wooden stalls and scents that were honest and familiar—hay and earth, and the musky smell of the animals themselves.

"Eva's kept it well," Max said as they moved away from the door.

"It means everything to her," Sam said, and she understood that there was nothing else behind the statement. Nothing meant to inspire guilt or confrontation. It was merely the truth, and everyone in Schomberg knew it.

Eva kept the farm going for future generations, hoping it would stay in the family for another hundred years. But with Brian gone, the only one left to pass it on to was Max. And she doubted that Peter would ever be tempted to muck stalls for a living. Especially now that he was photographing celebrities.

They walked on in silence, Max peering into empty stalls, knowing most of the animals would be outside now that the Bizarre was over. Time was, her father had kept dairy cows in this section of the barn, but the names and breeds tacked above the stalls were all new to her—xebu, pygmy goat, potbellied pig.

She knew nothing of them but assumed they'd be a big hit in Eva's new petting zoo. Right up there with face painting, hay rides and Maple Syrup Days.

When they reached the door on the north wall, Sam went through first. Her family had kept sheep there when Max was growing up, but now three ostriches stood behind a fence, all of them turning to see the intruders.

"That's Laverne." Sam pointed to the tallest bird. "And over there is Shirley."

"Which means my mother will name the male Squiggy."

"I hope not," Sam said. "For his sake."

The ostriches watched them a moment longer, then Laverne lost interest. She stepped back from the fence and opened her wings wide. The spread was at least six feet across, the feathers a glossy white and black.

Hats, Max thought, and felt her cheeks grow warm.

Then suddenly the ostrich rose up, shaking her wings and waving them as she walked back and forth across the pen, reminding Max of a chorus girl.

"Laverne is a show-off," Sam said matter-of-factly.

Then the male moved off and Laverne chased after him, dashing around in front and making him stop while she started all over again—bobbing and weaving, her wings stretched out as she did an ostrich shimmy for him.

Max shook her head. "She's not showing off, she's strutting her stuff." She glanced up at Sam. "Laverne is flirting with Squiggy." She turned back to the ostriches and frowned. "I take that back. She's not just flirting, she's throwing herself at him."

The male watched Laverne for a moment, raised his

head, lowered it, then wandered over to the feed box on the other side of the pen.

But Laverne was not easily discouraged.

"This is embarrassing," Max said, moving closer to the fence as the hussy chased him across the pen and lowered herself to the floor. "Oh, Laverne," Max called. "Don't do this."

The bird ignored her, and when the male raised his head out of the feed box, she spread her wings again, fluttering the feathers while weaving her neck back and forth seductively.

Max groaned. "What is that? The dance of the seven feathers?"

"Whatever it is, it's not working," Sam said, chuckling as the male dunked his head into the bin again and wandered off with a mouthful.

"What's wrong with him?" Max muttered, grabbing hold of the wires as Laverne jumped up and chased him again. "And what's wrong with her?" She rose up on her toes. "Laverne, you don't have to do this. You're young. You're lovely—"

"And very tall," Sam called.

Max shot him a nasty look. "Stay out of this," she said as the bird started her dance one more time. "Laverne, have some pride."

But Laverne kept going, doing her best to lure Squiggy, to show him that she was there for him, to let him know she cared. And Max's heart did a silly little flip when the male took a step toward her.

Just when it appeared that all would be well, he was distracted by something shiny at the top of the fence. A mere trick of the light, but it was enough to have him walking the other way, leaving Laverne in the lurch yet again.

Max shook the fence. "Oh, that's so typical. The least little distraction and he's gone. Wandering off, doesn't even call—" She stopped herself and headed for the door. "I need some air."

She glanced back in time to see Shirley reach over and pluck a feather out of Squiggy's back.

The male jumped and Max nodded. "Way to go, Shirl," she called, and noticed Laverne standing alone by the fence now, watching him from a distance.

Max swallowed a lump in her throat, not even sure when it had started, and scowled at Sam as he came toward her. "Why are men so dense?"

"Not all of us are," he said, catching the door as she went through.

"Oh, no?" Max crossed over to the stairs. "I had it, you know."

"Had what?" Sam asked, his hands outstretched and his brow furrowed—the very picture of male confusion. Rather like the ostrich with the missing feather.

She grinned and started climbing. "The Cinderella shoe."

FIVE

The loft had always been treated like an attic, the place where boxes and old furniture were stored. A crib, a highchair, old headboards, a sofa. Castoffs of a family growing up. And against a wall, a stack of plastic boxes and tubs, some quite new by the look of them, but with a fine layer of dust nonetheless.

At the front of the loft, a door opened out over the driveway. Max gave it a push, letting in fresh air and enough light so she could make out the labels on some of the boxes: CHRISTMAS. ODDS AND ENDS. RECEIPTS 1983. She turned away and headed back to the door, thinking that she'd help her mother clean out some of the junk before she left. It would give her an excuse to hide, a place to lie low until Peter arrived.

Holding on to the door frame, she leaned out, way out, enjoying the familiar giddy feeling as she looked down over the paddock, the shed, the river winding its way past the house and the picket fence that surrounded the house and gardens that made her mother so proud.

The hickory trees on the front lawn were taller now, the dogwoods fuller, but otherwise the view was the same, and she found herself searching for landmarks. The spot where she'd learned to throw a ball. The rock that was "home" when they played flashlight tag. And the tree where she'd built a clubhouse of her own—Brian and his friends be damned. It had still been there when she left but was gone now, and she wondered when her mother had finally taken it down. Or who had done it for her.

She felt Sam behind her and turned to see him at the top of the stairs. "Why did you have the shoe?"

"Because she looked like such a twit in that blue dress, I couldn't stand it." Max pulled herself back inside the loft, back to where it was safe and the ground solid beneath her. "I'm surprised you don't remember."

On a whim, she crossed over to the boxes and read more labels. RECEIPTS 1984. REPORT CARDS. PICTURES/MAX. PICTURES/BRIAN.

She hesitated a moment, then reached out, pulling Brian's box from the stack and carrying it back to the door. She blew the dust from the top, watching it dance in the sunlight for a moment before being carried off on a breeze. Then she sat, letting her legs dangle over the edge as she always had. And Sam came and sat with her, his long legs swinging beside hers as she lifted a corner of the lid.

"Are you sure you want to do this?" he asked.

"I guess I'll find out," she said, so softly she almost didn't hear it herself. But she held back for a moment all the same; giving her heart a moment to catch up before lifting the lid up and off.

Brian smiled up at her. That same wicked grin in a face of wide blue eyes and a strong, stubborn jaw. She made herself breathe as she took out a handful of pictures and sifted through them. Brian on the baseball field. By the Christmas tree. In her treehouse? She laughed even as her eyes stung and she kept going, glad now that she'd done this; thinking, for the first time ever, that it might be nice to take some home.

She stopped, finding the shot she was looking for: Sam

and Judith, going to the dance in Kleinburg. And time had not made the dress any less ugly.

She held the picture out to Sam. "See what I mean?"

He winced. "I do now. But I still don't understand why you took her shoes."

"Because I was jealous," she said, taking the picture back and studying it more closely. "I wanted to be the one on your arm as you went through the door. The one on her way to the ball." She paused, smiling at the fresh young faces in her hand. "So I hid her shoe. Just one. Two would have been obvious. I blamed it on the dog, but my mother saw through me." She sighed dramatically and laid the picture with the others in her lap. "Sadly, Eva's feet and Judith's were about the same size, so the night was saved, depending on how you look at it." She laughed and put the pictures back in the box. "As silly as it sounds, I had a crush on you back then."

His hand was cool on her wrist, his breath warm against her ear. "What happened?"

"I outgrew it," she said, but couldn't look at him, afraid that he'd already seen the blush in her cheeks or felt the quickening of her pulse, and that they both might mistake it for more than it was.

She curled her fingers around the box so she wouldn't be tempted to curl them around his hand instead. "I should go and rescue Eva," she said, and was relieved when he drew away and leaned back, not pressing her for details or explanations she wasn't ready to think about yet.

She was pulling her legs up, preparing to leave, when she spotted the corner of a book near the bottom of the box. She froze, then her legs settled back of their own accord as she reached inside and carefully lifted out the book.

"What is it?" Sam asked.

"A wedding gift," she said, running her fingers over

the cover, not quite believing what she'd found. "For Gwen."

"Are you sure?"

She nodded, remembering. "I was with Brian when he bought it," she said softly, the gold lettering as clear and bright as the day she'd helped him pick it out. "Love poems mostly, with some erotic short stories for interest. I'm surprised you've never seen it."

Her palms were oddly damp and she wiped them on her skirt before flipping back the cover. "Let me read you the dedication." The back cracked softly as she opened it up, and she knew right away that whoever had put the book away had never opened it, or looked inside. Had never read what her brother had written.

Which was perhaps just as well. The words were nothing special or outstanding. Just Brian's barely legible scrawl across a yellowing page—the simple declaration of one man's heart. And Max felt her own break as she read the words out loud. " 'For Gwen. My love, my life. My heart and my soul. Forever.' " She gave her head a shake and snapped the book shut. "That farm boy really had it bad."

"He loved her," Sam said, reaching over to pull a picture from between the pages.

Max couldn't help smiling when she saw it.

Brian again, with Gwen this time, on the porch swing. The two of them smiling, laughing. Gwen tall and willowy, undeniably beautiful. *Like a princess,* Max thought. Just as she had the day she snapped the shot.

"I loved her too," Max said. "In fact I wanted to *be* her, to be them. They were like Romeo and Juliet to me, young and beautiful and so much in love. It made me ache to think of them not being together always."

She took the picture from him, needing to hold it, to see if there was something she hadn't noticed that day. Something in Gwen's eyes or her smile that should have warned them. But all she saw was a radiant young woman and Brian—happier that summer then he had ever been in his life.

Sam watched the play of emotion across her face—anger, confusion, but beneath it all, a longing so real, so powerful, it was all he could do to keep from reaching for her again.

"I couldn't wait to be in love like that," she continued. "To want someone so badly that nothing mattered except being together. Just holding each other, touching each other."

"But you outgrew that too," Sam murmured.

"Yes," she said, meeting his gaze as she set the book in his lap. "And if you're lucky, one day you will too."

He shook his head. "That's not likely to happen."

"Ah, such faith, and after all that's happened too." She rose and carried the box back to the stack by the wall. "Tell me something, Sam. The woman you were engaged to, the one who left, did you love her?"

"Yes," he said, an image of a classic blonde, cool and sexy, flashing through his mind as he got to his feet. "At the time."

And he still had the ring to prove it. Sitting in a velvet box in his top drawer, tucked under the socks, like a haircloth coat for his heart.

"But it didn't get you to the altar, did it? All that love and nowhere to go." She folded her arms as he came closer, the chip on her shoulder almost a boulder now, daring him to knock it off. "Yet you still believe you need it."

"I know I do," he said. "And so do you."

He didn't take time to think it through, he simply bent to her, tipping her chin up and closing his eyes. Then he kissed her, softly, gently, the way he should have all those years ago.

He felt her stiffen again and was sure she'd pull away,

but then she was kissing him back, her hands reaching up, hesitant, wavering, her fingertips barely brushing his face.

He drew back a moment, for the first time in years unsure and wondering. Her eyes were still closed, her lips slightly parted. Waiting?

Her eyes fluttered open and her fingers curled back, touching her lips while she stared up at him, wide eyed, vulnerable, breathless. He wasn't ready for the rush of pleasure or the powerful need right behind it. He let his hands move around her waist, drawing her to him, pressing her close. And felt himself tremble when he bent to her again.

It was like every kiss she'd ever dreamed, ever imagined. Hard yet soft. Rough yet gentle. And deepening slowly, lazily, his clever tongue parting her lips and coaxing hers out to play.

It should never have started and shouldn't go on. There was Peter to think of, and the ring, of course. And the charm she wore to make everything right. But all she could think of was Sam, and this moment—and a kiss that should go on forever.

There was no Tap Room anymore, no past, no ghosts. Just this moment, with nothing to stop her from pushing her fingers into his hair and drawing him down. No reason not to arch her neck and press her breasts against him. And no way to resist when his hands slipped down over her hips.

The blast of a horn jolted them both, snapping them apart. They stood, eyes locked, as they tried to breathe, to think, to cool the need. And like dust in the sun, it forever drifted away.

"This did not happen," Max said.

"Seemed pretty real to me."

"Well, I can't remember it at all," she said, knowing it was a lie as she crossed back to the door. She held on to the frame again, more for support than fun, and stood well back from the edge.

Judith's car was gone, and in its place Max saw a taxi; the driver hauling bags out of the trunk while a woman with long dark hair, tight blue jeans and high-heeled mules dug into her purse for the fare.

Sam came to stand behind her. "Do you know who that is?"

Max nodded. "Peter's assistant. And my best friend." She raised a hand to wave. "Delia. Up here."

Delia Rosini spun around, frowned, then slapped the money into the driver's hand. "Where have you been?" she hollered. "I must have dialed your cell phone a million times since my plane landed."

Max winced as Delia swung her purse over her shoulder and struck out across the grass, on course to the barn and a twisted ankle if she didn't slow down in those shoes.

"Why is she wearing those?" Sam asked.

"She's from Staten Island," Max said, and felt herself smile. "It's her birthright."

"I mean, it's just not like you not to answer your phone," Delia said, then stopped and shook a stone from her left shoe before continuing on. "I know you're upset and Peter's an ass, but that's no reason to hole up in the barn and turn your phone off. Besides, there's nothing to worry about anyway. I have a plan to fix everything." Delia shielded her eyes with her hand as she drew up in front of the barn. "So are you coming down or not?"

"Be right there." Max turned to find Sam watching her, but she couldn't read what was in those dark eyes.

"What do you suppose her plan is?"

Max shrugged. "Chocolate first, and after that it's anyone's guess. But whatever she's got up her sleeve, I know I'm in good hands. Delia can fix just about anything."

And when it came to matters of the heart, no one knew

more than Delia. The woman dated more men in a year than Max would date in a lifetime. With her exotic good looks and easy manner, Delia turned heads wherever she went. While she referred to herself as "happily between men" at the moment, Max had no doubt that Mr. Right would find her one day too. Just as Peter would find Max—guaranteed.

She bent her head and hurried over to the stairs, letting the Tap Room and the ghosts take their proper places again, so she could take hers with Peter.

"So, between the plan and that love charm, I guess it's safe to say that Peter will be here in a matter of days," Sam said.

Max paused with her hand on the railing. "More like hours."

Sam nodded as he walked toward her. "I'll wish you luck then."

"Thanks."

He came to a stop about a foot away from her, that odd expression still on his face. "I'll see you around then."

"Yeah, see you around." She made herself start down the stairs, afraid that he might touch her again. And she might never leave.

"Max."

She stopped, looked back. And he smiled at last.

"For what it's worth, I had a crush on you too."

"Don't you ever worry me like that again," Delia said, wrapping Max in a hug before stepping back and looking her up and down. "You look good for a devastated woman." Her eyes narrowed. "Glowing, in fact."

"Country air," Max muttered, taking Delia's arm and herding her back toward the house, not wanting to think about glows or crushes, or what any of it meant. "What are you doing here anyway?"

"I quit last night, so I had a little time on my hands this morning."

Max pulled up short. Delia was Peter's right hand, the one who kept his appointments straight and his accounts current. He'd be lost without her, but worse, Delia would be in trouble without the job. "Why would you do that?"

"I had to."

"Why would you think that?"

Delia started walking again. "Because you're my best friend and what he's done is inexcusable. How could I go into the studio and pretend everything is fine when all I really want to do is smack him?" She bent to take another stone out of her shoe. "It would just be too hard."

"But what are you going to do about a job?"

Delia smiled and pitched the stone at the barn door. "The way I see it, once you two are back together again, the boss's wife might just help me get my job back."

Max laughed. There was always a satisfying logic to Delia's madness that never failed to cheer her. "How did you find out what happened, anyway?"

Delia dropped the shoe and shoved her foot into it. "The idiot left a message on my machine. 'Don't forget to send out the invoice for the Clayton job, and by the way, Max and I aren't getting married.' "

Max tried to swallow, quite sure there was no trace of a glow on her face anymore. "He said it just like that? We're not getting married?"

Delia gave her head a disgusted shake. "He said he needed to regroup, to think. The usual stuff men say when they bail out of a relationship. But you guys are good together, a real team. Peter needs you, and I'm sure that once he comes to his senses, he'll be here."

"And you have a plan to ensure this?"

"The Peter Plan," she said. "Not fully formulated, I grant you, but definitely in the works."

Max laughed and touched the little red charm as they walked. Even if Iona's magic couldn't bring the right man, at least it had brought her the right woman—guaranteed. "Thanks for coming," she said.

"No problem. But I know it's short notice, so if there's no room—"

"Eva doesn't have any guests for the next two weeks, so there's plenty of room. And if I know my mother, she'll be happy to meet you."

"If you're sure . . ." Delia said, stopping to turn in a circle as she gave the farm a quick once-over. "This is nice, by the way. Very Laura Ingalls. And the llamas are a nice touch. Exotic yet somehow homey."

"If you like that, you're going to love the wallabies," Max said, but Delia's attention was already fixed elsewhere.

"Hello, gorgeous," she said, peering over the top of her sunglasses as Sam stepped out of the barn. She sighed deeply, theatrically. "I finally know how they keep them down on the farm."

He gave Delia a nod and a grin, then he looked directly at Max and she watched that grin change; slowly, almost imperceptibly, until it was no more than a small, sexy curve of the lips—the same one she'd seen just before he told her about his crush.

"Who is that?" Delia asked.

"Sam," Max murmured as a wave of warmth rolled over her, holding her down and making it hard to breathe.

Delia eyed her curiously. "Someone special?"

"No," Max said, pulling herself back, remembering who she was, who he was and, more importantly, where they were. Schomberg was his home, not hers. And one kiss didn't change a thing. "He's just an old friend."

"I should have such friends," Delia muttered.

"You want a ride over to the house?" he called, motioning to Ben's pickup in front of the barn.

Delia opened her mouth, but Max jumped in first. "We'll be fine, thanks," she called back, pleased that her voice hadn't failed her. Now if her knees would just hold up—

"Speak for yourself," Delia said, pouting now as he crossed to the truck. "I've never been in a pickup with a cowboy."

"He's not a cowboy. He owns a Tap Room in town."

Delia pushed her sunglasses up on her nose. "And me without my tap shoes."

Max laughed and set a brisk pace to the house. They were just passing the paddock when Sam pulled up at the back door of the house, grabbed Delia's bags on his way to the stairs and carried them inside. He emerged a moment later with Ben in tow, still saying good-bye to Eva.

Max froze, then grabbed Delia's arm and yanked her back behind the fence.

Delia and the llamas stared at her. "What is wrong with you?"

"My mother." Max flattened her back against the slats and slid down to the ground. "I haven't told her about Peter. I know it's wrong and all that, but—"

Delia held up a hand. "Save it. I wouldn't tell my mother until I was sure it was really over either. If your mom is anything like mine, you'd have been in blind date hell within twenty-four hours." She hunkered down beside Max, pulled a small gold box from her purse and flipped open the lid, revealing Max's favorite truffles— dark chocolate and smooth as silk. She held the box out to Max. "Besides, you'd worry her for nothing. Once the Peter Plan is in place, he's as good as here anyway."

As good as here. Max settled back as she bit into the chocolate, figuring now was as good a time as any to tell Delia about the love charm.

* * *

"When the moon smiles, huh?" Delia licked the last of the chocolate from her fingers as they headed up the back steps to the house. "What exactly does that mean?"

"I'm not sure," Max admitted. "But she said I'd know it when I saw it."

"Well, it was a full moon last night, so we'll keep an eye out."

Max paused before opening the door. "Be honest; do you think I'm being ridiculous?"

"About the charm, no. About making me stand here in these shoes any longer, yes. Now open the door."

"Not a word about the charm either," Max whispered as they stepped inside.

"Got it," Delia said, then kicked off her shoes and sniffed the air. "Something smells good."

"Trout." Eva's voiced floated in from the kitchen. "Caught it fresh this morning." She came around the corner and smiled at Delia. Not the practiced hostess smile, Max realized, but the real thing—warm and welcoming. And as Max made the introductions, she wondered why she'd never noticed the difference before.

"You caught the fish?" Delia asked, already on her way to the stove.

Eva motioned out the window with her flipper. "In the river."

"I went fishing once," Delia said.

While they talked lures and bait, Max sat down at the counter and took a long look around, pleased to see that here at least, her mother had managed to let go of the past. Glass-front cupboards had replaced dark wooden ones, and avocado appliances had given way to stainless steel. The walls were whitewashed and the linoleum floor was now gleaming hardwood that carried through to the dining room, where a pine trestle table was set for two—

blue striped placemats, fresh flowers, sparkling crystal. One setting where Max had always sat, the other at what she assumed was still Eva's usual spot. She slid the stool back and stood up. A bit formal for lunch perhaps, but Peter would have appreciated the props.

"Max told me you were a good cook," Delia was saying, her nose over the skillet.

"She did?" Eva glanced over at Max while she nudged the sizzling fillets around. "Well, she used to put me to shame, I can tell you that. Always took first place at the fairs. Cakes, bread, didn't matter what she set her hand to. Hasn't she ever cooked for you?"

Max rolled her eyes. "How many times do I have to tell you—"

"I know, I know," Eva cut in. "Nobody eats what you cook." She pointed the flipper at Delia. "Well, take it from me, they used to. Max's buttermilk pie was a real favorite around here. Her father and Brian couldn't get enough of it."

Delia lifted her head. "Brian?"

"Her brother." Eva looked at Max, then went back to pushing the fillets around. "I'm surprised she never told you about him."

"It never came up." Max headed for the dining room. "I'll set another place."

Max opened the hutch and took out a bread plate, a dinner plate, a cup. The cup was a delicate robin's egg blue with a red rose painted on the bottom—a surprise for the cup holder when the tea was gone. The dinner plate was pink and white, while the bread plate was a soft leaf green. Everything in the buffet was like that, odd and old, a mixture of junk and antiques really, collected over the years at garage and rummage sales. While nothing matched, it all blended somehow, lending Eva's table a style and grace that no amount of planning could have achieved. And would be as out of place in Max's apartment as Peter would be in the barn.

She turned her back on the buffet and studied the table. Two places remained, and the only problem now was who Delia would be—Brian or Max's father.

"Max, I've got it," Delia whispered from the kitchen doorway. She checked over her shoulder as she stepped into the dining room. "It came to me as soon as Eva went out to pick herbs. I was asking her about the B&B business, what it's like, how she promotes herself, and she showed me this." Delia held out a copy of *Mountain Living* magazine. "You should see the ad in here for some bed-and-breakfast called Sweet Tree."

"Judith Anderson," Max muttered, setting the dishes down as she took the magazine.

The Sweet Tree ad was a quarter page, full color, obviously a professional job. The house looked majestic rather than merely large, the gardens careless and romantic instead of meticulously planned. Peacock Manor had more charm in the tiniest nook than Sweet Tree had in all five thousand square feet, but no one would ever know from the picture.

"Where's Eva's ad?" Max asked, searching the pages for more B&B advertising and wondering just how much competition her mother had these days. Not thinking about why it should matter to her, knowing only that it did.

"There isn't one," Delia said. "Which is where the plan comes in. Have a look at page one-eighty-one."

Max skimmed past the recipes, the features, the how-to's, searching for the right page. But it was the shot of Ben by a copper kettle that stopped her. And the picture of Sam beside a jukebox that held her.

She lifted the magazine higher, opened it wider, not sure at first if it was the same one. But how many Wurlitzer 2300S jukeboxes could there be in the world? She studied the picture closely. That had to be the same one that had sat in the O'Neal living room next to the television for as long as she could remember. She had to smile, remembering the cherry Cokes Sam's father would serve while hits from the fifties played back-to-back, and Brian and Gwen danced.

Delia peeked over her shoulder. "What are you looking at?"

"Nothing." Max quickly turned to page 181, pushing Sam and his jukebox aside as she scanned the copy.

The magazine was putting together a special bed-and-breakfast guide for the region. Ad space was limited but still available—and expensive.

Max laid the magazine down. "Eva has to be in there."

"She's planning on it, but with something small. You ask me, she needs something bigger, splashier." Delia lowered her voice as the back door opened and closed. "And that's when I thought, hey, Peter could do one for her for free."

Max laughed and closed the magazine. "He could ride the llama too, but neither is likely to happen."

"Don't bet on it." Delia grabbed her arm and hauled her into the living room. "All we have to do is come up with a layout that screams Southern charm, and I guarantee you Peter will be here to take the pictures."

Max went to the hutch for silver. "You need to eat. You are definitely light-headed."

"Max, this can work. Peter loves everything about the Old South, always has."

"This is the first I've heard."

"I'm telling you, the man has serious antebellum fantasies. Hoop skirts, rapiers, the whole bit. Deep down, I think he'd like to be Rhett Butler."

Max tried to picture it. Peter waltzing, kissing her hand. She stifled a giggle as she opened the silverware box. "How come you know so much about his fantasies?"

Delia shrugged. "I guess because I've worked for him for so long. You pull enough all-nighters with a person, you learn things you never wanted to know."

What Delia said made sense, but Max couldn't help thinking of the nights she and Peter had spent in the studio, working on layouts, going over setups, making love. And never once had he mentioned a hoop skirt. Then again, she'd never thought to ask.

"All right, say we did this layout. What makes you so sure he'd come up to shoot it?"

"Because we'll let him know we don't need him." Delia drew closer, her smile so wide, so wicked, Max knew they were onto something good. "We make sure he accidentally gets a copy of the layout, but we put the name of another photographer on it. Someone he knows. Someone he hates."

"Wilhelm?" Max asked.

"Bingo," Delia said.

Max knew that Willy Steiner and Peter had been rivals for years. Just the sight of his name on a photo credit made Peter testy for days. The idea of him working on the kind of layout he'd like for himself would last even longer.

"He'll definitely call," Max said, warming to the idea. "And if Peter doesn't come, I'll pay Willy myself. I can't let my mother get excited about this and have it fall through." She took a place setting from the box and closed the lid. "But how do we know we can get him on such short notice?"

"He owes me," Delia said. "I'll call him tomorrow."

Max tapped a fork on the table. "This could work."

"This will work."

"Did you tell Max about the travel guide?" Eva asked

as she came through the door with a tray of serving dishes.

"Just a moment ago," Delia said, taking the tray from her. "We both agree that you need something bigger, splashier." She shook her head when Eva started to protest. "It won't cost any more than a small ad because Max and I will put the whole thing together, and Peter will shoot it."

Eva looked at Max. "Peter?"

"He'll be happy to do it," Max said, holding back a grin.

"If you say so." Eva gestured for them all to sit down. "So, what kind of ad do you have in mind?"

"Something that screams 'Come on down.' " Delia pulled out a chair and curled one leg under her as she sat down. "After all, people choose B&Bs for a homey experience, right?"

"And the food," Eva added.

"Then let's hit them with both," Max said as she sat down. "But first we need a theme. What says *Virginia* to you?"

While Eva spoke of horses, mountains and Civil War heroes, Max was already picturing a breakfast table in the garden, a rebel soldier and a southern belle in the background, blurry and romantic. Fine china and crystal, and Peter setting up his camera under the tree.

She watched Delia nodding and talking a mile a minute, realizing she was in neither Brian's seat nor her father's. She was in Max's place, which suited Max fine, since she'd always liked the view from her father's chair. She just hadn't seen it for a while.

As she reached for the water jug, she spotted the *Mountain Living* magazine on the floor, facedown, Sam and the jukebox safely tucked inside, out of sight. Which was just as well, because with Iona's charm and Delia's plan, she and Peter could be back on track and chugging toward the life they had planned in no time at all. And wasn't that exactly what she wanted?

Yet for all of her certainty, she couldn't explain the flutter around her heart as she slipped the magazine under her chair.

SIX

Two-thirty, and the lunch hour rush was already over. While the Tap Room was usually slow on Wednesdays, the ripple effect of the *Mountain Living* article was starting to be felt. Passing tourists, summer regulars, even a few skeptics from the next town over had made a point of stopping in Schomberg to see the town's new addition, filling enough extra tables to keep the skeleton staff hopping for a few hours. But now it was the lull before dinner. The tables were clean, the ashtrays empty and every TV was tuned to Michael's favorite soap—a tradition Sam hadn't seen coming.

While Michael and Kerri, the waitress, argued plot points with Ben, Sam sat at a table near the back, trying to ignore the three of them as he sorted through a box of his father's old 45s.

He'd found the box when he cleaned out the basement of his parents' house over a year ago, but he hadn't opened it until last night. Now he was going through the records one by one, hoping to find at least a few that were salvageable for the jukebox.

Each title had its own memory, its own significance—the Motown songs his mother had loved, the Beach Boys his father preferred—but he was already more than half-way through the box and had found only two that might play: "Lollipop" and "Blue Moon." He couldn't help wondering if Maxine still knew all the words.

He glanced over as Kerri pounded a fist on the bar for the second time in ten minutes. "Michael, that's ridiculous," she said. "Everyone knows that if Ashley leaves Straun for Baker, she'll regret it forever."

Ben shook his head and sipped at his beer. "I still say she should go back to Lewis."

Michael dismissed him with a flick of the wrist. "Lewis is history. Get used to it. And if Ashley doesn't go with Baker, she'll always wonder what she missed."

Sam sighed and dropped yet another record in the box. It was like being at Cy's for morning coffee, only louder. And more ridiculous.

"The sad thing is that you really believe that," Kerri said, then wandered over and plunked herself down at Sam's table. "Do you need some help here?"

Kerri was twenty-one, a single mom and deadly in a Schomberg Tap Room T-shirt. She was Tracy's oldest daughter, and while she still had her hair done at her mother's beauty parlor now and then, she had no intention of taking over the family business. Kerri dreamed of opening a pub of her own one day—an offshoot of the Tap Room, if Sam was willing.

To prove she was serious, she arrived early, stayed late and was always willing to do more. Sam only hoped the HELP WANTED sign in the window would bring in a dozen more like her.

"I appreciate the offer, but you've been here long enough." He slipped the record carefully into its paper sleeve and got to his feet. "Why don't you collect that little boy of yours and go on home? We'll be fine until the night crew gets here."

"If you're sure," she said, already heading for the door. "By the way, any of you guys playing ball Friday night?"

Michael folded his arms. "Only if I get to pitch."

"So we won't be seeing you then," Ben said, and deftly dodged the coaster Michael flipped at him.

Kerri paused on the top step and turned to Sam. "How about you? We could use a good first baseman again."

Sam was tempted. It was only a town league with loosely defined teams and a lineup that changed from week to week depending on who was available. But the games were fast and fun, and the players usually ended up back at the bar once it got too dark to see the ball.

Of course, if lunch that day had marked the beginning of a trend, the night crew could be in real trouble on Friday night. And Sam couldn't afford to have new customers leave disappointed.

He gathered up the two 45s and got to his feet. "I'd love to, Kerri, but until we get more staff, I have to be here."

"Well, I don't," Michael said, breezing past Kerri and down the stairs. "Think I'll go toss a ball around. Get ready for my turn on the pitcher's mound."

"There must be someone else," Kerri whispered, and Ben was on his feet, heading for the back door, mumbling something about spreading the word.

Sam crossed the floor and set the records on a table beside the jukebox. "Is Michael's pitching really that bad?"

"Not if you're playing cricket. But speaking of pitchers, I hear you've seen Maxine a few times."

He shrugged and bent down to plug in the machine. "Once or twice."

"She was always so good with a ball. Do you think she'd like to play?"

"You'd have to ask her."

"I could, I suppose. But then I was just the kid she used to baby-sit. Not really a pal. Not like you—"

"Forget it," Sam said, shoving the jukebox back against the wall harder than he'd meant to, making the carousel tremble and Kerri's eyebrows raise. "Kerri, listen," he said more gently. "I won't be talking to her any time soon, so if you want her to play, you'll have to call her."

"It was just a thought." Kerri turned and went down the stairs. "Well, tell her 'hi' if you do see her again."

"There is absolutely no chance of that," Sam muttered, then pulled himself a beer and carried it outside.

He sank down and took a long sip, thinking about the patio tables he'd ordered, where he'd put them on the sidewalk once the approval was final and how much he'd love to see Max pitch just one game before she left. But he wouldn't be the one to ask.

He hadn't seen her since that morning in the barn and had no intention of changing things now. It wasn't as though she needed him around anyway. Not with Delia there, and a plan—and the love charm, of course. For all the good it would do her.

After all, it wasn't love that she was after, was it? Just common goals, shared interests and a marriage where she could hide out for the rest of her life; telling herself it was what she wanted, when the truth had been right there in her kiss. A kiss that had never happened, according to Max, yet still lingered on his lips and in his mind—hot, sweet and filled with longing. A constant reminder of all that she was hiding from and why.

He raised the glass, taking another long drink. And now that he knew, what was he supposed to do? Rant? Rave? Hold her down until she realized she couldn't marry Peter simply because she was afraid to care too deeply, to want too strongly—to love someone as much as Brian had loved Gwen.

He sighed and leaned back against the door frame, knowing he couldn't do any of those things. He'd given his word to support her decisions, to be her friend. So he'd keep up the pretense for her at Cy's, send a gift when the time came and stay away from Peacock Manor.

Because if he saw her, he'd be sure to disappoint her again.

He wasn't sure what made him sit up, or what made him turn his head. There'd been no noise, nothing glimpsed from the corner of his eye. Just a sense, a tug, that drew him around in time to see a white sedan at the corner, by the hardware store. The car was ordinary by any standard, nothing that set it apart from any other that might pass through town. But as it turned right and headed the other way along Center Street, Sam was positive he'd seen it before. In the driveway at Eva's the night Max arrived.

Downtown Schomberg was built on a hill, and since the pub sat at the crest, Sam had an unsurpassed view of the road as it headed down to the river, and the old metal bridge at the bottom. A few old boys were there, a line in the water and time on their hands, and traffic was light, making it easy for Sam to follow the sedan's progress down the hill.

He hadn't seen the driver clearly and knew it could well be her friend Delia or even Eva at the wheel. But when the car started to slow halfway down the hill, Sam knew without a doubt that Max was behind the wheel. And she still couldn't bring herself to go over the bridge.

The van behind her hit the brakes and the driver leaned on the horn. But the white sedan slowed even more until it was barely crawling, prompting another blast from the van and a flash of brake lights from the sports car behind.

The old boys were watching the sedan now, waving the driver forward, and a group of kids had come up from the river to see what was going on. Sam set his glass down and took a few steps into the street, when suddenly the car pulled off onto the shoulder, made a U-turn and headed back the way it had come.

As the sedan climbed the hill, Sam wondered if she'd intended to go to the bridge at all. Or if she'd simply found herself there after a wrong turn—a tourist now in the place she used to call home.

But when she slowed at the first corner, Sam was sure it was no mistake. She couldn't have forgotten that the only things down that lane were Boyd's Plumbing, St. Luke's Church and the cemetery. But if she still couldn't cross the bridge, what made her think she could go in there? Especially on her own.

He took a few steps into the road, watching her signal light come on, hoping she'd change her mind. Knowing it would be best if he stayed away, and feeling in his pockets for his keys when she started into the turn.

He glanced over his shoulder at the empty pub, then back at the sedan. "Damn," he muttered, then locked the front door and trotted across the road to his truck. Ben would be back soon to open up again. And if he wasn't?

He swung open the door and hopped into the cab. He could live with a few unhappy customers.

With hands still trembling and damp, Max gripped the wrought-iron gate and gave it a shake. Locked, she realized, finally noticing the sign to the right—SCHOMBERG CEMETERY—CLOSED WEDNESDAYS.

A ripple of laughter, as unseemly as it was uncontrollable, bubbled up and threatened to spill over. So she lowered her head and pinched her lips together. After all, what would folks think if they heard that Maxine Henley had been laughing outside the cemetery?

Then again, she'd already made a pretty good spectacle of herself out there on the road. A grown woman on a simple errand—raspberries or strawberries, she wished she could remember which—suddenly frozen behind the wheel. Aware of the horns behind her, the faces in front of her, but unable to go any farther. Unable to cross the bridge where her brother had died.

So she let the laughter come, a little too loud perhaps, and definitely too high, but it was better than tears. And the wave of sweet relief that came with it was more than she'd hoped for, so she rode it all the way back to her car.

CLOSED WEDNESDAYS. She shook her head as she opened the door. Who knew?

Tossing her purse into the passenger seat, Max glanced over at the little white church, fairly sure it was empty on a Wednesday afternoon, then checked on Boyd's Plumbing across the road. She couldn't see anyone at the window, only reflections of trees and overhead wires in the glass. But she smiled and waved anyway, just in case. That way no one could say she was rude. Just crazy.

Couldn't cross the bridge. Couldn't go in the cemetery. She could hear them at Cy's now: That's just how she was after Brian died, remember? Just sitting outside the cemetery, day after day, but never once going inside.

Max looked back at the wrought-iron gate as the buoyancy deserted her, leaving her stranded there by her car, remembering now that the cemetery had always been closed on Wednesday. And somewhere deep inside, she must have known.

"But I would have done it this time," she whispered.

Then prove it.

She could almost hear Brian's voice, teasing her, daring her. But wasn't that how the fiasco on the bridge had started in the first place? Trying to prove to herself that she didn't have to take a back road. That she could use the main routes just like anyone else. And she'd been right—until she was halfway down the hill and found she couldn't breathe.

Her gaze drifted past the gate to the carefully tended flowers, the worn paths, the oak trees that were older than most people in the town. And the stones, of course—a haphazard blend of old and new, sagging and straight, not a sign of landscaping or memorial planning anywhere. Just a simple country cemetery where family names often spanned four generations or more, and the Henleys had a spot all to themselves, six rows back and to the right. Just sitting there behind a locked gate and a chain-link fence—the easiest kind to climb.

Climb?

She stepped away from the car, her eyes moving slowly along the width of the fence. She couldn't do it, of course. The very idea was absurd. What if she fell, broke a leg or worse. She could be laid up for weeks, unable to work. And how would she explain the cast to Peter? You see, honey, I was climbing this fence . . .

She screwed up her nose. Peter would never understand. While she still hadn't heard from him, she had every confidence that his cold feet would warm up any day now. Especially if Delia was right about his passion for the Old South.

They'd been working on the layout for the Peter Plan for days and had come up with an ad that was so blatantly antebellum, it made Scarlett look like a Yankee. But for all that Max believed the ad itself would be good for Peacock Manor, she couldn't help wondering what else Peter had kept from her. A love of ancient ruins perhaps? A stash of sci-fi comics he'd had since he was a kid? Did he even like sci-fi? And why didn't she know?

She waved a hand, as if brushing away cobwebs. What did it matter anyway? There would be plenty of time to fill in the blanks later. A lifetime, in fact. And based on everything she *did* know about him, Max was fairly sure that he would never understand why she climbed a fence. That sort of thing was risky, dangerous—downright irresponsible.

And yet . . .

She pursed her lips, her gaze drawn back to the fence. There were no barbs. No electric wires. The whole thing

couldn't have been more than six feet high. It was like
an open invitation to climbers. Not that she was one. Not
anymore, at least.

And it would definitely be trespassing. Possibly break
and enter.

A smile eased across her face. Break and enter at the
cemetery. Brian would love it.

Without stopping to think, to analyze, she grabbed her
purse and slammed the car door. This time, she was going
in. And Peter would never have to know.

She chose a spot about six feet from the gate and gave
the mesh a shake, finding it a little sloppy. Still, she put
a foot into one of the diamonds, confident that anyone
watching would call for help if the fence gave out. Then
she gripped the wires, shifted her weight and remembered she was wearing a dress—baby blue, tiny straps,
short. She looked down. Very short.

She cast a quick glance at Boyd's. Maybe she should
go home and change first. At least keep the state of her
underwear out of the discussion at Cy's.

But then she'd have to make excuses about why she
was going out and where she was headed; maybe ending
up with passengers on the return trip. And how could
she even make that return trip when Eva would know
that the cemetery was closed? Wait a day, her mother
would say, and how could Max possibly argue?

She turned back to the headstones and flowers. She
didn't want to wait. Not a day, not an hour. And as far
as Cy's was concerned, she'd already given them the
Bridge and the Gate . . .

She took off her purse and tossed it over the fence.
Might as well add the Climb.

The going was slow, her sandals being designed more
for walking than climbing. But as she threw that first leg
over the top rail, she noted with considerable pride that
her palms were dry and her heart pounding only with

exertion—right up until she spotted Sam strolling toward her, his hands in his pockets and a smile on his face.

Why him? she wondered, holding the rail tighter, pressing her toes into the mesh harder and doing her best to ignore the sudden warmth curling deep inside.

He stopped about a foot back from the fence, head tilted to one side, that smile still on his lips. "A lady would have worn jeans."

"And a gentleman wouldn't look."

He laughed and had the grace to turn his back while she swung her other leg up and over. "What are you doing here anyway?" she asked as she found a new toehold.

"Same as you, I guess. Just out for a walk and thought, hey, what a nice day for the cemetery." He checked her progress with a quick glance over his shoulder, then pulled a key from his pocket and wandered over to the gate. "So here I am," he said, then inserted the key in the lock. The gate swung open before him.

Max could only stare as he stepped through. "Where did you get that?"

He held up the key. "This?" He tucked it into his shirt pocket, then bent down to pick up her purse. "Barry over at Boyd's thought I could use it."

"Figures," she muttered and started down again, mustering her haughtiest tone when he came to stand beneath her. "Do you mind?"

"Not at all," he said, and reached up, wrapping his hands around her waist and swinging her down easily. Her back was to him when he set her on the ground, and he held on a moment longer, leaning in close to whisper in her ear. "So . . . do you come here often?"

"Give it up, O'Neal," she said, fighting a smile as she turned and laid claim to her purse. But all of her resolve melted when she looked up into those dark, laughing eyes. Here she'd spent the last four days trying not to think about him, assuring herself that life was easier without him, and in the space of a minute realized just how much she'd missed him. Missed his smile, his laughter and, God help her, his kiss.

Her gaze drifted lower, fixing on that wonderful mouth. Which really was too bad, since the kiss was a nonissue. Never happened, she reminded herself, and forced her eyes away.

"So, how long ago did Barry call to tell you I was here?" she asked and started to raise a hand to wave at unseen faces and prying eyes.

But Sam grabbed her wrist, his smile dimming as he stopped her. "No one had to call, Max. I saw you at the bridge."

She shook him off, embarrassed. "Quite a show, wasn't it? I'll bet Cy and his crew took notes." She swung her purse over her shoulder and raised her chin. "Tell you what, next time you're at the Deli, do me a favor. Let them know that Maxine is just fine, thank you, and they can all go to hell."

He caught her shoulder as she turned, making her stay, making her face him. "No one doubts that you're perfectly fine. They just worry about you. I worry about you."

He moved closer, and she laid a hand on his chest, trying to ignore the warmth of his skin and the beat of his heart. And wanting more than anything to pull him to her even as she pushed him away. "I don't need you to worry about me."

"I can't help myself." He lifted a hand and brushed the hair back from her face. "It's just something friends do."

She turned her back on the tenderness in his eyes, refusing to see anything beyond friendship, yet all the while thinking of worn-out crushes and ill-timed kisses. And what might have been if she'd looked him up years ago, when he was still in New York setting Wall Street on its ear.

Shoving the traitorous past aside, she focused on the present—the markers, the flowers, the here-and-now that she'd been in such a hurry for on the other side of the fence. And wondering when it was that she'd lost her nerve.

"Max," he said, and she held up a hand.

"I know what you're going to say, but this is something I have to do."

"Fine. But you don't have to do it alone." He offered his arm. "What'll it be? Once around, or shall we dally?"

She looked up, torn between heart and head. Wanting nothing more than to curl her fingers around his arm and let him lead, let him take care of her, but too afraid that it would only make it that much harder to stand on her own again when the moment was over.

"Just put the key by the gate," she said and took a step away. "I'll lock up when I leave."

He made no move to stop her this time and she wasn't ready for the moment of panic that gripped her heart and stilled her feet. But then she was moving forward again, determined to face this, and put Schomberg behind her once and for all.

She kept going, moving into the shade of the oak trees on grass worn down to dusty paths. Past the McDermotts who owned the farm a few miles west of Peacock Manor, and the Schmidts who'd started the planing mill nearly a hundred years ago. She glanced over at the O'Neals in the corner but turned left where the gray-green statue of Gabriel announced the final resting place of Schomberg's one and only millionaire—Jonas B. Warren, whose family had left town in disgrace over fifty years ago. The details escaped Max at the moment, but there was no doubt someone in town who could fill her in at any time.

She paused a moment, admiring the Williamses' bright

orange roses, and knowing that just one row over were the white and yellow daisies Eva had planted thirteen years ago for Brian.

Max raised her head, seeing the modest white markers of great-grandparents she'd never known; the larger shared pillar of the grandfather and grandmother she still missed. Noticing too the red marble with the inscription PUT THE COFFEE ON, I'LL BE RIGHT BACK—the words her father had said every morning as he went out the door. And finally allowing herself to face the black granite that was newer than all of them. The one that was Brian's.

Sam stayed by the gate, watching her. Remembering how she'd looked up on top of that fence not ten minutes ago—beautiful, triumphant and showing enough thigh to make his mouth go dry just thinking about it.

But now everything had changed. Now she looked so tiny, so vulnerable. And so goddamned brave he wanted to shake her. Why she thought she had to face this on her own was beyond him. But he made himself wait while she stepped over the little hedge that separated the Henleys from the Williamses. Hung back as she read the words on the granite marker, and even when she knelt down, pinching back the spent blooms on the daisies at the base of the stone. He even lasted until she got to her feet and turned her back. But when she put her hands over her face and cried, he was through with waiting.

She glanced up as he approached, then quickly bent her head again, wiping her eyes with one hand while she searched her purse for a tissue with the other. "Don't you have somewhere to be?"

"Not that I can think of," he said and kept his eyes on the stones, pretending not to notice while she sniffed and swiped at her tears.

"Liar," she said, without a hint of reproach in her tone. Then sighed and started to walk away. "But it's all yours at any rate. I never know what to do in these places anymore."

"Why? What did you used to do?"

She paused and glanced over at the stones. "When I was little I used to talk to them. We'd come every Friday night. Eva would tend the flowers, Brian would climb the trees in the churchyard and I'd sit right over there, talking a blue streak."

Sam smiled, picturing it. "What did you say?"

She gave a short, self-conscious laugh as she came back. "Lots of things. Jokes, usually, for my grandad. He loved knock-knocks. Then I'd bring my grandma up to date on what I was doing in school, and make sure my father knew just how bad Brian had been."

"I'm sure he loved hearing that."

"Not as much as I loved telling it." Sam saw the wonder in her eyes as a tiny smile curved her lips, and for a moment he glimpsed the girl she had been. "The strange thing is that I honestly believed that they heard me. Every word."

"And now?"

"Now?" She shrugged, the magic drifting away on a sigh that was all too adult. "Now I know better."

Sam nodded and looked down at the daisies. "I had a client once. An old guy from Japan. We got along well, and we'd often have a drink after our meetings, sometimes dinner. Then one day he invited me to have tea with his wife." He paused and glanced over at Max. "Only I didn't realize his wife was dead until he pulled into a cemetery."

"Seems rude," she said.

"I think it was more like an oversight," Sam said, and turned back to the daisies. "My client didn't say a word when we arrived, just took a basket from the trunk and carried it up a hill to a headstone under a tree. I stood there, feeling awkward as hell, while he spread a cloth on the grass, set out three teacups, a plate of biscuits and motioned me to sit. He said we were having tea with the spirits. Then he filled the cups, introduced me to his wife and proceeded to tell her all about his day."

"I don't believe you," she said, arms folded and eyes wary, obviously wondering where he was heading.

Sam laughed and bent to pluck one of the daisies. "Neither did anyone else who was there. Cars would slow down as they passed. And I remember the grounds-keeper kept circling—" Sam shook his head and walked over to where she stood. "The point is that we stayed there all afternoon, drinking tea and eating cookies. And by the time we left, I felt like I knew his wife."

"Sounds lovely, but you know what they say: East is east, and west is west."

"Too true," Sam said. "Which is why I'll have to change it slightly when I do it for Brian. I'll have to make it 'Happy Hour with the spirits.' "

He watched her eyes widen in disbelief. "You mean like a six-pack and a bag of nuts?"

"I was thinking chips myself, but nuts could work." He reached over, tucking the flower into her hair. "So, are you up for it?"

"I don't know," she said, her fingertips feeling for the daisy, ruffling the petals. Then she glanced over at the granite marker. "What do you think, Brian? You up for Happy Hour?" She looked back at Sam, the wonder returning to her smile. "He says he'd love it."

"Then it's settled." Sam stepped over the hedge to the path. "We'll hit the Kwik Way and be back in time for Happy Hour."

"I'd rather wait here."

"Oh, no," he said, laughing. "This is a joint effort. I'll get the beer, but you are definitely in charge of the nuts."

"I can't." She stood back, shaking her head. "Not today at least."

He watched her smile fade, saw her eyes cloud. But it wasn't until he saw her look over at Boyd's that Sam understood. She was thinking of the bridge, the key and Cy's.

"Max, come with me," he said softly. "It won't be as bad as you imagine. People are curious, yes, but only because they haven't seen you in years. Besides, what's the worst that can happen? A few heads turn? A few tongues wag—"

"A Judith Anderson clone holds me hostage in frozen foods."

"That could be bad. But it's not like you'll be there alone." He drew another step closer and held out a hand. "You and me at the Kwik Way. What do you say?"

"You and me," Max murmured, taking his hand and holding on tight.

SEVEN

Max handed the clerk at the Kwik Way a ten dollar bill and tried not to watch while he rang up the can of mixed nuts. She'd picked the large size, of course. Honey roasted and 25 percent cashews—the kind Brian always ate. But fortunately the clerk was young and wouldn't know that.

In fact, if her guess was right, the boy had no idea who she was either. It didn't mean that he hadn't heard all of the old stories, or the new installments. But at least he couldn't put her face to the name, so she took comfort in her anonymity and only wished that he would hurry.

She drummed her fingers on the counter while the young man flipped through a price list, searching, searching, only to turn back to the beginning and start all over again. Max sighed and glanced over to where Sam was checking out the latest videos, knowing it was just a fluke that they were the only customers in the store. And simply a matter of time before another car pulled into the lot.

"Hey, Gisella," the clerk hollered, waving the can above his head. "How much for these nuts?"

Max stared at the can as it moved back and forth, wondering if this wasn't a sign. A chance to say, "Forget it," and run, putting some much-needed distance between herself and Center Street. And definitely Sam O'Neal.

She watched him continue along the video aisle with the six-pack he'd already paid for, pausing here and there, picking up titles, putting them back; completely at home in the Schomberg Kwik Way. At ease with who he was and what he was doing, while she had never felt more awkward or self-conscious in her life—and all because she'd listened to Sam.

If she'd only thought it through a little more, only said no to the whole ridiculous idea of having a beer with Brian, she'd be lounging on the porch at Peacock Manor with a glass of iced tea, instead of checking the Kwik Way parking lot every few minutes, resisting the urge to duck whenever a car drove by. But that was the whole problem, wasn't it—the fact that she hadn't thought? She'd simply reacted, going on impulse and heart. And the look in Sam's eyes.

"Those are six fifty," the unseen Gisella called from the back, and Max's escape disappeared into the till with her money. The nuts were hers now. Undeniable proof that the man was a bad influence. And that Peter had better get there soon.

She heard the door open behind her and stiffened, waiting, wishing again that she'd just driven home when she had the chance. But the voices were those of teenagers, all talking at the same time. Yet oddly enough, not one of them was saying, "Oh look, there's Maxine Henley. Let's go ask her a million questions about her wedding."

The group went by to the magazines, not giving her so much as a first, let alone a second, look. Max watched them, more than a little humbled by her own imagination. And yes, she had to admit it at last, her own vanity. She glanced out the front window again, wondering if perhaps Sam was right.

"I told you everything would be fine," he whispered as he came up beside her.

She glanced up at him. Fine? When he was standing

so close that she could smell the sun on his skin? And looking straight into her eyes that way? And somehow knowing her better than she knew herself. Fine? She almost smiled. He couldn't have been more wrong if he tried.

She glanced away, lifting a hand to her chest and pretending to brush away lint but really feeling for the charm, and suspecting that he knew that too.

"Miss?"

Max blinked and saw the clerk looking at her, with only mild curiosity. "Your change," he said, laying some bills and coins into her palm while pushing the can of nuts across the counter. "Have a nice day."

"I'd rather have a bag," Max said.

"This will do," Sam said, reaching past her to pick up the nuts.

"Thank you for shopping the Kwik Way," the clerk called after them. "Nice daisy, by the way."

"Daisy?" She glared at Sam as she plucked the flower from her hair and dropped it into the trash on the way to the door. "Why didn't you remind me?"

"Because I liked it." He checked the clock as held the door open. "Come on, it's getting late."

"Late? It's barely four o'clock." And then she remembered the Tap Room, the pub. *Good food and drink in Schomberg.* He should probably be working, and yet he was there with her. Had been for hours. So who had been watching the shop?

She followed him across the parking lot to where their cars were parked. "We can do this another time. You should get back to the Tap Room now."

"It can wait a while yet." He set the beer in the back of the truck and opened the passenger door. "Get in. We'll drive back together. Unless, of course, you'd like to see the pub first."

Max wavered, one foot in the truck and the other on

the ground. This was what he did to her, she realized. Snuck up on her, kept her off balance. Yet, even though she knew she should wait until both feet were planted firmly before answering, she was already turning, picking out the front window of the Tap Room from the other shops on the street. "You mean right now?"

He shrugged. "Only makes sense, since you're already here."

He had a point, which was too bad. Because she'd promised herself that she wouldn't go to Schomberg's newest addition without Peter. Then again, Peter might prefer something a little more upscale, and she'd never have another chance. It wasn't as though she'd made a special trip, and so far she hadn't run into anyone she knew. Her lips pursed as she focused on the closer shops. Of course, it was impossible to tell who was watching. Or, on the other hand, who wasn't.

She brought her foot down, planted it beside the other, but it didn't help her decide. "It's almost the dinner hour. You'll be busy."

He laughed. "I wish."

The laughter sounded so real that someone else might have missed the slight edge or the shift in his stance. But Max caught both, and it gave her an odd jolt of pleasure to know that he couldn't hide from her either.

A million questions begged to be asked, but the moment was lost when he swung an arm over her shoulder, drawing her away from the truck. "Come on, I'll buy you a real beer, and you can tell Brian all about it while he makes do with the bottled stuff."

She held back. "I should go home. Peter might—"

And suddenly Sam was standing directly in front of her, an arm resting on each of her shoulders as he backed her up against the truck. She had no time to think, to react, before he was bending to her, leaning down until his nose was level with hers. His eyes lowered to her lips and she could only stare, even as her breasts warmed and her fingers clenched, convinced that he was going to kiss her again, right there in the Kwik Way parking lot—until he smiled.

"Relax, Max," he whispered. "It's only a beer."

"And you're buying." She gave him a shove and walked ahead, hearing him laugh and smiling herself.

Sam would never be predictable, would never be safe. And wasn't that part of the appeal? Part of the crush, the madness, the reason her heart still beat too fast all these years later. But it wasn't what she wanted. Not anymore. And she told herself that over and over as they walked up the hill.

There were people on the street—a woman in front of the post office, a man coming out of the barbershop, two kids and a mom buying ice cream—but the coast was clear all the way to the Tap Room. Max kept going, head down and moving fast, glancing in the shop window as they passed the Looking Glass but turning her face away as she passed Cy's, feeling more exposed than she'd expected, despite the fact that Sam was there beside her.

The door to the Tap Room stood open, and he went up the stairs ahead of her. But Max couldn't resist just one quick look. She paused at the top and spun around just in time to catch three faces peering over the café curtains at Cy's. She didn't recognize any of them, but judging by the speed at which they dropped, Max assumed they knew exactly who she was.

As befitted a local celebrity, she swung both arms up over her head, hoping at least one of the faces caught her pose before she swept into the Tap Room.

"Ben does that routine better," Sam said.

"I didn't have time to practice." She dropped her arms as she cast a quick glance around the empty pub. Then she dropped her purse on the closest table, visibly relaxing as she wandered, eyes wide, taking in everything at once: the bar, the television screens—now mercifully showing a wrestling match—and finally the copper kettles behind the glass walls of the brewery.

"Have a seat," he called and headed out to the kitchen to find out who had opened up the pub again. "I'll be right back."

"Take your time. I'll be fine," she called. "I like your place, by the way." He glanced back in time to see her standing on her toes for a better look at the kettles. "Much classier than I imagined."

"I'm a classy guy," he said, stopping to watch but keeping the conversation light, letting the relationship be what it was; knowing that as long as he stayed in Schomberg, there wasn't a chance in hell that it would ever be anything else.

"The wrestling match proves it." She flashed him a smile as she crossed to the wooden screen on the far side of the pub. "What's behind here?" she asked, already poking her head around to see.

"A dining room eventually. Right now it's not much."

"Just needs a little imagination."

And several hundred thousand dollars, Sam thought, but kept it to himself.

She smiled and walked over to the jukebox. "I was surprised when I saw the jukebox in the *Mountain Living* magazine. I'd assumed it was gone a long time ago." She ran a hand along the glass dome. "Does it work?"

"It better," he said, noticing now that the lights had failed to come on. He'd spent six months rebuilding the damn thing—new chrome, new glass, new tubes—and he hoped he hadn't jarred something when he moved it down the stairs last night. "Flick the switch and see what happens."

She reached around, obviously remembering exactly how it was done. Of course, she'd done it almost as many times as he had. Why would he think she'd forget?

He heard the familiar click of the toggle as she switched the machine off, then the satisfying clunk as the amplifier came back on. He waited, watching the fluorescent tubes flicker, and smiling when they came to life, filling the dome with bright white light and spilling a rainbow of color down the front of the machine.

Max looked over at him, delighted. "Do you have any records?"

"On the table." He pointed to the table behind her and started for the kitchen again. "There're only two, but I think they'll play."

He slowed when he saw Ben scowling at the bulletin board by the back door. "I can explain—"

"Explain this," Ben said, cutting him off as snatched a piece of paper off the board. "Since when do we serve 'burned orange chipotle sauce and charred baby bok choy'?" He slapped the page down on the counter in front of Sam. "And what's for dessert? Charcoaled chocolate cake?" Ben shook his head as he backed away. "What's the man thinking, anyway?"

"Sounds like tapas."

Both men looked over as Max came into the kitchen, but Ben was the first to speak. "What's a goddamned tapas? And why does he have to burn it?"

"Tapas are dishes served in small portions, like appetizers. And the charring is just a method of preparation." She gave Ben an apologetic smile. "It's very big on the West Coast."

"And are we on the coast?" he snapped, still scowling as he went back out to the bar.

Max stared after him. "I don't think I've ever seen him that mad."

"Stick around," Sam said, posting the sheet back on the board. "He hasn't seen Michael's idea for goat cheese biscuits yet."

"I gather Michael is your chef."

"Best in the county. That was very impressive, by the way." He folded his arms and leaned back against the counter. "You still know a lot about food."

She shrugged. "Peter and I do a lot of cookbooks, so I have to stay current." She strolled over to the stove, where pots of soups and sauces sat waiting to be reheated. She put a hand on one of the lids. "May I?"

"Be my guest."

She lifted the cover and peeked inside. "Carrot soup. Interesting choice."

"Michael's specials are nothing if not interesting. It's just too bad his vision and Ben's don't match."

She nodded as she leaned over the pot. "Creative expression in the kitchen running headlong into the traditional views of the owners. Happens all the time in this business."

Sam had no idea how often it happened, but he was definitely fascinated by the way she closed her eyes, leaned in close to the pot and inhaled deeply, as though it was a fine perfume instead of soup.

"That's why I always swore I would never work in any restaurant but my own." Her eyes popped open. "Can I taste this?"

Sam grabbed a spoon from a tray and handed it to her. "That's right, I remember now. You were going to open a place on the river. You even had a name for it."

"The Blue Ridge Café," she said with a laugh. "I thought it sounded so elegant. But that was before I knew how much work a restaurant would be." She took a bit of soup on the spoon, closed her eyes again and tasted. And for the first time in his life, Sam was jealous of a spoon.

"This is delicious." She set the lid back on the pot and carried the spoon to the sink. "Hot, spicy, but not exactly homespun." She stood with her hands on her hips while she considered the rest of the pots on the stove.

"And to be honest, I agree with Ben. People don't come to the mountains looking for California fusion."

"What are they looking for?"

"Tradition with a twist. Meatloaf without the fat. Like Mom made, only better." She turned to him again. "If you like, I can drop off a few trade magazines. Let Michael see for himself that comfort food is making a comeback."

"Is that what you'd serve if you had your own place? Comfort food?"

"If I had a place, the food wouldn't just be comfortable, it would be downright cozy. And the competition would be dead in a week."

"Nice to see you haven't lost that down-home killer instinct."

She grinned as they walked back to the bar. "Just be glad I won't be opening up next door."

"Where will you be opening?"

She shot him a curious look as she climbed onto a stool. "Nowhere. Why?"

"No reason." He took two glasses from the shelf and pulled a round of Ben's stout. "What does Peter think of your restaurant idea?"

She shrugged and grabbed a pretzel from the bowl. "I don't think he knows. We've never talked about it. I decided a long time ago that restaurants are too risky." She took a bite and pointed the rest of the pretzel at him. "Food styling, on the other hand, pays well, and I don't have to worry about how it tastes, just how it looks. I cook it, Peter shoots it and I throw it away." She reached for the glass as Sam slid it toward her. "Nothing could be easier."

"Or safer. Or drier." He held on to the glass until she looked up at him, forgetting how useless it was to argue. "Just like everything else in your life."

She released the glass and sat back. "Don't start."

He wavered, giving serious thought to backing down, to letting it go. But he couldn't. Not after he'd seen her in his kitchen, eyes closed, savoring that single spoonful of soup. She'd been lost for a moment, excited by the aroma, the texture, the taste, just as she'd always been when she cooked, and the Blue Ridge Café had been as real in her mind as it was now, only she wouldn't admit it anymore.

Bit by bit, she was losing herself. Shedding everything she'd been to create someone new. Someone who took the safe road, steering clear of all the highs and lows in life and in love. He studied her, wondering if Peter knew she didn't love him. Or if he loved her. Or if the man had any idea not only of what he was losing, but what he'd never had.

"I'm not starting anything, Max," he said, sliding the beer toward her again. "It was just an observation." He reached under the bar for a couple of coasters and slipped one under her glass. "By the way, there's a baseball game on Friday night. Just local talent, nothing formal. They could use a pitcher." He set his own glass down across from hers. "You interested?"

She kept her eyes down. "I'd like to, but—"

"But you can't." He paused. "I didn't think so." Sliding his beer to the side, he leaned his elbows on the bar, studying her as she took a small sip. "Does Peter know you were the star pitcher?"

"It never came up."

"Does he even know that you played ball? Or that you took home blue ribbons from the county fair? Or tried to save your brother's life? Does he know any of that?"

"No. Are you satisfied now?" She set the beer down and swiveled the stool. "I should be going."

He laid a hand on hers, not intending to hold her, just needing her to look at him once more before she left. "You told me before that when you're with Peter, nothing of Schomberg exists. Not baseball, not the café, not even your brother. So tell me now how that happens, Max. Tell me how you can work with a man, sleep with him, even be prepared to marry him, but your past, what you were and who you loved, never once comes up in conversation, because I'll be damned if I understand."

"It's how I want it, all right?" She jerked her hand away and slid off the stool. "I spent a long time trying to make sense of what happened here. Trying to figure out what went wrong, and how my brother came to be such a fool." She crossed to the window and stood with her back to Sam. "Even after I left, I kept thinking, wondering, driving myself crazy, until I met Peter. He wasn't interested in where I'd been or what I'd done, only what I was going to do next. I found it refreshing and threw myself into the future instead of dwelling on the past. I put the whole thing behind me and went on as though my life started the day I moved to New York."

"But it didn't work, did it?"

"It did until I came back here. Which is why I can't wait to get away again." She turned and walked to the table where her purse lay. "But I don't imagine you can understand that either."

He walked around the bar, putting himself between her and the door, afraid he'd lose her forever if she left now. "Why would you think that?"

"Because you're the home boy now, aren't you? The conquering hero returned. And if you think that's not hard for me to figure out, think again."

"There's no need. I know it surprised the hell out of me when I decided to stay. I can only imagine what you must think."

"Can you?" She looked up at him, all the betrayal he'd seen that first night right there in her eyes again. "Then tell me, Sam, what was the lure, the siren song that you just couldn't resist?"

"There was no lure," he said and walked over to the jukebox, sure for the moment, at least, that she wouldn't run. "Just an empty house that needed cleaning out after my father died."

He watched her shoulders sag. "Oh, Sam, I'm so sorry—"

"Don't be. It was over a year ago. You had no way of knowing."

"But today, in the cemetery . . ."

"I waved as I walked by." He smiled. "They always liked you."

"Your mother too?" she asked.

"Seven years ago. My father was never the same after that. He let the house go, put the jukebox in the basement and that was it. I tried to get him to move to New York, but there was no talking to him." He unlocked the glass dome and lifted until it clicked into place. "You know my dad."

She nodded as she came toward him. "Only too well."

"When he died, I came back to sell the house, but it took longer than expected to clean it out, sell everything." He picked up one of the records from the table behind him and pulled it out of the paper sleeve. "I had an offer on the jukebox, but when the guy came to pick it up, I couldn't take the money. I don't know why. So I hung on to it, and kept lowering the price on the house. Once it was sold, there was no need to stay, but I kept hanging around, going back to the tavern, missing my flights. My fiancée and my office were both calling, asking when I'd be home. I was about to book a ticket when it occurred to me that I'd been happier during those weeks in Schomberg than I'd been in a long time. And I couldn't shake the idea of turning the tavern into something more. Making it the kind of gathering place it had been years ago."

Max was at his side now, watching as he slipped the

record into the slot on the carousel. "How did you break it to your fiancée?"

"Gently," he said and smiled at her. "Very gently. But when Caroline saw the town and the tavern, she couldn't do it."

He could still see the night he'd brought her into downtown Schomberg: Caroline Skinner, a New York lawyer, rendered speechless. Her cool demeanor shaken, quite possibly for the first time in her life, as they walked along Center Street. But he hadn't really been surprised when she caught the next flight out and had made no attempt to stop her, to compromise; knowing instinctively that it was for the best.

"She thought she was marrying a stockbroker," he continued. "Not a bartender. She was a corporate lawyer, a good one, and she couldn't see herself schlepping beer in some Virginia backwater for the rest of her life."

"Even though she loved you?" Max asked, and he knew where she was heading.

"It wasn't enough," he admitted. "We needed common goals as well."

But there was no triumph on her face, no sign of a battle won. Only a sadness he couldn't understand, for a love that couldn't last.

He closed the dome on the jukebox and locked it. "So Caroline went home, I stayed here and the rest, as they say, is history."

"And you're happy," she said, watching the carousel turn and settle back into place.

"Yes, I am."

"Being here doesn't make you think about Brian, then? Or Gwen?"

"All the time."

"Really?" she said, but he knew she didn't believe him.

"Come on, Max. Do you think it was a private grief you had going that summer? Brian was my best friend.

And in all the years I'd known him, I'd never seen him as happy as he was with Gwen. I thought love was the best thing that ever happened to him. After he died, I hated this town just as much as you did. When we made that pact to leave and never look back, I meant it. I wanted to forget everyone and everything, and make damn sure no one ever hurt me the way Gwen had hurt Brian."

She glanced down at the selector buttons. "Is that why you never wrote?"

He closed his eyes and drew in a long breath. "You don't know how sorry I am about that."

She lifted her head and seemed surprised. "Why would you be? If the situation had been reversed, I probably wouldn't have written you either."

He doubted that but saw no point in quibbling.

"I'm curious," she said, "about your plan not to get hurt. What did you do?"

He shrugged. "I put my heart on hold and I coasted."

"Until you met Caroline?"

He rubbed a hand over his jaw, embarrassed. "Even then, I'm afraid. To be honest, I wasn't feeling much of anything for anyone or anything until I came back here."

Her eyes held his, steady and unwavering. "No regrets then?"

"A few," he admitted. "I miss the jazz clubs, real bagels. And my brand-new, twelve-cylinder Aston Martin roadster." He sighed. "I loved that car. But I couldn't picture it with chains on the tires in winter."

Her smile came slowly. "Does ruin the mystique."

"How about you? Any regrets about life in the Big Apple?"

"None," she said too quickly, then lifted a shoulder, let it fall. "Okay, a few. Now and then."

"Any you'd care to share?"

"Not a chance." She reached for her purse. "I should be going."

"Suit yourself." He pulled a quarter from his pocket and slipped it into the coin slot. He glanced over as it dropped. "I thought you were leaving."

The purse slid back down to the table. "I've got a few minutes," she said, watching with open interest now as the selector light flashed on and he pressed A1.

Never had he known it to take so long for a record to lock into position and the tone arm to move forward. And never had he held his breath while a record hissed and crackled—only breathing again when the first notes finally played.

" 'Blue Moon,' " Sam said as she stepped closer to the jukebox. "It was your favorite, wasn't it?"

She stared up at him. "How did you know that?"

"Because it was the only time you were ever quiet." He smiled and dodged the punch she threw. "Every time that song played, you'd move closer to the jukebox and pretend to be doing something else, but I knew you were listening to every word, every note. I just didn't know why."

Her gaze slipped to the jukebox. "I wanted it to be me," she said softly. "I wanted to be the one that love found in the moonlight." A wry smile curved her lips as she turned back to him. "And I wanted so badly for someone to ask me to dance."

He took her hand and pulled her close. "Then dance with me now. For all the times we never did."

EIGHT

She moved into his arms and he brought her in close, feeling the softness of her breasts and the curve of her belly as she pressed against him; fitting herself into all the empty spaces and making him want more of her, need all of her.

She tucked her head beneath his chin and he danced her around the wooden divider into the section that would one day be the dining room. It was darker here, the windows small and shuttered. Slivers of sunlight slanted across the floor, and they moved between them, finding it easier here to forget about Brian, the bridge, the very things that should have kept them apart, made their steps awkward and faltering. But they moved as one, swaying to music that seemed far off now, distant. More like a song remembered than one playing nearby.

Sam stopped before the music ended and she lifted her head, not understanding. So he whispered her name as he dragged her closer still, and there was no denying the answering heat in her eyes as she rose to meet him. He bent to her then, touching his lips to hers, lightly at first, then harder, deeper; as though he had every right to hold her, kiss her, and be kissed in return.

She drew back, catching her breath as she raised a hand, tracing the lines of his face with her fingertips. Across his cheekbones to his jaw, along his jaw to his mouth; her touch so light, her concentration so complete, it was as though she was discovering him for the first time. And finding exactly what she was looking for right there in front of her.

She brushed her thumbs across his lips, a simple act made intimate as her own lips parted, as if feeling his kiss all over again. The music finished, wrapping them in a silence broken only by a moan that might have come from either of them as he bent to her again.

He covered her mouth with his, kissing her with a new intensity that startled them both, even as it thrilled. She wrapped her arms around his neck, holding him fast as she tilted her hips, seeking him out and finding him hard, ready. Sam slid his hands down and pressed her closer still, knowing it was foolish to want her this way, to need her at all. She was still waiting for Peter and would leave in an instant if that phone of hers rang. Yet he was lost in the feel, the smell, the taste of her, and couldn't find a way to step back.

Max knew it was wrong. Knew she should leave now, take herself home, call the man whose ring she wore. Yet how could she walk away when she could barely stand on legs grown weak with wanting Sam?

He held her with one hand while the other slipped between them, seeking a breast, a nipple. She gasped at that bold first touch, then moved against him, wanting more and glad when he lowered one strap of her dress.

He kissed her neck, her shoulder, the spot at the base of her throat where her pulse was strong and rapid. She let her head fall back, delighting in the heat of his mouth, the shiver across her skin and the sudden change in his touch—urgent now, almost rough as he pulled down the other strap and lowered her dress to her waist.

Her bra was lacy and sheer, the charm clearly visible.

"Enough of this," he said, his voice low, harsh, scraping across her flesh as he slid the charm from its hiding place and let it flutter to the floor. And before Max could form an argument, his mouth was on her breast, and there was nothing to do but feel.

It had been building for days, this tide, this wave. And while she'd never thought of herself as aggressive, never known herself to be bold, she gripped his strong arms and arched back, demanding even as she offered. And smiling at the sweet, low moan that came only from him, knowing he wanted her as she'd always dreamed he would.

He'd asked her earlier what was the worst that could happen, and as he turned his attention to her other breast, Max realized that this was it. Not the kiss. Not even the touch. But the fact that she could start falling for Sam O'Neal all over again. Falling into a love that had nowhere to go and no way to survive, and all because the man she was waiting for was taking too long to find her.

Desire pooled and burned as he started to lift her skirt, and it was only the sound of footsteps in the pub that stopped them. As if jolted from a dream, her sensuous haze gave way to reality.

"Sam?" a male voice called from the other side of the screen.

"Night staff," Sam muttered, turning them around so his back was to the screen, shielding her with his body while she hurried to cover herself.

"Sam?" the man called again.

She cast a quick nervous glance at the screen, but Sam only shook his head, his eyes still on her lips, her throat, her breasts; making her legs weak even as she slid the dress up into place.

"Ben?" the voice continued. "Anybody?"

Max squeezed her eyes shut, her face hot as the footsteps receded and his voice grew fainter. She heard the clang of a pot and knew he'd gone into the kitchen, giving her a way out.

But instead of letting her pass, Sam reached for her hand. "Max—"

"I have to go," she said, and tried to push past him. But he held on, making her stay.

"Don't you dare say this didn't happen," he whispered. "And don't you try and tell me that it was wrong either."

"Not wrong?" She almost laughed. "Sam, I'm engaged."

"To a man you don't love."

She jerked her hand free. "That doesn't change a thing."

"Doesn't it?" He took a step toward her, his eyes dark and searching. "Look at me, Max, and make me believe that you shiver when he loves you, and smile when he trembles at your touch." He stopped directly in front of her. "Convince me of that, and maybe I'll believe that you're not still waiting for love to find you in the moonlight."

He reached out, his fingers curving around her waist, drawing her back. And she felt herself go to him too easily, too willingly.

"And what if I am?" she said, breaking away, putting distance between them. "What if I admit that there's this small part of me that wants to believe in love songs and poetry? And that deep inside, I do want to be found? What happens then, Sam?"

"Then I'd find you," he said so matter-of-factly that for a moment she couldn't breathe, couldn't move, as the fantasy took shape in her mind.

But it fell apart just as quickly as another voice, another set of footsteps materialized on the other side of the divider. Female this time, calling his name while glasses clinked, silver rattled and the volume on the televisions was cranked up again.

The Schomberg Tap Room was officially open for business. And Max wasn't naive enough to believe that

Sam would ever have time to look for her once she was back in New York. Their time had already passed, and Peter's was running out fast.

"You really do need some new lines, O'Neal," she said, but the laugh she had planned wouldn't come. So she went straight for an exit line instead. "Thanks for the beer." She bent to pick up the charm and edged toward the divider. "I think it would be best if we don't see each other anymore."

"Max, wait," Sam called after her, needing to make her stay, to show her that they could make it work. And wondering what he was thinking about when he swung around into the pub and saw all eyes were on her already. The waitress, the night cook, even Michael, who had undoubtedly dropped by to make sure that Ben hadn't scratched the pine nuts off the evening menu. And all brows raised even higher when they spotted Sam right behind her.

"Max?" Michael asked. *"The* Max whose fiancé is taking pictures of Elvis for a cookbook as we speak?"

"That's me," she said, her cheeks growing red and her hands clenching at her sides.

"I'm Michael," he said, then glanced at Sam. "I thought she'd be taller."

"And I thought you'd have more hair," she said.

Michael stared at her for a moment, then looked back at Sam. "I like her."

"So do I," Sam said as she went to pick up her purse. "Max, please—"

"Does anybody know where these belong?" the waitress said, holding up the can of honey roasted nuts.

"Give them to Sam," Max said, and glanced back at him. "Just be sure to say hello for me."

He was about to protest when a middle-aged couple came through the door, clutching a rolled up copy of *Mountain Living* magazine. They stood just back from the reservation desk, looking from Michael to Max to Sam to the waitress. "We're here for a glass of Ben's Weissen," the man said, then lifted the magazine. "Page one-fifty?"

The waitress snapped to attention. "Of course, come in. Table for two?"

"I have to go," Max said and headed for the kitchen and the back door.

"I'll see you out," Sam said, but the front door opened again and the rest of the night staff straggled in. The busboy, the bartender, another waitress, all calling hello and asking about specials—each one needing something from him.

"It was nice meeting you," Michael called after her. "We'll talk another time."

Sam started for the kitchen, hoping to catch her, but the front door opened yet again. More customers, a table for six, locals this time and regulars at Cy's.

"I'll take care of this," Michael said and waved the group over to a corner table. "You'll never guess who I just met," he said as they approached.

And Sam could only shake his head as he turned back to his pub, his world, and the front door swung back again. "Welcome to the Schomberg Tap Room," he said, and froze with a hand on the menus.

"Hello, Sam." A woman stood at the door. Freckled, youthful, her hair still long, still that wonderful fiery red.

She smiled and gestured to the front window. "I noticed the help wanted sign." She paused as the conversation stopped and all heads turned. She backed up a step. "This was probably a mistake."

Through the door behind her, Sam saw Max slipping away, going back to her car, her future.

The woman waved a hand as she backed up a step. "This was a mistake. Forget I was here."

"No," Sam said, "come in." He smiled and offered a hand. "How have you been, Gwen?"

"Did you get the raspberries?" Delia hollered from the kitchen as Max closed the front door behind her.

She stared at the carton of strawberries in her hand. A fifty-fifty chance and she'd guessed wrong. But then, it had been a day for bad choices all around. Why should this be any different?

"Funny you should ask," she called back, kicking off her shoes and sniffing the air as she walked. The house was filled with the rich aromas of garlic and onions, chocolate and cinnamon, oranges and lemons. While there was always something baking or simmering at Eva's, this was different, more complex, exotic. Delia had been talking about trying her hand at recipe development for days, and Max could only assume that she'd finally made good on the threat. And hope that strawberries would fit into the new grand scheme.

"I decided strawberries would work better," she said, holding them before her like an offering as she made her entrance into the kitchen. "They have a universal appeal that raspberries lack."

Delia glanced over as she shook salt into a saucepan on the stove. "You forgot, didn't you?"

"Thanks for the vote of confidence," Max said, but hung back in the doorway, taking in the sinkful of dishes, the counter covered with open bags, boxes and canisters, and the stove buried under pots and pans with a recipe taped to the range hood. It was food stylist hell, but Delia's eyes were bright, her movements brisk, and Max had to admit that she looked like she was having fun.

"It has nothing to do with confidence," Delia said, picking up a pen and adding a line to the recipe. "I just know how preoccupied you've been." She tossed the pen aside and reached for the pepper. "And since Peter prefers strawberries it was a natural slip."

"That must have been it," Max said, keeping her head down as she squeezed the carton into the only available spot on the counter, afraid that Delia might somehow see the lie.

But how could she tell her the truth? How could she explain that it hadn't been Peter on her mind at all? That the man she was planning to marry had taken second place to Sam, and a love song. And a silly promise that wouldn't go away.

I'll find you.

As lines went it was a good one, right up there with *I'll never leave you,* and *I'll always love you*—two of Gwen's favorites, as Max recalled.

But Sam had never been good with lines, and she couldn't think of a time when she'd ever known him to lie. Which was unfortunate, because it only made it that much harder to forget, and confused her even more.

She'd spent half a lifetime convincing herself that love and passion were anything but vital to the success of a relationship. She knew the latest divorce statistics and had done extensive reading on the merits of arranged marriages. It had taken years to build up good solid reasons to ignore the poets, the song writers and the greeting card makers. She'd been so sure that she would never fall victim to fantasy the way Brian had. Yet, in a matter of days, Sam had taken everything she knew to be true and turned it upside down; leaving her wondering, floundering, searching for a way back.

So she focused on the pots and bowls, the aromas and mess—things that made sense, that she could understand and put right. "Does my mother know what you've done to her kitchen?" she asked, "Or was she responsible for most of it?"

"I'd say she made about half. Seemed like every recipe

she has calls for three different bowls, two pans and a zester." She glanced over at Max. "We've been working on simplification."

"May you have more luck than I ever did." Max leaned over for a look at what Delia was stirring. "What have you been making here anyway?"

"This is a barbeque sauce for dinner, but everything else was an experiment for the photo shoot. Pancakes, sausage, eggs, home fries, all the breakfast classics. And bowls aside, I have to say that Eva is fabulous to work with. My mother is a tyrant in the kitchen, always wiping up and putting away, but your mom just lets it roll off her."

Max nodded and reached for a spoon. "She gets caught up in it. We used to have these marathon cooking sessions that started right after breakfast. She'd sift and strain while I fried and boiled, and by the end of the day you were lucky if you could even see the counter. But dinner was generally interesting." She shot Delia a grin. "And the men always cleaned up."

"Your father must have been a progressive male."

"He just liked to eat." She dipped a spoon into the pan and tasted. "Needs a pinch of dry mustard," she said, then straightened and dropped the spoon in the sink. "I'm sorry—"

"No, it's fine. I knew something was wrong." Delia nodded at a casserole on the counter while she searched for mustard among the bottles. "Try that one and tell me what you think."

Max took a quick step back and pulled an apron from the hook by the stove. "I think I need to start the dishes, since there are no men to clean up anymore."

"That will be remedied very soon." Delia switched off the heat and plucked a courier's receipt from the clutter on the counter. "The ad layout went to Virginia Beach this morning, along with a letter on Eva's stationery, thanking Wilhelm for his input and asking him to forward the contract as soon as possible." She rubbed at a bit of mustard, then handed the sheet to Max. "I sent the whole thing same day delivery, which means Peter should have it by now. So keep your cell phone charged, because it could start ringing at any minute."

Max shook her head as she read the receipt. "I'm not so sure. He's bound to know it's a setup the minute he sees the letter." She laid the receipt on a canister and pulled the apron over her head. "I mean, how many times does something bound for Wilhelm just happen to fall into his hands?"

"I thought of that. So I included a note from me, telling Peter that I'm temping for Wilhelm now, and as a goodwill gesture for all the years that he and I worked together, I thought I'd let him see exactly what he's losing by being such an idiot. You, and the shoot. Once he reads that, it will only be a matter of which flight to catch."

Max stared at the pots in the sink for a moment, then looked over at her, voicing for the first time what had been on her mind for days. "But what if he still doesn't want to get married? What if he only wants the shoot?"

Delia laughed. "Honey, believe me, there is no chance of that. Not after what I heard today."

"You talked to him?"

"No, but I did call his voice mail." She shrugged and dumped the strawberries into a colander. "I wanted to remind him that the telephone and the electric bills are due today, otherwise he'll forget. You know how he is with his bills. Anyway, the point is that when I heard his message, I knew the man was a mess. He kept pausing, stumbling over the date and even the fax instructions."

"What does that prove?"

Delia stared at her. "That he's miserable, what else? The man practices those messages over and over before he records them, and he has never, ever stumbled. Not

THE PUBLISHERS OF ZEBRA BOUQUET

are making this special offer to lovers of contemporary romances to introduce this exciting new line of novels. Zebra's Bouquet Romances have been praised by critics and authors alike as being of the highest quality and best written romantic fiction available today.

EACH FULL-LENGTH NOVEL

has been written by authors you know and love as well as by up and coming writers that you'll only find with Zebra Bouquet. We'll bring you the newest novels by world famous authors like Vanessa Grant, Judy Gill, Ann Josephson and award winning Suzanne Barrett and Leigh Greenwood—to name just a few. Zebra Bouquet's editors have selected only the very best and highest quality romances for up-and-coming publications under the Bouquet banner.

YOU'LL BE TREATED

to tales of star-crossed lovers in glamourous settings that are sure to captivate you. These stories will keep you enthralled to the very happy end.

4 FREE NOVELS
As a way to introduce you to these terrific romances, the publishers of Bouquet are offering Zebra Romance readers Four Free Bouquet novels. They are yours for the asking with no obligation to buy a single book. Read them at your leisure. We are sure that after you've read these introductory books you'll want more! (If you do not wish to receive any further Bouquet novels, simply write "cancel" on the invoice and return to us within 10 days.)

SAVE 20% WITH HOME DELIVERY
Each month you'll receive four just-published Bouquet romances. We'll ship them to you as soon as they are printed (you may even get them before the bookstores). You'll have 10 days to preview these exciting novels for Free. If you decide to keep them, you'll be billed the special preferred home subscription price of just $3.20 per book; a total of just $12.80 — that's a savings of 20% off the publisher's price. If for any reason you are not satisfied simply return the novels for full credit, no questions asked. You'll never have to purchase a minimum number of books and you may cancel your subscription at any time.

GET STARTED TODAY –
NO RISK AND NO OBLIGATION

To get your introductory gift of 4 Free Bouquet Romances fill out and mail the enclosed Free Book Certificate today. We'll ship your free books as soon as we receive this information. Remember that you are under no obligation. This is a risk-free offer from the publishers of Zebra Bouquet Romances.

Call us TOLL FREE at 1-888-345-BOOK
Visit our website at www.kensingtonbooks.com

FREE BOOK CERTIFICATE

YES! I would like to take you up on your offer. Please send me 4 Free Bouquet Romance Novels as my introductory gift. I understand that unless I tell you otherwise, I will then receive the 4 newest Bouquet novels to preview each month FREE for 10 days. If I decide to keep them I'll pay the preferred home subscriber's price of just $3.20 (a total of only $12.80) plus $1.50 for shipping and handling. That's a 20% savings off the publisher's price. I understand that I may return any shipment for full credit–no questions asked–and I may cancel this subscription at any time with no obligation. Regardless of what I decide to do, the 4 Free Introductory Novels are mine to keep as Bouquet's gift.

BN040A

Name _____

Address _____

City _____ State _____ Zip _____

Telephone ( ) _____

Signature _____

(If under 18, parent or guardian must sign.)

For your convenience you may charge your shipments automatically to a Visa or MasterCard so you'll never have to worry about late payments and missing shipments. If you return any shipment, we'll credit your account.

☐ Yes, charge my credit card for my "Bouquet Romance" shipments until I tell you otherwise.
☐ Visa ☐ MasterCard

Account Number _____

Expiration Date _____

Signature _____

Orders subject to acceptance by Zebra Home Subscription Service. Terms and Prices subject to change.
Order valid only in the U.S.

If this response card is missing,
call us at 1-888-345-BOOK.

Be sure to visit our website at
www.kensingtonbooks.com

BOUQUET ROMANCES
Zebra Home Subscription Service, Inc.
P.O. Box 5214
Clifton NJ 07015-5214

once in all the years I've known him. I tell you, the man's a mess. Once he gets that package, he won't be able to get on a plane fast enough." She smiled and shoved the colander under the tap. "Which means wedding bells will be ringing in Manhattan."

Max watched Peter's favorite berries jostle and bounce under the spray. "I'm not so sure anymore."

Delia turned suddenly, the colander dripping on the floor, her smile gone. "Oh God, Max. Don't you dare get cold feet on me too."

Max shook her head and twisted the taps. "You really want that job back, don't you?"

"Yeah, that's it."

Something in her tone made Max glance over again. But Delia had set the colander on a canister and was busy tearing off hulls. "Look, all I want is for you and Peter to be happy."

"Me too." Max sighed and searched under the pots for a plug. "How can something that sounds so simple be so complicated?"

"I think it's a rule. When it comes to love, nothing shall ever be simple."

"Love has nothing to do with it," Max muttered as Eva came through the back door, a grin on her face and an empty box in her hands.

"Those pots can wait," she said. "You have to come out and see the table first."

Max accepted a kiss on the cheek as her mother breezed by. "You set it up already?"

Eva set the box down and shoved her hair out of her eyes. "In the garden, by the peonies. I got this lovely mesh tent from Dianne down the road—you know she has all those fancy things for entertaining—and I couldn't wait to see how it's all going to look. I figured I'd call a few people, see if they'll come by and join us for dinner . . ." She tipped her head to the side and studied Max's face. "You got some sun. Were you outside a lot?"

Max shrugged. "Only between errands."

"But you were gone so long." Eva paused, obviously hoping for more, and flashing a quick, bright smile before the silence became awkward. "Come see the table when you get a chance," she said and disappeared into the hall, leaving Max to admire her restraint.

Who knows? she thought as her mother went up the stairs. Maybe this time, they would part friends.

She turned to find Delia watching her closely. "I was wondering the same thing. Why were you gone so long today?"

Max sighed but had to smile all the same, finding it interesting that being friends with Delia meant no restraint at all.

Max counted off on her fingers. "Well, let's see, I nearly caused an accident on the bridge, broke into a cemetery and gave serious thought to having sex with a tall, dark man in a very public place."

"If you don't want to tell me either, that's fine." Delia went back to hulling berries.

Max squeezed detergent onto the pots, not at all surprised that Delia didn't believe her. The Max she knew was a careful driver, worked twelve to fourteen hours a day, had never broken into anything or had sex in the daytime.

Yet there she'd been, Maxine Henley, professional food stylist and all-around practical gal, dancing cheek-to-cheek and mouth-to-mouth with Sam O'Neal—a woman Max barely recognized herself, lost in a love song and a fantasy. And on the verge of making the biggest mistake of her life.

"If you stand there staring at the sink much longer," Delia said, "I may start believing there really was a tall, dark stranger."

"A stranger would have been easier," she said softly, and was grateful when her mother came back into the kitchen before Delia could ask any more questions.

Eva held up two crystal glasses as she went by. "I'd almost forgotten these were upstairs in the trunk. We'll have to go through it before you leave. See if there's anything you'd like to have, now that you're getting married." She paused at the door and smiled at Max. "By the way, I love being a prop girl."

"You're a natural," Delia said.

Eva laughed and pushed open the door with a hip. "Hold the praise till you see the work."

"We'll be there in a minute," Delia called after her, then turned to Max. "If she ever moves to New York, I'll set her up in the propping business myself."

Max pulled the apron over her head and hung it on a hook. "Don't hold your breath. Eva will never get out of this place."

Delia followed her down the back stairs. "Does that bother you?"

"Wouldn't it if she was your mother?" She waved a hand in a gesture that encompassed the entire farm. "Take a look around. What do you see?"

"Mountains, llamas." She smiled. "A very crazy dog."

Max turned in time to see Columbo racing around the empty paddock, ears flapping and tongue lolling, running as though all the hounds of hell were chasing him.

"See what I mean? Even the dog can't take it here." She shook her head as they walked around the side of the house to the garden. "There's no future in this town or on this farm. Just a lot of hard work and old memories."

NINE

Eva stepped back as they approached the tent. "Well, what do you think? And be honest."

Max shook her head in amazement as she entered the little nook her mother had created in the garden. Delia hadn't exaggerated. While Eva's eye for detail was always evident in whatever she set her hand to, she had outdone herself for the ad.

Two chairs draped with crisp white linen flanked a round table. On the back of one hung a bonnet, and on the other a sword. The crystal goblets were filled with iced tea, the flowers abundant and the food overflowing—ample proof of the joy that Eva took in having people sit at her table. From pancakes and biscuits to sausage and eggs, everything about the setting said sit down, relax and enjoy—exactly the impression they needed to create.

"This is going to work out beautifully," Max said, already shaking off Sam and the farm as she clicked easily and gratefully into work mode.

She might be confused about everything else in her life, but here there were no questions and no gray areas. Max was good at her job, knowing at a glance what had to be done and precisely how to do it.

She walked the length of the table, making a mental list of what she'd need to make everything look mouthwatering, irresistible—picture perfect. "With a half-page ad," she said to Eva, "we should be able to include not only a table shot, but closeups of at least two individual dishes. It's just a question of which ones."

She reached for the stack of pancakes and gave the plate a half-turn. "These always say breakfast to me. We'll need about forty for the shoot, but they'll need to be fluffier." She glanced back at Delia. "Maybe we can work some extra baking powder into the recipe, or a couple of egg whites—"

"That will ruin the taste," Eva said.

"But not the look," Max said, already sliding the jug of maple syrup to one side. "We can't use this, of course, or the butter. I'll need some dark corn syrup and I'm sure I've got a squeeze bottle in my kit. We'll freeze the syrup and some margarine and hit them with a blow torch just before the take. That way it will look like the butter is melting slowly and the syrup is in the process of spreading and running over the side—"

"What are you talking about?" Eva cut in. "Corn syrup and a blowtorch? I've never heard of such things."

Max glanced over at her. "Mom, this is advertising, not reality. Everything needs to look better than real."

"But can't you just put the food out fresh and snap the picture quickly?"

Max shook her head and moved on to the biscuits. "It doesn't work that way. The lighting has to be set up and Polaroids taken before we even put the film in the camera. Believe me, I know what I'm doing." She turned back to Delia. "The biscuits are good, but we need them to look piping hot. I'll bring the hypodermic and we'll inject some water—"

"You're not injecting anything into my biscuits."

Max shrugged. "It's either that or a few calcimated metal chips tucked inside. Both will give a good steam effect—"

Eva snatched up the basket of biscuits, holding them in front of her like a shield. "You may know what you're doing, but the question is how you can do it. How you can take perfectly good food and poison it, turn it into nothing more than . . ." She paused, obviously struggling. "Props."

Max backed away from the table. "Why are you so surprised? It's what I've been telling you for years. Nobody eats what I cook, not because I won't let them, but because they can't."

Eva stared as though seeing her for the first time. "I guess I just never believed it."

"Mom, it's not that bad," Max started, but the opportunity to explain, to justify was lost when Ben appeared at the gate.

He nodded to Max and Delia, then turned to Eva. "You want to come and see the truck for the petting zoo?"

"Yes," she said, softly at first and then louder. "Yes, I do." And she ran, still clutching the basket, as though they'd both just been rescued.

Delia picked up one of the glasses of iced tea and held one out to Max. "She didn't have a clue about the blow torch, did she?"

"Apparently not." Max sighed and sipped at the drink. "I've tried to explain what I do, but you could say that Eva and I don't always communicate well."

"So I gather." Delia watched the ice in her glass as she swirled the tea. "In fact, I'd say you don't communicate well with anyone."

"What is that supposed to mean?"

Delia looked up. "Only that I've been your friend for years and I never knew you had a brother until I came here."

Max shrugged. "I don't talk about him much."

"Eva says you don't talk about him at all. Not even to her."

Max gave her head a disgusted shake. "Let me guess: She gave you a guided tour of his room, complete with full descriptions of all trophies and pennants."

"She showed me a picture," Delia said softly. "And she told me that he was a wonderful young man."

"He was," Max said, her voice sounding distant and flat even to herself. "Bright, funny—"

"Then why do you pretend he never lived?"

Max looked over at Delia. There had been no censure in her voice, nor was there any in her eyes. She was simply waiting, giving Max the benefit of the doubt and a chance to explain. And it was then that Max realized how appalled Delia must be.

She had been born into a close-knit Italian family, and all four daughters still ended up back at her parents house for dinner every Sunday. While Delia fought with each one of them, her three sisters were so much a part of her life that Max felt she knew each of them intimately, even though she'd only met them once or twice.

How could Max hope to make her understand about Brian?

"How could I ever pretend he never lived," she said at last, "when I miss him every day?"

"Eva said he was killed in a car accident when he was young."

"Eighteen." Max set down her glass and turned her back on the table. "He was eloping. Did she tell you that too?"

"She mentioned a girl. Gwen somebody."

"Harper. Red hair, freckles, a smile you would have loved." Max knew her own smile was tight and bitter, and she started back to the house, too restless to stand still any longer. "Gwen was one of the summer girls," she said as Delia fell into step beside her. "The kind who comes in June and leaves in September, and is off-limits to the local boys. But that didn't stop my brother from falling for her."

Max slowed as they approached the back steps, her eyes moving up to the balcony above the sunroom, and her bedroom beyond. "Of course Gwen's father wouldn't let Brian near her. She was going to Harvard, going to be a lawyer just like her daddy, and he didn't want some farm boy getting in the way, confusing the issue. But Gwen didn't mind slumming, for a while anyway."

"Max, I'm sorry. I shouldn't have pried—"

"The whole thing was like something out of a movie," Max cut in, surprising herself; discovering that she wanted to keep going, wanted to tell Delia exactly what had happened. But she had no idea why. The only thing she knew for certain was that she wasn't ready to go into the house, wasn't ready to stand still just yet.

She headed for the gate. "It was a summer of romantic rendezvous and stolen kisses. But every stolen moment required a go-between, someone to help Gwen escape, and that was where Sam and I came in."

Delia drew her head back. "The cowboy?"

Max nodded and opened the gate. "I carried the notes and made the phone calls, and Sam drove the truck. We thought we were so clever. So sure we were fooling everybody, when we were fooling no one. The whole town knew and took sides. That's what they do best here in Schomberg. Discuss other people's business." She gave a short, harsh laugh as they crossed the driveway. "And believe me, the Henleys made for some good conversation that year.

"Some said Gwen's father was wrong, others insisted Brian was nothing but a troublemaker. And things really heated up once somebody suggested that Gwen might be pregnant." She looked over at Delia. "Ah, you didn't hear that, did you?"

Delia shook her head. "Was she?"

Max shrugged and kept walking. "Who knows? But it didn't matter anyway. They were already planning to run away and get married. She was going to meet him at the gas station at midnight. We were all there, and right on the stroke of twelve, her father walked into the station. Gwen must have told him where we'd be, because he had this big smile on his face when he told Brian that she wasn't coming. She'd left that morning to get ready for school. He laughed and called Brian a fool, said he must be crazy if he believed that she'd actually throw away everything she had to live with him in some Virginia backwater. Then he handed back the wedding gift Brian had given Gwen the day before. Told him she'd been touched, but there was only so much room on her keepsake shelf for summer flings. That's when Brian went after him."

She stopped in front of the empty paddock and stared out across the fields, blind to the llamas and goats, even the ostriches. Seeing only Brian, furious and unbelieving, and still in love with Gwen.

"It was good that Sam was there," she said softly, "because I think Brian would have killed the man. Sam kept pulling him off again and again, screaming at him to forget it, forget her. She wasn't worth it." She paused and tried to moisten her lips, but her mouth had gone dry. "That's when Brian turned on Sam, went at him like a crazy man. And I just stood there, frozen, still not believing she had done this. Not Gwen, anyone but Gwen." Max drew in a shaky breath, suddenly fifteen again and watching her world fall apart in slow motion. "Then Brian hit Sam so hard he nearly passed out, and that's when I finally moved. Brian ran for the truck. Said he was going to find her, make her tell him to his face that she didn't want him. I went after him, tried to stop him. I even stood in front of the truck, told him he could run me over if he wanted to, but I wasn't moving."

Delia closed her eyes. "Max, stop—"

But Max couldn't hear her, because the truck was there in front of her, Brian revving the engine while Sam hollered at her to get out of the way.

"Turned out, he didn't need to run me over after all. He just backed up, swerved around and took off. I ran after him, but he was going too fast. Last thing I saw was his truck skidding on the curve at the bottom of the hill. And all I heard was the crash."

Delia touched a hand to her arm, bringing her back. Max looked over at her.

"He went right through the guardrail. The river was down. It was mostly just rocks. They said he died instantly. A blessing, is what the police called it. But in all this time, I have never felt blessed."

She lowered her head and started walking again. "They said it was a clear-cut case of youth, anger and speed. They didn't even drag Gwen back and make her explain, make her tell us why in God's name she left him standing there. And why she'd ever told him that she loved him." She looked over at Delia. "I still wonder if there was something I missed, some warning I ignored—"

"Max, you can't blame yourself."

"But I was with her almost every day."

"You were a kid. What about Sam, your mother, Brian himself? What did they see?"

"Gwen," she said softly. "Just Gwen. On the porch, by the pond." She sighed as she looked around. "There isn't a spot on this farm that doesn't still say Gwen. And I can't figure out for the life of me why my mother stays."

"Because it's her home," Delia said, as though that was enough.

"Or maybe she's just stuck." Max looked over as Ben and Eva came around the side of the barn, each with a wallaby strapped to their chests. "Stuck with ghosts and memories that won't let go, and keep her from moving on."

Delia followed her gaze. "He likes her, doesn't he?" she said. "Ben, I mean. He likes your mother."

"He loves her," Max said, not sure where it had come from but knowing it was true.

"From the look on her face, I'd say your mom likes him too."

Max watched her mother smile and touch a hand to Ben's arm, wondering idly where she'd stashed the biscuits. "She has for years. For all the good it does either of them."

Delia nodded. "Like I said, matters of the heart are never easy."

Max paused, considering, as Eva and Ben continued on around the barn, the two of them oblivious to her, Delia and the dog bearing down on them. "You may be right, but the problem between Ben and Eva has more to with the head than the heart. My mother made up her mind that she won't be unfaithful to my father's memory and that's that. It's called carrying a torch to extremes."

"I know the feeling."

Delia's sigh was soft, but it was enough to draw Max around. "You're carrying a torch? Why didn't I know that?"

Delia frowned. "Did I say I was carrying anything? I only mentioned that I know what it's like when you can't let go of an old love, or even an imagined love. One that never happened but might have, if something had been different." She shook her head and gazed out at the meadow. "Those are the worst."

"Because you can't stop asking, 'What if?' " Max said. "What if you'd met sooner, or later—"

"Or not at all."

"Not at all would be best," Max agreed, wondering

how much easier life would be if she had never run into Sam again.

If she'd never heard his voice or laughed at his jokes. Never felt the heat of his skin or the beat of his heart. And how much simpler everything would be if she'd never tasted his kiss. A kiss that made her want to hold on tight, even when she knew she had to let go, because her future lay elsewhere, with a man she didn't love but needed in ways that Sam would never understand.

"Never would definitely be best," she said. "And if you ask Ben, he'd probably say the same thing."

Delia shook her head. "I doubt it. No one could look at a woman the way he's looking at your mom right now and regret meeting her."

Max saw what Delia meant. It was right there in his eyes, his smile and the tender way he touched her. And as she turned back to the house, Max felt her heart break for what would never be—for Ben. For Eva. For herself.

TEN

By eight o'clock Friday night, the Tap Room was almost crowded and the beer was flowing nicely. Satisfied that the night crew could handle things on their own for a while, Sam tossed his glove into the backseat of his pickup and drove to the ballpark.

But he smiled as he pulled into the parking lot. At last, a chance to hit something. Lord knew he'd been wanting to do just that for the past two days.

He switched off the engine and squinted at the baseball diamond. As far as he could tell, nothing was being thrown or hit out there. The bunch of them were sitting on the bench, smoking and talking, while the little kids played tag between the bases.

Sam grabbed his glove from the backseat and jogged across the field, determined to put some life into the game. But the closer he got, the more apparent was the reason for the apathy. Never had he seen such a poor turnout. There weren't more than a dozen players, and all of them were men. Howard from the real estate office, Jeff from the hardware store, Ben, Michael and a few of the other regulars. But none of the women were there, not even Kerri or Tracy, and the number of kids playing on the field was less than half the usual.

Sam slowed to a walk, wondering when everybody else would get there.

Ben raised a hand in greeting as he got to his feet. "You're just in time. Hand him the talking stick Howard, and let the male bonding begin."

Howard laughed and tossed Sam the bat. "We promised ourselves that if even one more person turned up, we'd play."

"And thank God for that." Michael pulled the ball from his glove and headed for the mound. "I thought I'd never get to pitch. Okay, Sam, you're on the blue team. Blue is batting, Red is out in field."

"Lord have mercy," one of the men muttered as six of them straggled out to the diamond.

"Where's everybody else?" Sam asked as he joined Ben and Jeff on the bench.

"This is all we're going to have tonight." Ben pulled a pack of gum from his pocket and held it out to Sam. "Gum?"

"No thanks," Sam said, wincing when Michael threw the first pitch. "What do you mean, there won't be more? Where're Kerri and her friends? And don't you usually get more men out than this?"

"The women are at the shower and the rest of the men are home baby-sitting."

"Back up a bit. What shower?"

"The one for Maxine," Jeff said, shaking his head when the batter had to leap out of the way of the next pitch.

"A shower for Max?" Sam sucked in a hissing breath as Michael wound up again. "What kind of shower?"

"Wedding, of course." Ben rubbed a hand over his mouth as Michael walked the next batter. "Tried to stop it, but you know Judith. Once she gets an idea in her head—"

Sam stared at him. "Judith Anderson is holding a shower for Max? Since when?"

"Since Wednesday morning," Jeff said. "She called

the house and told my wife they couldn't let Max leave without a proper wedding shower. She only had Friday night open, so they got everything together, spread the word and took the whole shebang out to the farm. They were hoping it would be a big surprise to Max."

Sam nodded. "I'm sure it was."

Jeff rose for his turn at bat. "They figured it would be easier than trying to get Max to go anywhere else. Like taking the mountain to Mohammed, is what my wife said." He glanced back as he walked out to the field. "Judith thought they should kidnap Max, but they pooh-poohed that idea quickly enough."

"Probably a good thing," Sam said, trying to picture Judith kidnapping Max and living to talk about it.

"They had a quite a turnout too," Ben said, scowling as Michael lobbed one right over the batter's head. "Seems everybody's looking forward to seeing Max again."

"I'll bet they are," Sam muttered. "So when did you find out?"

"When I went home this afternoon. There was a message on my machine from Kerri, telling me she wouldn't be at the game tonight after all. Seems she only found out when she got home herself."

"Did Eva know?"

"I couldn't reach her on the phone, so I went over to warn her. She hadn't heard a word about the plans, but there was no way to stop it. And maybe just as well. Get it over with." He tipped the bill of his cap down so he didn't have to watch the game, or Michael's pitching, anymore. "I was still at the farm when they started pulling in. Longest line of cars I've seen in a long time. Looked like a caravan."

"Or a funeral. How did Max take it?"

"Now that was interesting. She and that friend of hers made a beeline for the car when she realized what was happening, but Eva caught up with them, brought them both back." Ben smiled at the memory. "From the look on Max's face, you'd have sworn she was being led to a firing squad."

Sam nodded. "I can hear the drums from here. But she doesn't blame Eva?"

"Or her friend. I have to say that Delia tried her best to get her out of there, but she can't run for beans in those shoes. Can't figure out for the life of me why she wears them."

"It's her birthright," Sam said and looked over at the field where Michael was throwing just short of the plate this time.

The smartest thing he could do right now would be stay where he was, warming the bench until it was his turn to bat. She'd made it clear that she didn't want to see him. And he'd told himself over and over again that it was better that way. What did they have in common anyway? Nothing but a past she wanted to forget and a few hot kisses he couldn't forget for the life of him.

There was no doubt about it; he should stay right where he was. But the more he thought about Max and a wedding shower, the worse Michael's pitching became.

"You know," he said to Ben, "I think we really could use a new pitcher." He gathered up his glove and got to his feet. "I'm just going to slip over and see if Max wants to play."

Ben smiled. "I figured you might."

" 'I can't believe I'm doing this.' " Judith looked up from the page she was reading and added, "In bed."

Max groaned and blew at the strands of yellow and white ribbon that dangled in front of her face, while all around her women chuckled and smiled. A few even laughed out loud, obviously not having been out of the house much over the last ten years or so.

It was round two of Judith's favorite shower game, Honeymoon Openers—a game no one had mentioned to Max.

Without informing her, Judith had taken down the first words Max uttered when she stepped through the gate, sat in the chair and opened each gift. Now she was reading them back and tacking on "in bed" at the end of each line—a game Max figured must be particularly popular among shut-ins.

"Are we ready?" Judith asked, waiting for silence before reading the next line. " 'Oh God, take me now,' " she said, then raised a hand as if leading a band, and the whole bunch of them called out, "In bed."

While the women laughed and sipped their coffee, Max sat back and studied Judith. She stood in the center of the circle of women, just a few feet from Max's "seat of honor," looking cool and elegant in a floral print dress, her hair tied back in a neat little bun, her makeup light and flawless. When she spotted Max watching her, she smiled and sent her a little wave. Max smiled and nodded, knowing she should be gracious. But for all that she appreciated the trouble Judith had gone to in putting together the shower, Max still was not convinced that the woman's motives were entirely friendly. Especially once she started in on Honeymoon Openers.

But as effective as the game was, the humiliation had not been complete until the hat—a lovely pink paper plate festooned with the bows and ribbons from the gifts Max had opened. It now sat atop her head at a jaunty angle, tied securely under her chin with narrow curly ribbons dangling in front of her face like a veil.

Tradition, Judith had called it.

Revenge was what it felt like. Perhaps for the way Max had snubbed her at the farm the other day.

And to make matters worse, every other woman had gone along. Passing the bows, cutting the tape, then pronouncing the whole mess "cute" and snapping endless pictures—recording for posterity the humbling of Maxine Henley.

Judith waved the page of one-liners. "Are we ready for more?"

Max rose and slipped quickly between the chairs; smiling, nodding, excusing herself when necessary and finally making it around to the front porch.

Surprised to find herself alone, she plunked down on the top step and tried to untie the knotted ribbon under her chin, convinced that showers were like root canals—to be endured in silence, while clinging to the hope that it would all be over soon.

But even as she struggled with the bow, Max knew that most of the women had come in good faith. Arriving in cars, trucks and vans loaded with tables, chairs and food, they had brought the mountain to Mohammed, as one of them kept saying. And from Mrs. Mathews, Max's old baseball coach, to Kerri Jordan, the girl she used to baby-sit, everyone there seemed genuinely happy to see her.

No one had mentioned either Brian or Gwen, focusing instead on Peter and the celebrity cookbook, the wedding plans and when he would be arriving. Despite Max's own discomfort, their questions were nothing more than normal curiosity, and the congratulations rang true.

The fact that there was nothing to congratulate was not their fault. And Max had done her best to remember that when she'd opened their gifts, feeling a little more guilty each time she folded back the layers of tissue to reveal a tea cosy or an afghan or a pair of pot holders. Nothing sophisticated or trendy, just simple gifts from the heart, meant to help her turn a house into a home. And the best Max could do was smile and help Delia keep track of who had given her what, in case they all needed to be returned.

Later, when dinner had been served, they'd sat at long tables, laughing and talking, their plates piled high with everything from potato salad and fried chicken to stuffed grapes and tabbouleh. The scene was like something out of a Rockwell picture, only it was real. There was no prop girl, no special effects man. No one hollering, "Bring in the kids," or "Okay, cue the dog." This was life in Schomberg, with a rhythm that was ageless. And Max began to understand what it was that had drawn Sam back.

But she was the outsider now, neither a chic daughter from the subdivisions nor a mother from the farm. Belonging nowhere, afraid to relax, to enjoy, weary from keeping her guard up, yet afraid to let it down because she might slip, might tell a wrong lie about Peter.

"I think we could use a few more pictures," Judith called. "Where is that girl?"

Max sighed as she rubbed the back of her neck. And Judith was only making a bad situation worse.

Delia cast a quick glance over her shoulder as she came around from the garden. "You have my word that I will never do this to you. A little wine, a nice meal and no hat."

"I'll hold you to that," Max said, making room for her on the stairs. "Did you get all the presents listed, just in case?"

Delia patted her back pocket. "Right here, but all you'll need it for is thank-you cards."

Max plunked her chin on her hands. "I'm not so sure anymore. Peter's got the envelope by now, and he still hasn't called."

"Well, the moon hasn't smiled yet either, has it?"

Max glanced up at the sky. "It's too early to tell."

Delia started to protest when Judith's voice drifted

around from the side of the house. "Where's Maxine? It's picture time."

Max sighed and got to her feet, but Delia was already on her way down the stairs. "You need a break," she whispered. "Go on inside for a bit and I'll cover for you."

Max hesitated. "You sure?"

Delia shooed her away. "Positive. Just go."

"Thanks." Max glanced back when she reached the door. "And if you get a chance, grab that list of Openers."

Delia flashed her thumbs up. "Consider it done. Now go and relax."

Grateful, Max slipped through the front door and up the stairs to her room. She'd hide out for a few minutes, stash the hat and go back to the party, hoping she remembered exactly what she'd said about Peter.

She was trying to untie the knot at her throat when she heard a noise at her balcony door. Columbo had taken to sleeping in her room these past few days, and she crossed to the door, expecting to find him there, wanting in. But he wasn't on the deck or the stairs. She assumed she'd heard wrong and went back to working on the knot when she heard it again—a single tap, unmistakable this time.

She moved closer to the sliding door, cupping a hand on the glass for a better look at the deck. But still there was nothing on the other side.

"Maxine, it's picture time."

It was Judith, her voice carrying up the stairs from the porch. Resigned, Max turned, still tugging at the knot, when she heard it again, a distinct tap on the glass—like someone throwing stones.

She went back to the door and looked down at the deck this time. Sure enough, three small white pebbles lay on the planks. Curious, she slid the door open and tiptoed across the boards to the railing.

She leaned over and had to smile.

There stood Sam, white pebbles in his hand and a foolish grin on his face. She tried not to wonder how he'd known she needed him, or how he'd found her. But she couldn't stop the rush of pleasure that came with seeing him there.

Couldn't stop it, no. But she could definitely ignore it.

She rested her hands on the railing and tried to look bored. "What do you want, O'Neal?"

He bounced the stones in his hands. "Someone said that the baseball diamond is only a stone's throw from your yard."

She pursed her lips, fighting a smile. "But you had to see for yourself?"

"How else would I know for sure?" He tossed the pebbles back into the garden and dusted the sand from his hands. "I like your hat."

She laughed then, at him, at herself, at a situation that was too silly to be taken seriously, suddenly feeling like Juliet and Roxanne and every other woman who had ever been wooed on a balcony. But if he started to sing, she was leaving.

Besides, he wasn't wooing her, he was annoying her, distracting her, keeping her from thinking about Peter—something she would do well to remember.

She tugged at the ribbons, finally working them free. "What are you really doing here?"

"I came to see if you changed your mind about playing ball."

She dropped the hat on the deck and ran her fingers through her hair. "It's getting too dark for baseball."

He glanced over his shoulder at the setting sun. "It wasn't when I left," he said, and looked back at her.

"Why don't you come on down and we'll talk about it on the way to the park?"

"Maxine?" Judith called, then Delia said, "Leave the girl alone, she's probably in the bathroom."

Sam folded his arms and gave her that grin she knew too well. "Unless, of course, you'd rather put that hat on again and go back to the party."

Max frowned, thinking of the lies and the excuses and all those earnest faces. "I don't think I could get the bow right again."

"Then come out and play." He smiled and came up the stairs. "We really need a pitcher."

Max looked back at the door even as her feet took her to the top of the staircase. "What will I tell them?"

"Nothing." When he reached the top step, he took a folded piece of paper from his pocket. "Put this on the hat and let's go."

He stood eye-to-eye with her now, daring her, tempting her, making her feel more alive than she had in years.

"Come with me, Max," he whispered.

Max moistened her lips. It was now or never. Hat or baseball. Sam or Judith.

She snatched the paper out of his hand and dashed back to drop it on the hat. All evening she'd lied—to herself, to her neighbors, to her friends. But this was honest, this was real, and it was exactly what she wanted to do.

She felt light and free as she hurried back, running on her toes as though she was dancing. And when she might have stopped to think about what it meant or where it would lead or what anyone would say, he grabbed her hand and ran, taking her with him down the stairs and across the grass to the back gate he'd left ajar.

"Maxine, are you up here?" Judith called.

"In the bathroom," she called back, and laughed when he swept her up in his arms.

She held on tight all the way to his truck, burying her face in his neck and breathing in the warm, friendly scent of his skin. "What did the note say?" she asked as he set her on the front seat.

"Transaction canceled," he said, and closed the door. "It was an ATM receipt."

He started the truck and they bounced across the field, the windows open and the wind in her hair as he took her away from the house and out to a trail that ran through the woods—the one Eva used for sleigh rides in the winter.

The car slowed to a crawl, then a stop, and he looked over at her. "You're right, it's too late for baseball."

Max leaned back against the seat and looked over at him. He was turned toward her, one hand resting on the steering wheel, the other across the back of the seat, the carelessness of the pose at odds with the tension in his face, the set of his jaw, and the deep, fathomless black of his eyes.

Max felt that familiar warmth all over again, the one that started deep inside and uncurled slowly, steadily. She shifted on the seat, knowing she should ask him to take her back. Or maybe into town for a very public cup of coffee. Someplace where there would be no chance for him to sit too close, or touch her skin, or kiss her the way she'd been thinking about since the moment he climbed the stairs to rescue her. The way she was thinking about right now.

There was no doubt in her mind what she should do. Yet when he reached out and ran a finger down her cheek, she heard herself whisper, "Then just drive," and couldn't think of a reason to change her mind.

ELEVEN

He dropped the truck into gear and Max leaned over to switch on the radio, twisting the dial until she found something slow and bluesy while he continued along the trail. She sat back, eyes closed as the music washed over her, not thinking about where they were heading or what she was going to do when they got there, until he turned right at a fork in the road. Then she opened her eyes and glanced over at him, knowing exactly where they were.

The water in the pond lay still and golden in the last rays of the sun, and Max sat forward, ducking her head slightly so she could see the full sunset through the windshield. They'd come into the pond from the back way and weren't far from the house now, but no one would see the truck through the trees.

Sam switched off the engine and pushed open the door. "Come on. It's better from the dock."

Spring had started out hot and dry and stayed that way into the first days of summer, making quick work of the mosquitos that might have made an evening under the stars more of a test of wills than a pleasure. As they walked across the grass to the dock, the only sounds were crickets and bullfrogs, and the gentle lap of the water against the canoe.

The sun dipped below the horizon, leaving the sky streaked with shades of rose, peach, amethyst and indigo, and as she stepped onto the dock, Max knew that some-where, the moon was already looking down on them.

Sam kicked off his shoes and sat down on the dock. "So how was the shower?"

"Strange." She sat down on the edge and put a hand into the water, ruffling the surface and watching the cir-cles spread out into the growing darkness. "I hadn't ex-pected to enjoy seeing everyone, yet I did. And oddly enough, I was glad Peter wasn't there. Not because I was embarrassed, but because I wasn't. I'd been part of din-ners like that years ago and was touched that they had gone to so much trouble for me. But all I could imagine was Peter snapping pictures and thinking about where he could sell them. Quaint country charm to the highest bid-der. And I didn't want him to have that chance." She looked over at Sam. "Not much of a fiancée, huh?"

Sam shook his head as he lay back, his arms folded behind his head. "It has nothing to do with being a fi-ancée. It has to do with who you are and where you came from, and the need to hold onto some part of the past."

She nodded, her eyes skimming over the broad expanse of his chest to the taut plain of his belly, down the length of his legs to the tips of his toes. And finding him watch-ing her with open curiosity when her gaze returned to his face. She sucked in a quick, embarrassed breath and turned her attention back to the water. "Like you and the Tap Room."

He smiled as he sat up. "Although there's no need to go that extreme. A few cuttings from your mother's gar-den would probably do just fine."

"You've really taken a risk haven't you?"

He stared out at the water. "Let's just say that if a client had come to ask my advice on this particular in-vestment, I'd have told him to run the other way."

She smiled. "You never were very good at following advice."

"Especially my own." He ran a fingertip along the side of her leg. "But they're planning to build a new resort about twenty miles from here. Once that goes in, the town should see some spillover business, which will help spread the word."

"But it will only be tourists," she said, tucking her legs up under her dress. "What you need is a steady clientele. What you need are Judiths."

He sighed and leaned back on his hands. "Judiths?"

"People from the subdivisions and the cities. People who will look for the Schomberg Tap Room even in the winter."

Sam shook his head. "They'll never make the trek."

"They will if you come up with something irresistible."

He tipped his head to the side. "For instance?"

She got to her feet and glanced back at the house. "Brewery tours and special tastings. Gourmet nights in the dining room with special foods that you never offer on a regular basis. Dishes that are unique and different and can only be experienced at a tasting. And naturally, each course is accompanied by a sample of Ben's latest creations, served in small, tastefully designed glasses." She gave a solemn nod. "I can feel a cookbook in this."

He smiled at her. "I'd need a dining room first."

"So what's the holdup?" She kicked off her shoes and sat down again. "You've got the kitchen, and you've got Michael. All you need to do is create the right ambience."

"That takes furniture and money."

"It doesn't have to be expensive. You scour rummage and garage sales, you refinish and recover. Just like the jukebox, you rebuild and make it new."

"I was planning something more formal."

"Formal is fine in the city, but not here. You want tourists in shorts and T-shirts to feel as comfortable as the guy in the suit who drove straight from work to meet his wife for dinner. And that means casual yet refined. Not an echo of the pub, but not the kind of place where laughter doesn't feel out of place either." She put one leg over the side and dipped her toes in the water. "Think of Eva's house; nothing matches yet everything blends. That's what you want. The kind of place that will make the locals feel at home and drive a Judith crazy trying to copy it." She gave a nod of approval. "This is very exciting."

She was what was exciting. Maxine Henley with her soft skin and her hard nose, charging the air between them with energy and ideas. Visions so vivid, so real, he could see them as clearly as she could. He just couldn't see her staying long enough to make them come true.

"I could use a consultant." He waited until she looked over. "You're not looking for a job are you?"

Her face clouded, the excitement, the vibrancy fading, taking the dreams along.

"If Peter doesn't call, I might be. But not here. Not in Schomberg." She put her other foot over the edge of the raft, dipping more toes in the water. "I don't suppose you'd consider opening a branch in New York? They say Chelsea is the hot spot for eateries these days."

"Chelsea," Sam said, picturing boutiques and galleries, celebrities and ingenues. And trying to picture the Tap Room there, stuffed between the bodegas and the bistros, working hard to be an eatery when it was really a simple country pub. And ending up as lost and out of place as he would be himself now.

"I didn't think so," she said, interpreting his silence for exactly what it was, and removing the burden of a reply. She lowered her foot a little deeper into the pond and sighed. "What I wouldn't give to be in that water."

"So do it."

"I'm not wearing a bathing suit."

"Does it matter?"

She laughed and glanced over at him. "You're the one who used to skinny-dip here, not me."

"How did you know that?"

"I saw you." He raised a brow. "Just once," she added, then lowered her head and tried to hide a smile. "It was August and hot, more humid than tonight. I couldn't sleep, so I grabbed my bathing suit and a flashlight and came down here to cool off. But I heard you and Brian laughing and talking about a hundred feet ahead of me. So I switched off the light and followed."

"What were you planning to do?"

The smile widened. "Take your clothes while you were in the water, of course. Brian was already swimming by the time I arrived. But you were still dressed and standing on the raft, as though you'd changed your mind. I couldn't get to Brian's clothes with you there, so I started back. Then all of a sudden you peeled off your shirt and dropped it on the boards." She shrugged a shoulder. "So I sat down and waited for the rest."

"But you didn't expect me to turn around, did you?" It was his turn to smile when her eyes widened. "I knew you were there. I'd seen the lights flick on in your room as Brian and I were walking along the side of the house. When I heard the rustle in the bushes, I figured it was you. And when you didn't come out, I assumed you'd come to watch, so I decided to put on a good show."

"You certainly did that," she said, avoiding his eyes as she dipped a hand into the water again.

"I remember thinking you'd run when I started to undo my belt. But you didn't. I also remember thinking that what I was doing was wrong. That I should call out and say I knew you were there."

She lifted her face, meeting his gaze. "Why didn't you?"

"Because I liked knowing your eyes were on me. That's why I took my time shedding those clothes. It was agony in that heat, and Brian kept hollering at me to hurry. But I wanted to do it slowly, to see how long you'd stay, how long you'd watch." He paused, remembering. "You surprised me."

"I surprised myself," she said, her voice barely a whisper.

He rose, taking her with him. "Then surprise me again. Come swimming."

She pushed him away with a laugh. "Are you crazy?"

He started to undo his shirt. "Probably. But the water's warm and it would be a shame to waste this beautiful night."

She slapped her hands over his, stopping him on the second button. "You can't be serious. All those people are still up there. My mother, Delia—"

"And the party is still going strong." He lifted her hands, kissed each palm, and started in on the buttons again. "Chances are, they haven't even missed you yet."

"Thanks a lot."

"It's not an insult, just a faint hope that we've got a bit of time left before they start hollering your name from the porch."

She nodded, knowing they would definitely holler as she watched the V at the front of his shirt grow wider, deeper, hinting at well-defined muscles and a mist of dark hair that led her eyes down, down . . .

She jerked her head up. "I have to leave."

"You're blushing, aren't you?" He turned his back and pulled his shirt out of his jeans. "Okay, this time no one looks." He glanced over his shoulder and frowned. "Do you mind?"

She swung around, smiling at the path. He was right

about it being a beautiful night, and the water was indeed warm. And it wasn't as though they'd left a trail of crumbs for anyone to follow . . .

She gave her head a shake and folded her arms. "I am not doing this."

His breath was hot and unexpected against her ear. "Then how come you're still here?"

She snapped her shoulder up but had no answer as he dropped his shirt into a soft puddle by her feet. She listened to the unmistakable sound of a belt buckle loosening and knew that in another moment he'd be naked. Sam wasn't the type to play games or start something he didn't intend to finish. He meant to swim, to cool off in the pond. She could join him or not, it was that simple.

But what about her? What was she starting? "And what about Peter?" she whispered, realizing too late that she'd spoken out loud.

"He can join us when he gets here."

She heard the smile in his voice and wanted to smack him.

"And what exactly would I tell him? 'Hi, honey, the water's fine. Just jump right in with me and this naked man—' "

"Friend."

"Sam, please. I think we passed that point a while back. Which is exactly why I have to go."

"Max," was all he said, but she knew he wasn't smiling anymore. "Go if you want, but first be honest. You've never been skinny-dipping, have you?"

"Of course I have," she said, the very soul of indignation. But the effect was lost since he wasn't looking, and she felt her shoulders sag under the truth. "All right, so my childhood was lacking."

"And what are you going to do if Peter never calls?"

"I'll go home," she said, the answer coming quickly, easily because she'd already accepted the possibility that

Delia was wrong. That Peter was neither miserable nor distracted, just busy. And he might keep on thinking forever.

"So either way, you'll leave," Sam said. "Go back to your apartment, your studio, your work."

She shrugged. "Life as usual."

"And you still will never have skinny-dipped." He drew in a deep breath and let it out slowly. "Well, if you ask me, that seems like a terrible waste of a beautiful summer evening."

She looked down, watching a bug skate across the surface of the water. Then froze, listening to the unmistakable sound of a zipper lowering. "So," he said as his jeans hit the floor, "do you need a hand with that dress?"

"Just keep your back turned," she said, laughing as she tugged the dress over her head and dropped it on the pile of clothes at their feet.

She glanced down at the love charm still in place over her heart. She moistened her lips, then pulled the tiny red pillow from its hiding place and bent down to tuck it into the folds of her dress.

"You're not peeking, are you?" he asked.

"Of course not," she said, unhooking her bra and feeling her face warm as she let it fall on top of her dress.

Officially, nothing had changed. She was still engaged, with the presents to prove it. And if that phone rang, she'd go with Peter, back to New York and the life they'd planned. But right now, she was going to swim naked in the moonlight, and damn anyone who tried to tell her it was wrong.

"You're not peeking either, are you?" she asked as she stepped out of her panties.

"Yes."

She froze a moment, then folded her arms over her breasts and checked over her shoulder. He stood half in darkness, half in pale and watery light, captured forever in her mind like a black-and-white photograph, a moment to be brought out years from now when she would remember him just this way. Strong. Hard. Male.

His arms hung at his sides, as though there was nothing to hide, then his eyes met hers and began a slow, frank journey down the length of her back to her hips, her thighs, lingering a moment on her feet before traveling up again, making her legs weak even as her pulse grew stronger, more urgent. She saw his mouth tighten, his eyes narrow, and took pleasure in seeing what she did to him.

"Do you have any idea how beautiful you are?" His voice was low, hard-edged, and a wicked smile curved his lips as he came toward her. "And Peter is a goddamn fool."

She turned and he covered her mouth with his, no preamble, no seduction, just a need that matched her own, making her dizzy with its force and power.

Then he lifted her into his arms and tossed her into the water. "That's for watching all those years ago," he said, and smiled when she came up sputtering.

"I'll get you for that," she called.

"God, I hope so," he said and leapt in beside her, sending a wave of water over her head again.

"How do you like it so far?" he asked, that edge of passion still there, stronger now as he pulled her to him, supporting her while she shoved her hair out of her eyes and wiped her streaming face.

"I haven't had time to find out," she said and he kissed her hard, then laughed and swam away, floating on his back, naked and beautiful in the moonlight.

She swam after him, long, powerful strokes that felt good and right after days of inactivity. The water was warming now, passing over her body like a caress, shocking at first, then soothing and relaxing. And she rolled over, floating on her back as he did and staring up at the stars, hearing nothing but the beat of her heart and the lapping of the water around her.

He surfaced beside her and she struggled to cover herself and keep afloat at the same time, making them both laugh as the awkwardness gave way to practicality. She thought he might come to her then, but he ducked and was gone, leading her in a game of hide and seek. She followed his lead and they chased each other, diving and surfacing, laughing and splashing like children. Then he stopped suddenly and floated her in his arms, kissing her slowly, deeply, reminding her that they were anything but children.

She pulled back before the need became too stark, too hard to deny, treading water as she watched him swim with purpose now, cutting through the water with ease and grace; knowing it wouldn't be long before he was back, reaching for her, wanting her.

With Peter, sex was fine, sometimes interesting, but usually orchestrated or not at all—just something neither of them seemed to need often. But Sam was sexual by nature, completely at home with his body. And hers.

She swam to the raft and climbed out, suddenly shy, shaken. The air was warm but the breeze raised gooseflesh on her wet skin, making her shiver as she reached for her clothes.

He came up the stairs after her. "You're cold," he said, taking her hand and lifting her to her feet.

"No, I'm fine," she said, and tried to cover herself with her hands.

"Max, look at me," he said, his voice low and soft, and she raised her eyes, feeling her face warm as he wrapped his shirt around her.

His hair was still wet and slicked back from his face, emphasizing the strength of his features, the length of his lashes. He looped his arms around her shoulders, drawing her close. She moved to him and tipped her head back, sure that he would kiss her. Then suddenly he scooped her up and she squealed, thinking he might throw her in again. But he shushed her with a look, then started to carry her away from the dock, and she realized he was heading up to the truck.

"It's softer here," he whispered, setting her in the backseat and climbing in after her. And Max heard herself giggle as he closed the door and gave her that wicked smile, just before he eased her back on the seat.

She stiffened, feeling silly all of a sudden, stretched out there on the backseat of a pickup. With Peter there was always wine and food, and soft music. Then Sam reached into the front seat and there was music in the truck too—a real hurtin' country song. And she had to laugh as he sat back, singing the chorus in the worst down-home twang she had ever heard.

But Max's laughter caught and her blood warmed when he stopped singing and smiled that wicked smile. Who needed wine? she wondered as his hands pushed her shirt open. And who could think about food when all she wanted was that wonderful mouth on hers?

She reached up, some part of her knowing this wasn't like her, and the rest not listening as he brushed feathery kisses across her forehead, her eyelids, her cheeks, her lips. She sighed and pulled him down, seeking his lips while the heat swirled and pooled low in her belly.

His hand was on her breast now, hot against cold, and she arched into him, loving the way his breath came, quick and shallow as he kissed a path from her ear to her throat, and farther to her breasts.

His mouth closed on her nipple and she ran her fingers into his hair, holding him fast and wondering again what it was about Sam that made her want, made her need as she'd never needed any man.

Her experience was limited and only ever after due consideration and thoughtful conversation. But with Sam there was no time for thought or discussion. There was only sensation—friction and heat, wet and dry—and a feeling that she was on the edge of something. That all she had to do was step too close and she'd lose herself in this man who was serious and teasing, charming and rude; always changing, keeping her off balance so she couldn't pin him down. Couldn't say *this is Sam*. Because he was always so much more.

Was this love? she wondered, a sudden shock moving through her as he stroked her thighs and parted her legs. Because if it was, she wanted no part of it. Yet as he moved a hand between her legs, finding her ready and shamelessly wanting, how could she stop herself from falling over that edge? From ending up like Alice, tumbling down the rabbit hole to a place she didn't belong, with no way home. In a love that had no future, just like Brian, just like her mother.

What is it with the Henleys? she wondered as she lifted her hips, giving, taking, she wasn't sure which anymore as the first wave washed over her, through her and brought her back to the surface, sweating, gasping and not nearly finished.

He moved over her, and she welcomed him, feeling him hard against her belly. "Max," he whispered, and she covered his mouth with her hands, afraid he would say something now to push her over that edge. Make her fall in love. And once she had, how would she find her way back again?

"Don't talk," she said, looking into his eyes, seeing the heat, the hunger and something deeper, more tender, almost vulnerable. As though she was looking into his very soul and seeing fear. Of her? Of himself? While she struggled to put a name to it, her body responded, rising up, wanting to take him deep inside, where they would both be safe.

"Are you sure this is what you want?" he asked, still

holding back, trembling with the effort as his eyes begged for answers. She moved against him, letting silence be her answer, telling only herself that it was all right. That she could have this and nothing would change, and knowing it to be a lie. He was changing her even now, opening a heart that she had guarded for so long it frightened her now to think of that fall. So deep, so unforgiving. With nothing at the bottom to catch her.

It was then that she heard it. A voice drifting in through the back window, faint beneath the music. He heard it too, and rose, switching off the radio and sitting perfectly still, trying hard to control his breathing as they listened. It wasn't one voice at all but many, all of them hollering her name. She didn't get it all, but the gist was clear. Max. Peter. Phone.

Sam didn't ask if she wanted out. Just swore and opened the door—one short, punchy word that summed everything up nicely. Then he reached back into the truck, offering a hand, helping her up, looking away this time, giving her back her privacy.

He walked ahead of her to the dock, pulling on his jeans and keeping his back turned for real this time as she dressed. She rifled through the pile, one ear tuned to the path, knowing it was foolish—no one would look for her here—but nervous all the same. Her fiancé was on the phone and she was pushing her feet into her underwear on the dock. Difficult to explain at the best of times. And this was definitely not the best of times.

She didn't know why but her eyes stung and her throat was suddenly dry. Frustration, she told herself, fumbling with the clasp of her bra and biting her lip to keep from making a sound while Sam just stood looking out over the water, his breath calm now, his back rigid. And she could only guess what was on his mind.

She pulled the dress on, pushing it down while she searched the raft for the charm. Almost wishing the damn thing had fallen through the cracks and floated away. But there it was, by his left foot. The gold threads glistening in the moonlight.

She bent, picking it up quickly and pushing it into place as she left the dock.

"I'll drive you back," he said, turning to follow.

"I'll walk."

He swung open the driver's side door. "You can't walk all that way in the dark. Now get in the truck."

"I can't get in the truck," she said, trying to swallow the dryness in her throat. "It won't look good for the two of us to arrive together. And you know how they love to talk."

He stared at her a moment, then tossed his shirt in the truck. "Suit yourself."

And suddenly what had seemed wonderful and right was now merely dirty and cheap. He started the truck, and Max called herself every kind of fool and more as she stumbled up the path; scolding herself roundly for getting too close to that edge. For almost falling for a man she couldn't have and shouldn't want, when the perfect man was waiting for her on the end of the telephone line.

And counting herself lucky as the truck roared off across the field, kicking up dust and startling the llamas and ponies in the loafing barn.

"Thank you, Iona," she said out loud, then glanced up to see the moon peeking over the trees. A Cheshire Cat grin if ever she'd seen one.

TWELVE

Jealousy. Sam had never tasted it until last night on the dock. Had gone his whole life without knowing anything as cold and bitter as the feeling that had crept over him as he stood on that raft, listening to her dress. Hearing her fumble with clasps and straps and seeing tears of frustration on her lashes as she hurried up that path.

Embarrassed because she'd let her guard down and simply been Max—laughing, passionate, carefree. And so beautiful it made him ache just to look at her. Made him want to hold her there, warm and naked beside him, until she faced who she was and what she wanted from life, from love. From him.

Max might think him an incurable romantic, but Sam had never been one to kid himself, to imagine things that weren't there. But neither was he one to doubt the truth when he saw it. And last night the truth had been right there in her eyes—that tiny spark of wonder or hope or whatever the poets might call it. But as far as Sam was concerned, that light was love, plain and simple.

She loved him, or wanted to, just as much as he wanted to love her, believing in spite of everything that they could make it work. Find a way to compromise, to change. And he had no words to describe the pain that had gripped his heart as he watched that light fade, snuffed out before it could really catch hold, and all because Peter had called.

Peter the fiancé, the fool, the pain in the ass who would take her away from the farm, the memories and him. And she would go too, letting herself slip right back into a life that was familiar and painless, and kept her numb from the heart down—because the idea of love scared her to death.

As he sat now on the fence outside her house, a cup of takeout coffee in his hand and the morning sun on his face, Sam felt that bitter taste return—twice as strong, and every bit as useless. Because there was nothing he could do to stop her.

"You going to help with these animals or sit there and stew?" Ben called.

Sam glanced over to where Ben was herding two of Eva's goats up the ramp and into the back of a gooseneck trailer.

"I'm not stewing, I'm thinking," Sam said and slid off the fence, dumping his coffee into a trash can on his way to the truck.

Ben scowled as he approached. "I've seen you think before, and what I'm seeing now is definitely not thinking."

Sam scowled back, knowing he should have stayed at home. He was only torturing himself by being there, and the old man had been testy since dawn. Growling and snapping like a little dog on a short leash, nearly taking Sam's head off when he asked what was wrong.

But he'd promised to help get the petting zoo rolling, and he wasn't one to go back on his word. And if he was honest, there was some perverse part of himself that hoped Peter would pull in while he was there, just so he could see for himself that the man was real.

So he ignored Ben and picked up the clipboard from

the ramp, ticking goats off the list as they clomped into the trailer.

"What's next?" he asked as Ben came back out of the barn.

"Potbellied pig." He glanced over at Sam as they walked. "And no jokes. He's very sensitive and Eva doesn't need a sulky pig at the mall."

"Heaven forbid," Sam said as he opened the gate to the paddock.

The llamas looked over expectantly, but the sheep ignored them, as if knowing their place in line. Goats first, followed by the pig and then the sheep. The llamas would go in the second compartment, and the ponies in the third.

Eva and Ben had loaded up the portable pens, feed and bedding yesterday, then double-checked everything this morning. Another half hour and the Peacock Manor Petting Zoo would be on the road, heading for their first official engagement. With luck, she'd find more bookings as the summer wore on, not only helping the animals to earn their keep, but also spreading the word about Peacock Manor a little farther, sparking interest in the hayrides and the corn roasts and anything else Eva could come up with.

Sam shook his head as he snapped the lead on the pig. It never failed to amaze him what people would do to hold on to the things they loved.

Once the sheep were loaded and the first compartment closed, Ben turned to Sam again. "So, what are you thinking about so hard anyway?"

"Rummage sales." Sam looked over as they walked back to the paddock. "You any good at refinishing furniture?"

"Not me, but my brother does a fair job." Ben snapped a rein on the llama's halter and she stepped out, head high, leading rather than following, to the trailer. "Why? Do you have something you need done?"

"Not yet." Sam glanced up at Max's window. "It was just an idea."

Ben stopped, and he and the llama looked over at Sam. "You know you're barking up the wrong tree, don't you?"

"With rummage sales?"

"With Max." Ben and the llama turned away and kept walking to the trailer. "She's going to marry that guy and you'd be well advised to stay out of it."

"I don't know what you're talking about—"

"Don't even start." Ben pulled up short and the llama looked none too pleased with either of them. "Everyone knows she came back to the shower with wet hair, and you were seen driving off with no shirt and your hair plastered to your head."

Sam drew back as if he'd been punched. He'd assumed no one had seen him. A clean getaway, he'd thought, hoped. "Who told you?"

"I heard it at Cy's, where else?" He took a step closer. "I ran damage control as best I could. Told them you were helping to get the animals washed down for the petting zoo and must have come out on the losing end."

Sam nodded his thanks, but Ben just waved it off. "What in God's name were you doing with that girl?"

"Skinny-dipping," Sam said, knowing it wouldn't go farther, not even to Eva if he asked Ben to keep it there. "She'd never been, so I took her. Just two friends going for a swim."

Ben's mouth pinched as he studied him. "And that's why she was up all night, walking around the front lawn in the dark? Because everything was so innocent. Just two friends and a goddamned naked swimming party."

"You don't understand—"

"I understand that Eva called me at three in the morning, worried sick because Max was out here talking to herself, mumbling about smiling moons and beer with the spirits and a whole lot of other nonsense." Both Ben and the llama stepped closer. "That girl had enough to worry about when she came here. What with Gwen being back, and an idiot fiancé, and that bridge still haunting her. I swear, if you did anything to hurt her, anything at all—"

"Ben, I'm in love with her."

Ben's jaw snapped shut and the llama could only stare.

He'd known last night, of course, and hearing himself say the words out loud made it more real, but no less impossible.

"Does she love you back?"

Sam looked down at his feet. "I think she does; in fact I'm sure of it, but what difference does it make? You said yourself she's going to marry Peter."

Ben shook his head. "How can she do that if she loves you?"

Sam smiled at his confusion, understanding it completely. "Because she's Max. And she's convinced herself that love killed Brian and she doesn't want any part of it."

"Just like her mother's convinced herself that there's only one love for every lifetime."

"And she's already had hers."

"Fifteen good years," Ben said, but Sam knew it was Eva talking. Ben rocked back on his heels and looked down at his feet. "So what are you going to do about it?"

The llama stepped closer, eyes wide, waiting.

Sam shrugged and stroked her ears. "What can I do? You know as well as I do how she feels about Gwen, the bridge, the whole town in general. That doesn't leave a lot of room for negotiation."

"Impossible situations. I know them well." Ben sighed,

sounding weary and defeated, and the closest to sixty that Sam had ever known. "And I don't blame you for giving up so quick." He looked over at the house as Eva came through the back door. "Because I'm about to do the same thing myself."

Max shoved the door back and followed her mother down the stairs. "But why do you have to go today? Why can't you do it next week?"

Eva paused and looked back at her. "Because the mall has designated this as Pet Week. Next week will be Beauty Week. Potbellied pigs do not belong at Beauty Week." She smiled and cupped a hand on Max's cheek. "Besides, you and Peter can use the time alone."

Max frowned. "What is that supposed to mean?"

Eva threw up her hands and started walking across the lawn. "Not a thing. Only that you haven't seen each other in almost two weeks, and you probably want to spend some time alone."

Max trailed along behind. "Of course we do. Why wouldn't we?"

"No reason at all," Eva said, her bright smile looking forced as she went through the gate.

And no wonder, Max thought, knowing she'd been impossible all morning, whining and snarling at every turn. She'd love to get away from herself if she could. But it was only because she hadn't slept, and Peter was coming. And she did not want to be alone with him. Not yet, not today.

"What if you sent the Jenkins boys with Ben?" she called, and raced to catch up to her mother.

Eva slowed and turned to her. "Max, will you stop? You're just nervous. It's natural after what happened, but everything's going to be fine now."

Max eyed her. "Fine now? What is that supposed to mean?"

Eva dropped her head back. "All right, you win. I know that Peter broke off the engagement, does that make it easier?"

"He didn't break it off," Max said, folding her arms and staring out at the paddock. "He just wanted time to think, to adjust. And how did you know anyway?"

Eva's eyes softened. "You're my daughter. I can tell when you're lying or covering up. And I can tell when you're hurting." She gave her head a small, sad shake. "I understand why you didn't tell me, how confused and embarrassed you must have been. But now he's on his way and the two of you have a chance to make things right. And you don't need me around to make him feel awkward."

"Which is exactly what I said to myself this morning," Delia said as she came across the grass, no longer tottering on heels, but walking solidly on a pair of Eva's flat, sturdy runners.

A practical Delia, Max thought with a smile. Who'd have guessed?

" 'Delia,' I said, 'the last thing Max needs is a fifth wheel.' " She grinned as she drew up beside them. "So I have come to help with the petting zoo. If that's okay."

"Love to have you," Eva said, putting an arm around Delia's shoulder and turning toward the trailer. "The llamas have grown quite fond of you, you know."

Delia nodded. "I thought I could feel this bond growing—"

"Delia, wait." Max held out her hands when she and Eva turned. "Please don't go. I need you."

Delia shook her head, her grin softening as she came back. "You don't need me anymore," she said, her voice gentle, almost wistful as she took Max's hands in hers. "You'll be fine, you and Peter. Great, in fact." She gave her fingers a squeeze. "That was some plan, huh?" Then she smiled brightly and turned back to Eva. "The ad was my idea, did you know that?"

"It was truly inspired," Eva said, then glanced back at Max. "By the way, Sam has invited us all to dinner at the Tap Room tonight. A little engagement party."

Max shook her head. "That's not a good idea."

"He promised it would be a private table, just for the five of us, but I insisted he join us, so now it will be six."

"Mom, I don't want—"

"Maxine, don't fret. He promised it would be private and you know that Sam always keeps his word."

"Not always," she muttered, an image of him watching her on the raft lodging in her head. Her mother looked at her curiously so she laughed and waved a hand. "Kidding, kidding. But I still don't think we should go."

"Nonsense. I won't be home in time to cook dinner anyway, and we all know what you'd do to it, so the Tap Room is the logical conclusion. I think he said eight, but you could ask him," Eva added as she and Delia walked away, leaving Max alone by the fence.

"I'll be sure to call him," Max muttered as Columbo wandered over from his favorite spot under the trees and nudged her hand with his nose. Max knelt down and scratched his ears. "Looks like it's just you and me."

"I'll stay if you like."

She raised her head, hearing the same rich voice she'd heard inside her head all night.

"I'll be fine," she said, knowing it was a lie the moment she looked up and saw his face.

The tiny lines around his eyes were more pronounced this morning, and there was nothing playful or teasing in the set of his mouth. He looked tired, spent, but she found no pleasure in the knowledge that he hadn't slept either. What was the point of both of them being miserable if there was no solution?

He got down on one knee to scratch the dog's other ear, putting Columbo into a state of unrivaled bliss. It was easier, she supposed, with the dog between them. Something to look at besides each other, and occupy hands that might forget where they belonged.

She risked a glance at him again and caught him watching her. But he didn't look away, made no attempt to hide, and she had to turn first, knowing she wouldn't be fine until she was back in New York.

"You look lovely, by the way."

She nodded and mumbled her thanks as she rose. She'd taken care when she dressed, choosing something new—electric blue, spaghetti straps—from the holiday collection that had stayed stuffed in her suitcase until four o'clock that morning, when she'd tired of walking and started ironing instead, proving just how bored she was.

But the dress had looked better without the wrinkles. And it was nice to know that the effort had been appreciated.

"I brought you something," he said, and came toward her.

She held back, wary.

"Hold out your hand." He smiled when she held back. "It won't bite, I promise."

She opened her hand and he placed a glossy black ostrich feather in her palm. "I figured you might want to think about that hat, now that Peter's on the way."

"I just might," she said, and pushed through the gate, heading for the porch with the feather, signaling the dog to follow. But he'd rolled on his back in front of Sam, looking for a belly rub.

"So what happens now?" Sam asked.

He was still patting the dog, but he was looking straight at her.

"What do you think happens? Peter arrives, I go home. It's pretty straightforward."

"He wants to get married after all?"

"That's what he said on the phone last night. He wants to meet my mother, set a date, all the things we planned weeks ago."

"And you simply pick up where you left off then, is that it?" Sam rose and came through the fence, his steps slow, measured. "Forget that he broke your heart and left you stranded—"

"He needed time to be sure—"

"And what about you, Max? Are you sure now?" He stopped in front of her, his voice softening, matching his touch as he reached out, cupping her cheek in his hand. "Are you positive this marriage is what you need?"

"What I need is to go home," she said quietly and drew away, fighting the urge to lean into a touch that was still too fresh in her mind, making her forget what it was that she wanted to say, and why. "I need to see my apartment, the studio, Peter behind a camera. I want to put my life back the way it was—"

"And pretend that nothing happened here? Make believe we never touched, never kissed, never came so close to making love that I can still taste you, still smell you on my skin—"

"Why are you doing this?" She turned, walking backward now, moving toward the porch, away from him. "What is the point?"

"The point is, I love you."

She slowed and stopped, watching his eyes as he came to her. *So this is what love looks like,* she thought. Dark, tender, more than a little unsure. She knew now because she'd seen it before—last night, when he'd hesitated, holding back, needing to be sure she wanted him. How could he have doubted, when he was all she wanted even now?

Max felt herself on the edge again, slipping, slipping; about to fall down that long dark tunnel into a love she didn't want, couldn't use, when the right man was on his way. Driving up from Virginia Beach to start over, set everything straight, take them back to where they'd been. Back to trade shows and office furniture. All the things that still made sense if she thought clearly and logically, and stayed well back from the edge. And the only way to guarantee of that was to make sure Sam wasn't waving to her from the bottom.

So she folded her arms against the tenderness in his eyes, the heaviness around her heart, and prepared to go home. " 'I love you,' " she quoted, then smiled. "You say that easily, don't you? First to Caroline, now to me. Who will it be by Christmas?" She narrowed her eyes as she gave her head a shake. "I don't know, Sam. Sounds to me like you're still coasting."

She would see it that way, and with reason. Even he knew he'd fallen too hard, too fast, something that had only happened once before—the summer he turned eighteen and she'd been far too young. "I stopped coasting a while ago. And if you're not here at Christmas, I'll only be saying it to you on the phone."

"I doubt my husband would like that."

"If you get married."

"I will be married," she said evenly, then lowered her arms. "Besides, even if I'm not, what difference does 'I love you' make?"

"It's a good place to start."

She blinked. "Start what? You're not about to hang a 'For Sale' sign in your window, and there's nothing for me here."

"There's the Blue Ridge Café. Just a little place on the hill, serves comfort food—"

"Sam, don't."

"Can't you see it? Right beside the pub, all refinished

furniture and mismatched china." He risked taking a step toward her. "I said yesterday that I could use a consultant, but I was wrong. I could use a partner."

Her eyes narrowed. "I won't have a partner, remember?"

"Then I'll put that side of the building up for lease. See if I get any offers."

"I'm sure you will," she said, and he watched her look away, refusing to dust off old dreams, to get caught up in her own fantasy. "Schomberg could use a good bait and tackle shop."

"It can use the café more. You could build one, Max. Make it everything you talked about. All you have to do is stay."

"And risk running into Gwen at the grocery store?" She was off again, heading up the porch stairs and calling to him over her shoulder, "No thanks."

He followed to the stairs. "Why don't you talk to her, find out what happened that night?"

"Because I stopped caring about her side a long time ago. She never once contacted us, never spoke to my mother, sent her a note, nothing. Silence is like an admission of guilt, don't you think?"

"She was only eighteen."

Max paused at the screen door. "Old enough to use a phone. But if you're so interested, you talk to her."

"I tried to."

Her face remained neutral, but her fingers gripped the doorhandle. "You've seen her?"

"I probably should have told you before. She stopped in at the Tap Room, looking for a job. I didn't hire her, of course."

"Matters not to me," she said, but the air of indifference rang false.

"This may come as a shock to you, but it's not easy

for her to be here. People haven't welcomed her with open arms."

"Then maybe she'll leave. The fact remains that Brian loved her and she let him down. What more is there to know?" She swung the door open. "Love has a way of doing that, have you noticed? Lifting you up only to let you fall flat on your face. And I for one am not going down that slippery slope."

"Too late."

She glanced back. "Don't flatter yourself."

"I'm not. But I was in the truck with you, remember?" He sat down on the bottom step, listening to her march back across the porch and down the stairs as he made himself comfortable. He smiled up at her when she stood on the walkway in front of him. "So the question now is, what do we do about it?"

"You go away. That's what we do about it. Peter and I have everything I need—"

He held up a hand. "I know, I know, shared goals and common interests. Or is it the other way around?"

"Either way, it's a place to start. A solid one." She turned as a car came up the driveway. "That's Peter now. If you'll excuse me . . ."

"Just one thing—when he asks how your week was, what will you say?"

She glanced back at him. "I'll tell him I almost fell down a rabbit hole, but I'm just fine now."

THIRTEEN

Peter's car was as familiar as her own. Silver Jaguar, only a year old, always professionally detailed and shining. *Except today,* she thought, as the cloud of dust he'd created settled over the sports car, dulling the finish. But it didn't seem to bother him as he closed the door and looked over at her—a tall man, lean bordering on thin, with hair the color of summer wheat and a face that had made her write home to mother.

He came toward her, not with Sam's long, easy stride, but that of a man in a hurry. A city man: intense, focused, seeing only what was ahead of him. And right now, that was her.

She smiled, truly glad to see him. She liked Peter, always had. They'd met three years ago on a pasta shoot for a gourmet magazine, he the photographer in charge, she the stylist hired as a last minute stand-in. Initially leery of each other, she couldn't help but be impressed by his fresh approach to each shot. And when he saw what she could do with a forkful of linguine and a pair of tweezers, he'd asked for her business number. Perfectionists both, they'd quickly recognized each other as professional soul mates, and a successful partnership had blossomed into romance, of a sort.

Not the romance of poets and songwriters with irrational expectations and declarations of love. But a comfortable romance, one of substance and longevity. One built on—

She frowned and glanced over at Sam, suddenly restless and irritated and bored with the mantra herself by now.

"Khakis and leather loafers," he said so only she could hear. Then he turned and flashed her that smile she knew was trouble. "Very Chelsea."

"It's a good look." She turned away. "You should try it some time."

"Honey, I invented it," he said, and she laughed, couldn't help it. The idea of Sam in a deconstructed jacket and drawstring pants was just too hard to imagine.

But Peter wore them well.

"Baby, I am so sorry," he said when he reached her.

She moved into his arms, thinking how tired he looked and touched by the knowledge that he'd driven all night to be there so early.

They held each other for a moment, and Sam looked down at his feet, wondering when they'd go and why the man was patting her back, and whether or not she actually liked it.

He looked up in time to see Peter kiss her, if that's what it was. More like a peck really, the kind reserved for buddies, the kind Sam had given her on the night she arrived. Hardly appropriate for a fiancée.

Peter stepped back from her as though noticing Sam for the first time, and Max quickly made the introductions, ending with, "And Sam was just leaving."

"Any minute now," he said, smiling broadly at Peter as he shook his hand. "So how was the drive? Must have been a pleasure in a beauty like that."

"Always," Peter said, looking back at the Jag. "I've had that car a year and it's still a thrill every time I get behind the wheel."

"I know what you mean. I had an Aston Martin DB7."

"A DB." Peter gave a low whistle. "Hell of a car." He glanced over at Max, then quickly back at Sam. "I could probably stand out here and talk cars all morning, but if you don't mind, Max and I have some catching up to do." He smiled at her. "Did I tell you how fabulous you look?"

Sam had to give him points for that. And for holding on to her hand as though she might get away from him. Most of all, he had to give the man points for looking at her like he was surprised to see her standing there beside him—this beautiful woman he'd almost lost. And he couldn't help wondering if Peter did love her after all.

Sam tasted that bitterness all over again as he backed up a step, figuring the first place they'd head when he left would be her bedroom. Lord knew it would be his own first choice. His stomach clenched with the memory of her, warm and soft beneath him, and he wished he hadn't hesitated, wished he'd loved her when he had the chance—because it would never come again.

"I understand," he said, and moved back farther. "Don't forget, dinner at the Tap Room tonight."

Peter looked from one to the other. "Tap Room?"

"Sam owns a restaurant in town," Max said. "He's invited us for an engagement dinner, but if you'd rather not—"

"I'd love to." Peter smiled and held out a hand to Sam again. "Thank you. It will give us a chance to celebrate this engagement properly."

"That was the idea," Sam said, hoping his own smile was half as sincere as Peter's. And regretting now that he'd told Eva he would join them.

"I'll get my bags and you can help me get settled," Peter said to Max, then turned and jogged back to his car. "I want a full tour of the farm too. Delia told me there were llamas."

"And ostriches," Max said, realizing she was still holding the feather. She glanced over at Sam. "So I guess we'll see you tonight after all."

"Eight o'clock," he said, while Peter pulled his cameras and suitcases from his trunk—the mates to the ones Sam had carried for Max when she arrived. "I'll arrange a private table and get Michael to whip up something guaranteed to ruin Ben's night." He watched Peter slam the trunk and pocket his keys. "He seems like a nice guy."

"He is," she said, and looked over at him. "He really is."

"I guess I can forgive him the loafers then," Sam said, and shot her a quick grin, only to find it wouldn't hold. "I forget what it is that I'm supposed to wish the bride. Is it congratulations or good luck?"

"Good-bye," she said, and turned to smile as Peter approached.

"See you tonight," Peter called to Sam, who saluted him, then turned and kept going, across the driveway and the lawn to his truck.

"A dinner party," Peter said as he drew up in front of her. "That should be fun." He motioned to the bags. "Let's get rid of these, and you can take me to the llamas. What's with the feather, by the way?"

"It's for a hat." She turned and led him through the gate to the porch. "It's a long story."

"And this is a lovely spot," he said, giving the gardens a quick once-over. "I'll get some exterior shots for the ad as we walk around. I have to say that was a great layout. I knew it was more you than Wilhelm the moment I saw it."

"To be honest, it was mostly Delia." She held the front door open, surprised that they'd slipped so smoothly into the routine.

But wasn't that exactly what she wanted? The quick way home?

"Delia, huh?" He carried his bags into front hall. "You never can tell what she'll do next. Like up and quit on me, or send me something meant for Wilhelm." He smiled as they climbed the stairs. "She's not like you at all."

"I'm pretty predictable." She hesitated outside her door, then turned to him. "But there are a few things you should know. Things that happened this week—"

He set his bags down and took hold of her shoulders. "All I need to know is that you're not having any doubts now. That you really want to marry me."

"Of course. It's just that—"

"Then nothing else matters. It was a strange week for both of us. I was so afraid to come here, to meet your mother, to make the wedding real. But when you weren't with me in Virginia Beach, I missed you more than I ever thought I would. More than you can know."

She stared at him for a moment, then moistened her lips. "What exactly did you miss? What made you sure all of a sudden that we should get married?"

"There wasn't any one thing." He motioned to his bags. "Can we get these put away?"

"I'm sorry." She pushed the bedroom door back and led him inside. The bed seemed huge, ungainly, as though there wasn't even room to walk around it. She stayed in the doorway as he went to the dresser. "Take the two drawers on the left."

"I usually like the right." He shook his head and laughed. "Left is fine." He dropped his bags on the bed and drew back the zipper. "Where's your mother? I've been preparing for this meeting all the way up. Working on my impress-the-mother-in-law speech."

"She'll be back tonight, and you won't need a speech." She walked to the window, suddenly nervous, irritated but not sure why. "Just tell me what you missed about me, then. That should be easy."

Peter looked thoughtful as he lifted out a stack of T-shirts. "Little things mostly. The way you know what I'll need for a shot before I do. The way you're always prepared for anything . . ." He broke off and looked over at her. "How long are we staying? Not that I care. We've got a week left of vacation, but if you want to leave early I'll leave most of these packed."

"You missed that I'm well prepared?" She drew her head back. "Peter, a girl scout is well prepared too, but that doesn't mean you marry one."

He dropped the T-shirts and came around the bed. "I didn't mean it like that. It's just that working with another stylist showed me what an idiot I'd been. We're a well-oiled machine, you and me. We're the Hepburn and Tracy of food photography. The Gable and Lombard of cookbooks."

The Laurel and Hardy of love, she thought, then shook her head, wondering where that had come from. Love had never been the issue. And hadn't Hepburn and Tracy had a long and happy career together? A well-oiled machine, just like Peter had said.

Yet for all of her conviction, she couldn't keep from looking out the window when she heard Sam's truck pull away.

"I figured we'd get started on the food and interior shots tomorrow," Peter said, already back at the bed, carrying clothes from suitcase to dresser. "What shall I keep out for tonight for the party?"

"Something casual. The Tap Room isn't fancy." She glanced at the bed, then back at Peter. "You don't care then, about what happened this week; is that right?"

"Naturally I care. But I'm guessing you were furious with me, so I'm sure you went out, partied with the girls . . ." He laughed and looped two cameras around his neck. "And if that hat is any indication, you had a wild time."

She wandered over to where the beribboned hat hung on the chair back. "They threw me a shower." She looked down at the glossy black feather in her hand, then worked it in between two of the bows and picked it up. "They gave us some lovely gifts." She carried the hat to the mirror and set it on her head. The ribbons bobbed in front of her face, the bows were still ugly. Even with the feather, it wasn't quite a Monet. But maybe without the blue dress . . .

She dragged the hat off and set it on the dresser. That was definitely not like her, and Peter would be shocked.

His face appeared in the mirror over her shoulder. "What are you doing?" he whispered.

"Nothing." She ran a fingertip over the ostrich feather, then looked up at him again. "Peter, we have to talk about this past week. There are lies that I told, things that I did—"

"Because of me." He hesitated a moment, then reached for her, turning her around and pulling her into his arms. "I don't have a speech prepared for this, so I'm just going to wing it. You haven't said so, but I know you must have been hurt when I didn't call before last night. And I hope you believe me when I say that it wasn't the layout that brought me, although I'm looking forward to doing it."

"Delia told me you like the Old South."

He gave her a sheepish grin. "That woman has a way of making me talk about the silliest things."

"It's not silly," she told him. "And I do believe you're not here just for the ad. But it made me realize how little we know about each other." She touched a hand to his face, trying to replace in her mind the line of another jaw, the curve of other lips. "Why is that?"

He shook his head, his eyes searching hers. "We're just always busy talking about other things. Work, the studio—"

"Office furniture," she said quietly, then pressed a fingertip to his brow, easing the crease that formed when he frowned. "I've always liked the way we are." She lowered her head. "And that's why I have to tell you what happened—"

"Please don't," he said quietly, like a plea. "Max, I like the way we are too. Sure, we're preoccupied with work, but I love that too, and we've got our whole lives to catch up on all the little things." He reached into his pocket and pulled out his wallet. "Let's set a date right here, right now." He pulled out a card calendar and handed it to her. "Pick a date, any one you like, and it will be official."

Max stared at the calendar. "October is lovely with the colors."

"First Saturday in October, then." Peter smiled. "How does that sound?"

"Wonderful," she said and handed back the card, her throat oddly dry, tight. But why, when everything she wanted was right there? Her future stretching out just as she'd planned, with a flourishing career, a good man and a solid relationship. For there was no doubt in her mind that Peter would work as hard to build a marriage as he had a business.

They'd have a house, children, life insurance, a mortgage. All with no surprises, no risks and no tumble down a long dark tunnel. A safe and perfect life, far from Schomberg and a man who made her believe it was all right to have beer with the spirits, skinny-dip in the moonlight and dream old dreams of a place called the Blue Ridge Café. A place that never had, never would exist anywhere but in her mind.

So she swallowed the tightness and prepared to walk back into her life once and for all. But even as she leaned in to press a soft kiss to Peter's lips, she couldn't help wishing she'd stayed naked in the water just a little while longer.

She moved out of Peter's arms, took his hand and led him to the door. "You're right about us having time for the details. But right now is a good time to start with a few. The shower gifts are next door. In my brother Brian's old room."

Sam had pulled out all the stops, moving the screen from the front of the dining room to create a private nook in the corner of the pub and laying the table with his mother's silver and china—an ornate pattern of roses and gold edging, long hidden inside the box his father had packed and sealed and stashed in the basement with the rest of the memories.

Slowly but surely, Sam was pulling them out and dusting them off, salvaging what he could of the past for children who were yet to be born. Yet as he set the wineglasses by the plates, he could almost see them—a girl with wide blue eyes and a boy with dark hair. Both so much like the woman who would sit at the table tonight with the man she would marry. A nice guy who Sam couldn't bring himself to hate, even as the children in his mind gradually faded away.

He stood back, counting himself lucky that only six would sit down to dinner as some of the dishes had been broken in the box, and another person would have had to make do with regular plates from the kitchen. *Mismatched china,* he thought, and just as quickly pushed the memory aside.

He still wasn't sure what his intention had been when he first extended the invitation. Maybe just a chance to see her before she left. Or perhaps something more sinister—one last shot at breaking the engagement, of showing her the mistake she was making. But even though there was some truth there, he knew it wasn't the case anymore. Not after seeing them together.

They cared for each other; that much was obvious. And if life with Peter was what she wanted, then it wasn't up to him to try and take it away. So he'd raise a glass to toast the bride and groom, and get on with his life again.

He lifted his head as a sudden burst of laughter floated over the screen along with the music and chatter that made Saturday night one of his busiest. There were fifty-three people out there at last count; not capacity by any stretch, but a good mix of locals and imports from the subdivisions. Sam had thought about closing the pub for the night, but they were still too new and couldn't afford to turn anyone away. So he'd plunked some easy rock in the CD player, kept the volume down, and as he made his way to the kitchen, only hoped that Max would understand.

"No, no, no, " Michael hollered, handing off a plate of wings and fries to a waitress as he hurried over to the stove. "You must whisk lightly, quickly. Oh, for heaven's sake . . ." He snatched a saucepan out from under the night cook's hand and held it out of reach. "I'll finish the sauce. You take care of the burgers."

As the young man walked back to the grill, Michael lowered his voice and frowned at Sam. "That's the caliber you get when you hire off the street."

"He'll learn," Sam said, going over the menu on the board as he set the trays on the stack. "Goat cheese and leek galette?"

"An appetizer. Like pizza, only better. And guaranteed to annoy the hell out of Ben."

"Always nice to see a man enjoying his work." Sam tapped a finger on the page. "What's Saganaki?"

"You'll see," Michael all but sang as he hustled Sam

out of the kitchen. "Just relax and know that this will be a meal to remember."

"You're right about that," he said, checking the clock as he went back out to the pub and wondering where Ben was. He'd said he'd come early to finish in the brewery before sitting down to dinner. Sam glanced over at the kettles and tanks on the other side of the glass walls but saw no familiar figure in coveralls hovering over the controls.

He had no time to think further, however, as the front door swung back and Max stepped into the pub, followed by Peter, Eva and Delia.

Max wore red. Just short enough and tight enough to make him stop, take a breath. And remind himself that Peter had every right to have that arm around her.

Peter was talking, she was nodding, but she spotted him right away. Her eyes lifting, searching him out, as though feeling him there at the back of the room, watching her. But her smile was nothing more than cordial as he went forward to greet them.

He wasn't fast enough, however, and a few folks in the pub were there ahead of him, offering handshakes, hugs and congratulations.

While Max held back at first, he watched her slowly relax and make the introductions. Peter performed equally well, shaking hands and deftly sidestepping questions about his whereabouts for the past week and the celebrity cookbook. Max must have told him about the lie, the excuses she'd had to make to cover up for his absence. And Sam was glad that traces of guilt still lingered in the man's eyes every time he looked over at her.

As he started forward again, he noticed a few eyes on himself now—moving from him to Max and back again. So he made it a point not to look at her too long or too hard. Knowing that Ben's damage control on the rumors after the shower had not been enough to stop the stories from spreading, the speculation from growing. Another installment in the Perils of Maxine.

Yet for all that it frustrated him, he didn't believe there was anything malicious in the gossip or discussion. It was simply curiosity. A desire to see a bit of town history come to a close.

Brian and Gwen had been part of Schomberg lore since that terrible summer, their story repeated along with accounts of the blizzard of '73 and the hermit who used to live up on the mountain. Like it or not, Max was part of that story. But unlike the blizzard or the hermit, hers had yet to come to a conclusion. As Sam glanced around, he knew that was what they were waiting for, to see how things turned out for Max. By and large, they were all in her corner, and he wondered how long it would be before she finally figured that out.

Eva touched him on the arm, startling him. "Have you seen Ben?" she asked.

"Ben?" Sam glanced over at her. "I thought he'd be with you."

"He said he'd meet us here." She took a step back to the door, checked the street. "I've never known him to be late."

Hoping Ben wasn't ending it this way, Sam laughed and tried to draw her away from the door. "He's probably grabbing a burger over at Cy's."

She looked up at him, then glanced back at the window. "He did say that Michael would be cooking. If his reputation is anything close to what Ben tells me, there will be peanuts in the Jell-o."

Delia looked over at Sam. "Is he that bad?"

"Or that good, I'm not sure which." He offered a hand. "You must be Delia, the one with the plan."

"Guilty." She looked past him to where Max and Peter were shaking more hands, accepting more congratulations. And all the while Peter's hand rested comfortably on the small of Max's back.

Sam leaned closer to Delia and lowered his voice. "I'd say it was a success."

"He would have come without it," she said, her voice soft, almost wistful. "But I had to be sure."

Sam drew his head back. "Sure of what?"

Peter glanced over, catching sight of Delia, and Sam watched his smile change, grow more relaxed, easier.

"That he gets married," she whispered, then screwed up her nose, making Peter laugh and shake his head as he turned away. "They make a good couple," she said, and Sam wasn't sure who she was trying to convince, him or herself.

But before he could ask, she was gone, walking back to join Eva in her vigil by the window as Peter strolled over and slapped him on the shoulder. "I want to thank you again for having us."

"It's my pleasure," Sam told him, and only then allowed himself to look directly at Max. "Your table is ready."

"This is very nice of you," she said, and he wasn't sure which it was that bothered him more, the formality or the pretense.

The pretense, he decided. Both of them trying to make small talk and pretend the air wasn't humming between them.

"I should warn you that we are in a serious party mood," Peter said, bringing him back.

"Well, you've come to the right place," Sam said, leading them through the tables to the private nook at the back.

But Peter stopped suddenly and glanced around. "You know what, I think we should get things rolling right now."

He took a few steps past Sam and raised his hands.

"Can I have your attention a minute?" He reached back for Max's hand, and Sam watched her lower her head as Peter drew her forward. "As many of you know, Maxine and I are celebrating our engagement tonight, and we'd like you all to be part of it." He pointed to the bartender. "The next round is on me. Drinks for the house."

A cheer rose up and Peter turned to Sam. "Put it on a tab and I'll settle up with you later," he said quietly, then gave the screen a quick once-over. "And let's get rid of this, shall we? Make it a big party."

Max drew him to one side, out of the limelight. "But Sam went to all this trouble to keep it private."

He glanced over at Sam. "You don't mind, do you?"

Sam turned to Max. "Whatever you want."

He knew she was on the verge of refusing but then she shrugged and gestured to the screen. "Get it out of here."

"Grab the other side," Peter said, "and we'll get it out of the way. Can we do something about the music while we're at it?" He didn't wait for a reply, simply lifted a hand to signal the bartender. "You want to pick up the pace on the tunes?"

"No problem," he called back, and within seconds the pub was pulsing to a driving salsa beat.

Peter glanced around. "All we need now is a little room to dance."

Max shook her head. "Peter, this isn't a shoot."

He winced and turned to Sam. "I'm sorry. I'm way out of line here. But I would really love to dance with Max tonight."

Sam watched her eyes widen in surprise while waitresses hustled past with the free drinks. All around them, people were smiling, bobbing in time to the music—everyone waiting to see what Sam was going to do. What choice did he have?

He circled an area with his hand. "Let's get these tables out of here." And if he'd rubbed a lamp, he didn't think the service could have been faster. Within minutes the tables were stacked against the wall and a square of floor, maybe eight by twelve, sat empty.

Peter whooped as he whirled Max onto the dance floor, and soon more tables were being lifted to make room for all the couples who had joined them.

"Peter certainly loves a good time," Eva said, still watching the door. "Funny Max never mentioned it." She stretched up on her toes, leaned a little to the side. "Is that Ben?"

"I believe so." Relieved, Sam waved him over as Peter and Max came back to the table.

"This is definitely a good time." Peter wiped a hand across his forehead and signaled to a waitress. "Shall we order a pitcher of something for the table? Delia, help me out here."

She shrugged and reached for her water glass. "Ask Sam or Ben. What do I know, anyway?"

"Enough to make me glad you'll be back on Wednesday." Peter's smile dimmed as he looked at her. "You have no idea how much I missed you."

She nodded but didn't lift her eyes from the glass. "Yeah, it's hard to keep those bills straight."

He studied her a moment longer, then drew himself up and turned to Ben and Sam. "Gentlemen, what's good?"

"Depends on what you want," Ben said, and even Eva leaned in to join the discussion. Leaving only Max to notice when Delia got up and left.

She watched her weave through the tables to the ladies room, wondering why she'd snapped at Peter and why she'd left her purse behind. Slipping the strap of Delia's bag from the chairback, she rose and followed.

Max gave the door a push and peeked into the ladies room.

Delia stood alone at the mirror in a room that was

cramped and utilitarian at best, with clean white floors, tiled walls and a slightly disinfectant smell. Not the kind of bathroom Max would ever have in a place of her own. But then again, this was Sam's place, not hers. And it never would be.

She stepped through the door and held up the purse. "I figured you could use this."

Delia nodded and flipped it open on the counter, but she wouldn't meet Max's eyes. "That's a good party out there."

"It's amazing what a little music can do." Max perched on the edge of the counter and watched her in the mirror. "You never said how the petting zoo went."

"Fabulous. I swear, if I ever have property, I'll buy a llama." Delia popped open a dark red lipstick and leaned closer to the mirror. "Eva swears that if you pat a llama every day, you can't possibly be stressed."

Max laughed. "Eva also swears that her dog is highly intelligent, so be warned."

"Well, I believe her. In fact, I can't remember when I've enjoyed myself more." She waved the lipstick near her mouth as she spoke but never made contact. "So I thought I might stay on a while. Say to heck with filing and rent a room from your mother for the summer. Really pat the llamas."

Max stared at Delia in the mirror. "The whole summer? But Peter would be lost without you."

"He'll be fine," Delia said and dropped the lipstick back into her purse without using it. "Assistants are easy to come by." She gave Max a tiny smile. "It's love that's hard to find."

Max looked down at the sink. "So I've been told."

"But the love charm worked; Peter is here and we should get back out there and celebrate." Delia snapped her purse shut and headed for the door. "Because soon you'll be walking down that aisle. And then we can all relax."

Her last words were mumbled as she went through the door, said more to herself than anyone else and leaving Max more confused than ever.

"Delia," she called and went after her, catching up to her in the hall outside the ladies room. She was fiddling with her skirt now, tugging it down, smoothing it over her hips. Wasted actions, just like the lipstick. And so unlike Delia that Max reached out, laying a hand on her arm to stop her.

"Delia, what's going on?" Max asked, her voice softer than she'd expected, hesitant, although she couldn't for the life of her say why. "What do you mean, we can all relax?"

"It's just been so tense, that's all," Delia said. But Max noticed that even the too-bright smile was gone now, and Delia wouldn't look at her. "All this will-he-won't-he, and what happens if he doesn't come? It's just nice to know it's over and you'll be married."

Max followed her into the crowded pub, trying to understand what was in her voice, her manner. But it wasn't until Delia stopped just back from their table and changed direction, heading for the bar instead that Max knew, and she wondered how she could ever have missed it.

Max hopped up on the stool beside her, nodded to the woman on her other side, then leaned close to Delia and lowered her voice to a whisper. "You're in love with him, aren't you?"

"Were you out in the sun today?" Delia asked, forcing a laugh as the bartender set a mug of beer in front of her. But it didn't fool either of them.

Max moistened her lips and glanced around. "How long have you loved him?"

"This is so embarrassing. I never wanted you to know—"

"Delia," she said gently, "how long?"

Delia leaned back with a sigh. "From the first day I went to work at the studio."

Max shook her head, leaned her elbows on the bar, and tried to ignore the couple staring at them from the end of the bar. "Then why did you go out of your way to come here, to help me get him back?"

Delia's smile was small and wry. "Because he doesn't see me as anything but an assistant. Never has. I pretty much threw myself at him just before he met you. Dinner at my apartment, soft music, wine. But it went right over his head."

"Men can be dense," Max said, an image of Laverne and Squiggy floating in from nowhere.

"Then you came along," Delia continued, "and the two of you are so good together. The energy when you're working is unlike anything I've ever seen. And to make matters worse, I really like you. You're intense and focused, you know what you want from life and you get it."

"It looks that way, doesn't it?" Max said, so quietly she barely heard herself.

"So when he asked you to marry him, it was like a weight had been lifted. He'd finally be taken, really taken, which meant that maybe I could put the torch down and get on with my life."

"Max, Delia."

They looked over to see Peter at the side of the dance floor, his hands raised as if to say, "What's going on?"

"You'd better get back," Delia said as she waved back.

Max smiled at Peter and spoke to Delia. "Aren't you coming?"

"In a minute." She slid off the stool but made no move

to leave. "Do you think your mother would mind if I stayed on at the farm?"

"Mind?" Max laughed. "I know she'd love it. The two of you get along better that we ever did."

"I'll call home before I sit down, let them know I won't be back for a while. And figure out what I'm going to tell Peter." She paused and looked down at the ground. "I hope you believe me when I say that I'm happy for you."

Max nodded, amazed and humbled. And wondering how she'd come to be blessed with such a friend.

"Good, because I want you to know that if you ever get a line on another of those love charms and you don't tell me"—she raised her head and smiled—"I swear I will hunt you down."

FOURTEEN

Peter held a hand out to Max as she rounded the dance floor. "Is something wrong?"

She shook her head. "Delia's just calling home, letting them know when she'll be back."

Peter nodded. "She's very close to her family," he said as they walked, and Max couldn't help thinking that he wasn't quite as bright as she'd always imagined. How could he not know how Delia felt? Work with her day after day and not see it?

And how could she have spent the last week with her and have no idea until five minutes ago?

She'd hidden it well, Max decided, then paused and glanced back. Or was it simply that no one had been looking?

"Ben's volunteered to show us around the brewery," Peter said, his hand on the small of her back now, drawing her along to the table. The seats were empty, the pitcher of beer in the center untouched.

Peter peered through the crowd at the glass walls of the brewery. "Ben's already there with Eva." He turned back to Max. "I'll tell them to hold off a few minutes while we wait for Delia—"

"No, don't." Max knew she'd said it too quickly as soon as Peter turned back to her. And the last thing Delia needed was to have Peter's curiosity piqued. So she gave a careless shrug and pulled out a chair. "It's up to you, of course, but you know how it is when she talks to her sisters."

Peter frowned. "Could take hours."

"That's why you should go and I'll wait." She sat down and sipped at her water. "We'll catch up as soon as she gets back."

"If you're sure." But he was already on his way, calling to her over his shoulder. "We won't be long."

"Take your time," she said, then sat back, checking out the breadsticks, pouring herself a glass of beer, only too aware that she was now alone at the party.

She took in the table that Sam had set for them, seeing the details for the first time—the flowers, the candles waiting to be lit—and was touched by the care he'd taken. She ran a fingertip around the gold rim of the plate, lifted a crystal wineglass, the patterns as familiar now as when they'd sat behind the glass doors of his mother's hutch. The good dishes, treated with respect and reserved for special occasions. Thanksgiving, Christmas. And now her wedding.

She held the glass higher, watching the play of light and color through the pinwheels and thinking of Sam's mom and dad, jiving by the jukebox, necking in the kitchen—so in love after more than twenty years of marriage, it was no wonder Sam grew up believing love was the key to a lasting relationship, convinced that falling down the rabbit hole would lead to nothing more than a cozy little sanctuary, the essence of hearth and home.

But Delia had taken that trip, and where had it landed her? On the phone to her family, racking up the long-distance minutes because the man she'd fallen for didn't have the sense to love her back.

She sighed and set the glass down, catching a glimpse of the couple at the next table, smiling at her as though she was just the cutest little thing they'd seen in a long time. Assuming, no doubt, that it was wedding gowns and roses she'd been seeing in the crystal rather than long, dark tunnels and phone bills.

But who was she to shatter the fantasies of strangers? She would save that for her friends. So she smiled too and sat back, hoping the tour would wrap up soon.

She glanced over at the brewery, thinking she might join them after all, when she spotted Ben and Eva behind the glass, deep in conversation. A serious one, judging by Eva's stance and the fact that Ben wasn't looking at her. He was staring down at his feet or over at the kettles—a man of few words, making himself clear in gesture.

But whatever they were saying to each other was cut short when Peter came around the side of a kettle, pointing behind him to something Max couldn't see. Eva and Ben moved apart and focused on Peter, each one stealing a glance at the other now and then, but neither attempting to close the gap. The conversation was over but nothing decided, and Max could feel the tension between them from where she sat. *Ain't love grand?* she thought, and shifted her attention to Peter with a sigh.

He was by a stainless-steel tank now, climbing up on a step stool for a better look. She had always known that he was fascinated by details; it was part of what made him so successful as a photographer. But after their day at the farm, she also knew he had a black sheep sister, loved science fiction but never found time to read, and that he'd fired the stylist in Virginia Beach after she miscued with a blowtorch and nearly set the studio on fire.

That was moments before Delia's envelope arrived. And he'd been sure it was a sign.

She glanced over at Eva, thought of Delia—both in love and both miserable. And herself, on course to the life she wanted, and knew he was right. It was a sign.

Much like a smiling moon.

"What's a nice girl like you doing in a place like this?"

"You are hopeless," she said, smiling as she turned to find Sam picking up the pitcher and filling a glass.

"And you've been avoiding me." He motioned to her glass. "You want me to top that up?"

She nodded and watched him tip the pitcher up, knowing she shouldn't have been surprised. He simply wasn't the type to mince words or hide behind the weather or the price of feed. Not when he had other things on his mind.

"I thought it was wisest under the circumstances," she said, seeing no reason to be any less honest.

"You're probably right," he said, and flashed her a grin as he set the pitcher down. "Under the circumstances."

She knew she should excuse herself, go and find Peter, or drag Delia back from the phone. Anything to avoid being alone with him. But for all her own good advice, she couldn't bring herself to leave, to be cool and distant. Which was too bad, because he was nudging a chair back from the table, obviously preparing to join her.

She laughed at herself and reached for her glass, wondering where the danger could be in a room full of people.

He stood a moment, giving the room a quick once-over, acknowledging a wave or a smile, telling a harried waitress to take five once her tray of drinks was delivered, giving the bartender and the busboy a thumbs-up for keeping the music going.

He was made for this, she realized. For the people, the hustle, the challenge of building something to last. He was part of the town again, fitting in smoothly and easily in a way she never would.

"It's not exactly the evening I planned," he said as he turned back to her, "but people certainly seem to be enjoying your party."

She nodded. "Looks like you've reached capacity out there. Which tells me you need a permanent dance floor."

"Or Peter as social director."

Max shook her head and laughed. "Believe me, he's not usually like this. I don't know what's gotten into him."

"He's a happy guy. Like most grooms." He sat down across from her—a discreet distance she appreciated under so many watchful eyes.

Yet, ridiculously enough, she was aware that beneath the table, behind the cloth, his legs were mere inches from hers. All she had to do was move slightly to the left and they would be touching.

This was the danger, she realized. The draw, the instant response even in a room full of people, with her fiancé in plain view. So she shifted to the right, raised her glass to her lips and told herself she was only warm because of the beer; knowing from the way he was watching her that she hadn't fooled him either.

He leaned back with his glass, and she waited, wary now, hoping Peter, Delia, even the busboy, would happen by.

"So," he asked, "did you set a date?"

"First Saturday in October."

"Should be lovely that time of year."

"That's what we thought." She glanced over to where Peter had last been, feeling Sam's eyes on her still. "Of course, it doesn't give us long to plan, but Eva will help and there's always—"

"You're making a mistake," he said softly. "You know that, don't you?"

She turned back to him. "Sam, don't. Not now."

"Not now," he repeated, then took a long swallow of beer, wiped his mouth with the back of his hand and set his glass down hard. "Then when would be better, Max? When you're back in New York, putting hair spray on food and wondering if I ever found anyone to take that spot, to build your café?"

She slid the chair back. "I don't have to listen to this."

"Or how about later on tonight?" he continued, holding her down, pinning her to the chair with nothing more than his words, his voice. "When the party's over and you're lying in bed, making love to Peter and thinking of me."

She shook her head. "I won't be thinking of you."

He searched her face, her eyes, then a sad, slow smile curved his lips. "Yes, you will. The same way I'll be thinking of you. Because I love you. The way you laugh, the way you think. The way you feel when I touch you—"

"How can you say that? It's only been a week."

"Max, it's been a lifetime. I think I've loved you forever."

"Sam, please—"

"Please what? Please lie, tell you what you want to hear because anything else is too hard, too painful?" She saw him reach for her hand and catch himself, snatching up his glass instead. "Please sit here and smile at Peter, watch him put his hands on you and pretend I feel nothing?" He shook his head and leaned back, away from her. "I can't do that, Max, not anymore. Not when I want you so badly it hurts. And all I have to do is look at you to know you want me too." He drew in a breath and let it out slowly. "I love you more than you can know. And as hard as it is for you to believe, sometimes that's just enough."

She moistened her lips, met his eyes, and for one mad moment she wavered, right there on the edge all over again, ready to fall for this man who was so very wrong, and knew her all too well.

Then someone was calling her name, pulling her back,

saving her from herself. And she looked up to see Peter coming back at last.

Sam lifted the pitcher and cursed himself for a fool. He hadn't meant to start this. Had told himself he was only joining her because Peter had gone off and left her alone at a table set with candles and crystal in a room of beer mugs and pretzels. And he told himself now to just sit back, relax. Have a drink and toast her health. But even as he should be moving back, he felt himself moving toward her, unable to let go.

"Max—"

"Sam, I can't," she snapped, and then put a hand to her chest, laughing lightly because heads had turned. And he wished he'd closed the goddamn place down when he had the chance.

"Quite a setup you've got here," Peter said, looking from one to the other as he drew up to the table with Ben and Eva.

"It certainly is," Sam said, taking another long drink so he wouldn't have to watch Peter swing an arm across the back of her chair as he sat down.

"Was it something you always wanted?" Peter asked, and Sam almost laughed.

"Never," he said, looking over at Max. "In fact, it surprised the hell out of me."

"Oh God, here we go," Ben said and Sam turned, grateful for the distraction as Michael approached the table with a sizzling skillet.

Ben rolled his eyes. "He's burned something again."

Sam shook his head and had himself another drink. "It's part of the show." Just like everything else going on at the table.

"Ladies and gentlemen," Michael said, "this evening I have prepared a meal I call 'A Tribute to Love for Six.' " He gave the table a quick, disgusted once-over. "Someone is missing."

"Just go ahead," Max whispered. "She'll be back soon."

"Oh, fine," Michael said. Then he raised his arm and held the skillet aloft as he poured the contents of a small bottle over the top. "Specialties from the most romantic cities in the world. Rome, Paris, Niagara Falls." He chuckled. "Just kidding."

Ben groaned as Michael pulled a lighter from his pocket with a flourish. "We start our tour in Athens, for Aphrodite, goddess of love." He flicked the lighter, touched it to the skillet and thrust the pan into the air as a burst of flame rose up, prompting an equally enthusiastic burst of applause from the audience. "Saganaki," he called, turning to the dance floor. "Flaming cheese."

"Flaming idiot," Ben muttered.

Eva stifled a laugh and put a hand over his.

Ben looked down at her hand, but he didn't smile, didn't speak. Without warning he scraped his chair back and left the table.

"Saganaki for four," Michael said, as Ben kept going, heading for the front door.

Eva stared after Ben, Michael's flame sputtered and Sam knew Ben wouldn't be back. Not this time.

Smart man, he thought, and watched Eva start to rise, then sit down again and pointedly turn her back on the door—a stubborn Henley woman right to the end.

Peter leaned toward him again. "I hear you'll be expanding with a dining room soon."

"That was the plan." He glanced over at Max. "Just a small place, nothing fancy. And I had this idea for gourmet nights, and special evenings. But everything's on hold now."

Peter shook his head. "What a shame."

"It's a mistake, is what it is," Sam said, and he wasn't sure if he saw regret or resignation in her eyes.

"That certainly looks interesting," Peter said as Michael squeezed a lemon over the cheese and set the skillet on the table. Then he turned to Sam again. "Let us know when the dining room comes off hold. We'll come back for the grand opening."

"I'll look forward to that." Sam pushed his glass aside as he rose. "And be sure to bring the kids."

"Kids?" Eva looked over at them but couldn't keep from checking the door. "Are you two planning kids right away?"

Peter laughed. "Let's get through the ceremony first. Speaking of which . . ." He turned to Sam. "We'd like you to come up for the wedding, wouldn't we, Max?"

"That's not possible," Sam said, saving her the trouble. "Ben will be going, and both of us can't be away at the same time. Fact is, I can't even do this tonight." He stepped back from the table. "Congratulations again. I hope you'll be very happy."

Peter got to his feet. "You're not leaving?"

Michael frowned as he sliced the cheese. "Saganaki for three."

"There are a few things I have to do," Sam said and turned to say good night to Eva.

But she was standing now too, watching the front door as she picked up her purse, put it down, picked it up again.

"Eva," he said, and she looked over at him, her eyes wide, uncertain. "Go," he said. "Just go."

Eva stared at him, then looked over at Max. "Go," she said, and Eva tucked her purse under her arm and headed for the door.

"I only hope it's not too late," Sam said softly, then turned to Michael. "Don't forget the champagne."

He waved a hand. "With dessert, and you'll get none."

"I'll come by later if I have the chance." He managed a smile as he glanced back at Peter. "But you two have a good time."

Max watched him turn and leave. Watched him weave his way through the tables on his way to the kitchen, knowing he'd lied for the first time since she'd met him. He wouldn't be back again.

"Pass me your plate," Michael said, but Max couldn't move, could barely breathe. Yet it made no sense. He was Schomberg and pretzels, she was Manhattan and magazines. They wanted nothing the same, couldn't even live in the same place. They weren't meant to be, it was as simple as that. So why was it so hard to watch him walk away?

"Max, your plate," Peter said.

She looked over at him, her heart suddenly pounding too hard, too loud. Surely he could hear it. Yet his face showed nothing, no sign that anything was wrong beyond the fact that she hadn't picked up the damn plate.

"Would you rather just have a bite of mine?" he asked, concern creasing his brow, making her agitated and guilty at the same time.

There was the right man, the right choice, right there in front of her. He knew it, she knew it, everybody in the room knew it. Yet Sam was the one she wanted. Sam, with his dreams and his pretzels and his utter inability to deliver a pickup line, because she wasn't standing on the edge any more. She'd fallen hard. And as she looked along that tunnel, the one standing at the end was Sam.

Not for always, or forever, not for better or worse, because none of those things were possible. But for now, for tonight, while the moon still smiled.

She turned to Peter. "I can't do it."

He shrugged and put the fork down. "There'll be another course."

She shook her head. "I mean I can't marry you."

"That's it." Michael snatched up the skillet and headed for the kitchen. "I do not do Saganaki for one."

Peter stared at her. "Max, we've set the date. They've got champagne—"

"Let me ask you this." She put a hand to his cheek, felt herself smile. "Do you love me?"

He pushed her hand away. "Of course I do."

"How do you love me?"

"As in 'Let me count the ways?' " He drew his head back. "What kind of a question is that?"

She saw the confusion, the embarrassment—that horrible, awkward embarrassment because he had no answer. And she felt such tenderness for him in that moment, she might have persuaded herself she was wrong. That she could marry him after all. But she recognized the tenderness, the affection, for what it was, and understood what Sam had meant when he said it wouldn't be enough. Not anymore.

"Peter, be honest. Are you in love with me?"

"Max, be reasonable—"

She smiled and squeezed his hand. "It's okay. It really is. Because I'm not in love with you either. You were right when you called the first time, when you weren't sure we were doing the right thing. I just don't know why you changed your mind. Why you came back."

He hesitated, and she knew he was struggling with expectations and plans, and bottles of champagne. Then he sighed and drew her hand toward him. "I came back because I may not know about love, but I do know that I like you, I respect you. And I couldn't live with myself if I hurt you." He twined his fingers with hers and studied them there on the table. "For all that you're successful and independent, I always knew you were old-fashioned at heart, a romantic."

Max laughed. "Hardly romantic."

Peter smiled, the easiest, most genuine smile she'd seen on his face all night. "You're the most romantic woman I know. That's why you wouldn't live with me, or sign a prenup. Marriage and home are too important to you. I'd promised you both of those things, but when the time came, I let you down. And you have never once in all the years I've known you, let me down. That's why I came back. Because more than anything, I wanted you to be happy."

She nodded and looked over at the kitchen. "I will be. But not if we get married. Not when I'm in love with someone else."

"Sam, right?" She glanced back and he shrugged. "I guess I know you better than either of us thought." He drew his head back. "Are you staying here, then? Am I losing a stylist too?"

Max looked down at the ring on her finger. "I won't be staying. I can't."

"Then what are you going to do?"

"I have no idea." She pulled off the ring and held it out to him. "I just know that this is the right thing to do."

He stared at the diamond for a moment, then took it from her and glanced over his shoulder. "Now what do we tell them?"

Max turned to see faces watching them from the tables, the dance floor. Faces that quickly turned away while feet struggled to find the rhythm and glasses were too quickly raised.

She laughed and got to her feet. "The truth," she said, knowing they'd be talking about this at Cy's for a month anyway, and not bothered at all.

She turned in time to see Delia coming around the corner from the telephones. She grabbed Peter's hand and dragged him to his feet. "But before we say anything, tell me who that is over there."

He followed her gaze. "That's Delia."

Delia stopped and was looking at them as though she might cut and run at any second.

Max smiled, and Delia shook her head frantically, but it was too late for Max to turn back. She glanced over at Peter. "Do you know why she can get you to talk about the silliest things, and keeps you organized, and came all the way out here to make sure we got married?"

"Because she's my assistant?"

Max laughed. "Because she loves you."

"Me?" He put a hand to his chest. "Delia loves me?"

Max felt her heart squeeze at the wonder in his eyes. "She's loved you for years."

"I always thought I imagined that look," he said. "I never dreamed . . . I mean, I'm nothing like the men she dates. I'm not her type at all."

Max laid a hand on his arm. "But you're exactly the type she wants."

Peter was looking now, she realized. Looking at Delia and seeing everything he'd missed for so long. "And if my guess is right, you want her too. But if she walks out that door, you might just lose her forever."

Max watched him cross the floor, watched Delia back up, hands outstretched as she shook her head. Then she saw Peter reach for her, saw her move into his arms, and didn't need to see anymore.

She was off, heading for the kitchen, weaving between the tables, hoping Sam hadn't gone far, since this was probably not the time to ask Peter for his keys.

FIFTEEN

Max skidded to a stop at the kitchen door, looking from Michael to the night chef. "Which way did Sam go?"

"How should I know?" Michael said, still pouting as he pulled a tray out of the oven.

But the night chef pointed to the back door. "He slammed out of here about fifteen minutes ago."

"I think I heard his truck start," a waitress said as she came into the kitchen. She glanced over at Max as she grabbed a basket of nachos from under the warming lights. "But I can't be sure."

Max looked over at the back door, hoping the waitress had heard wrong. She might find him on foot but didn't have a prayer if he was driving. "I'll start with the parking lot," she said, and turned back to Michael. "Is that a galette?"

"Goat cheese and leek. Do you have any idea how far I had to go for a decent goat cheese?" Michael slapped the pan down on the counter. The cheese was brown and bubbling, the crust thin and golden. "What am I supposed to do with it now?"

"Wrap half," Max said, grabbing a plastic takeout container from the shelf by the warming lights. "Think of it as Paris-to-go."

"That's supposed to make everything all right?" Michael sniffed as he sliced the galette into four pieces, piled two into the box and sealed the lid. "What about the other half?"

"Delia and Peter are still out there celebrating." She picked up the box and raced to the door. "Why don't you serve it to them? Make the presentation beautiful. Lots of color."

Michael saluted. "Yes, ma'am."

She laughed and swung around. "And Michael, the next time you make Saganaki, be sure you've got crusty bread to go with it. Those bread sticks are completely wrong."

"I told him that," the night chef said, then pointed at the waitress. "Didn't I tell him that?"

Max had no time to listen to Michael's rebuttal, only time to find Sam. But as the screen door slammed shut behind her, she stood perfectly still on the step, realizing she had no idea where to start.

She felt for Iona's charm, forgetting that she'd stuffed it into her purse last night, right after Peter called; telling herself she didn't need it anymore, the right man was on his way—guaranteed. She lowered her hand, wishing she hadn't been so rash, wishing she'd left it for just one more night, until she glanced up at the sky. The moon was smaller than last night, fading just like the Cheshire Cat grin, and letting her know there was still time. Wherever Sam was, she would find him tonight.

She walked down the stairs and took a look around. The pub had once been an inn so, unlike most of the buildings on the street, there was a small parking lot out back and a driveway leading out to the road. The lot was dark, with only one halogen lamp on a pole in the middle. She walked between the two rows, searching for a dark green pickup in a sea of green, black and red pickups.

"He should have kept the Aston Martin," she muttered and started checking plates instead, bending as she walked and squinting in the half-light, hoping something would feel familiar when she read it.

She stopped, her fingers tightening on the plastic take-out container. Sure enough, the third green pickup on the left had a plate that seemed right. That was enough to have her spinning around and heading out to the street. If he was walking, she'd find him.

Warm Friday nights always drew a crowd down to Center Street. Summer people, locals, tourists, all strolling, window shopping or just sitting eating ice cream in front of Cy's.

The evening concerts, a tradition for over twenty years, had started up again on the front stairs of the post office. Blankets and folding chairs dotted the lawn, and even though it was dark, a group of earnest young men were still on the steps, playing their own arrangement of a Willie Nelson tune, the name of which escaped Max as she stepped out onto the sidewalk.

The audience was mixed, with little kids playing tag between the blankets under the watchful eyes of all the parents while the teenagers stood off to the side, too cool to join their families but needing to be part of the whole just the same. And it occurred to Max that if those boys were still playing when she found Sam, it might be nice to sit on the lawn and listen while they ate Michael's galette and laughed about how close they'd come to missing each other.

She darted across the road and up the side of the lawn, searching for Sam among the families, the couples, the groups of friends; seeing a few familiar faces, but not the one she wanted. At a loss again, she went back to the beginning, to the pub, and stood at the bottom of the stairs, checking first one way, then the next—trying to think like Sam, to figure out where he'd go.

To the left was the bridge at the bottom of the hill, with a little park, three picnic tables and an outhouse. A lovely spot this time of year, filled with people fishing, paddling and just lying around. Guaranteeing a good-size audience should she venture that way and try to cross the damn thing again. She sucked in a breath and looked to the right. Nothing half so interesting down that way. Just a few stores, a couple of old men sitting on the stoop outside the barbershop and the Kwik Way.

She headed right, away from the bridge—calling herself a coward and worse but sure Sam wouldn't have gone that way.

She hadn't passed more than a few doors when she stopped and turned around, drawn back by something she couldn't name, a tug that was too strong to ignore. She wandered back the way she'd come, checking the store windows more thoroughly this time, but not seeing him anywhere.

Confused, she looked across the road to Cy's. He couldn't be in there. But why not? Didn't everyone in town go to Cy's? Screwing up her courage, Max stepped off the curb and headed for the yellow and white door. But as her hand closed on the knob, she cast a glance over her shoulder to the pub. That was when she saw it. A single light on in the third-floor apartment he called home.

Max dashed back across the road, wondering how she could have forgotten something so basic and pulling up short when she reached the front steps. How did he get up there? She hadn't noticed a staircase inside the pub, but perhaps there was one running up from the storage room off the kitchen, and he'd slipped upstairs without anyone noticing.

She ran around to the back of the pub and was about to open the back door when she had a better idea. Picking up a handful of stones from the driveway, she walked backward until she could see the three third-floor windows. The rooms were dark, making it impossible to decide what each might be. She rattled the stones in her hand, set down the takeout box and hoped no one came out for their car in the next while.

She took aim, starting with the window on the far right, and tossed the stone, missing by about a foot. She frowned and flexed her arm a few times, glad now that she hadn't made that baseball game after all.

Then she wound up again and let it go, hitting the glass dead center. "Like riding a bicycle," she whispered and stepped across to window number two.

She waited a moment, imagining he'd heard the noise and was sitting up straighter, listening. Would he know right away? Or would it take him a while?

He'd know, she decided, and tossed another, smiling when she heard the distinctive ping on the second window. Excited now and moving faster, she lined up the third window and let the stone go, already crossing back to the first when she heard the tap.

One more stone, and another and another. Six in all and no sign of movement inside the apartment, no silhouette at the window. She opened her hand, her heart sinking as she let the rest of the pebbles drop and scatter at her feet. He wasn't home after all.

"You give up easily, don't you?"

"And you could have told me you were there," she said, smiling as she turned to that rich, deep voice.

He stood at the end of a dark green pickup—the one she'd thought was his—leaning back against the tailgate, one foot crossed over the other, looking like every fantasy, every midnight dream her female heart had ever known. And when he pushed away from the truck and came toward her, that heart beat a little faster with each step the man took.

"I could have. But it seemed a shame to interrupt when you were just getting your pitching arm back."

He stopped in front of her, not touching her in any

way, but close enough that she could breathe in the scent
of him, feel his warmth on her skin. She thought he
might reach for her, but instead he tipped his head back
to look up at the windows.

"Four out of six," he said. "Not bad at all."

"I hit five," she said, straining toward him, her eyes
drawn to his mouth, the tender lower lip, the perfect
curve of the upper; wondering how she'd gone so long
without feeling that mouth on hers. And how she would
manage when she was back in New York, his kiss no
more than a memory.

"The last one was just luck," he said, looking at her
closely now, at her hair, her cheeks, her mouth—the hunger building, growing steadily, as clear and sharp as her
own.

Yet he made no move toward her, and she lifted her
hands between them, anxious fingers reaching up. "So
where were you all the time I was warming up?"

"Lying in the backseat, wondering how long it would
be before you broke one. But as I said, you gave up
easily." He grabbed her wrists, holding her hands down,
away from him, the light in his eyes suddenly stern, hard.
"What do you want, Max?"

She stared at him, trying to keep her balance, to figure
out what had happened. "You," she said, as though it
was the simplest thing in the world to understand. "I
want you."

"Just like that." He let her go and stepped back, bent
to pickup the takeout box. "Where's Peter?"

She saw the doubt, heard the wariness beneath the
harsh tone, and understood. He'd made the first dozen
or so moves. The crucial one was up to her. "He's inside," she said. "With Delia."

"Delia." He studied her for a moment, then flipped
open the lid, tilted the box. "What is this?"

"Paris-to-go." He glanced over and she shrugged. "I

thought we could share it. Sit on the grass, listen to the concert." She made a vague gesture to the music floating down the driveway, then gave her head a shake. "Never mind."

He closed the box and carried it to the pickup, not looking back until he'd lowered the tailgate and made himself comfortable. "Why is Peter with Delia?"

"Because we're not getting married." She held up her hand as she walked toward him. "See, no ring, no fiancé." Her arm dropped. "No wedding."

No raised brows, or falling jaw either. Nothing at all to give him away. Just a single word in the silence. "Why?"

"Why?" She lifted her hands, let them fall. Searching for a way to hedge, to dodge, to avoid hearing him say "I told you so," and finding only one route open. The truth, because he deserved nothing less.

"Well, it's fairly obvious. I mean, you said it yourself. How can I marry Peter . . ." She took a breath and closed her eyes. "How can I marry Peter when I'm in love with you?"

He made no reply, so she had no choice but to open one eye. And she watched a smile ease across his face. "What did you say?"

She backed up a step, pointed a finger. "Oh, no. Do not smile that way. Nothing has changed."

"Everything's changed." He slid off the tailgate and held out a hand. "Come here."

She moved toward him, a little unsteady, a little unsure—of herself, of him. Of what he would want, and how much she could give, knowing she risked disappointing them both. But the truth had served her well so far, so she trusted it again as she took another step. "You know I can't stay."

"You've mentioned that."

"I still have a job. An apartment."

His smile broadened to a grin. "But no office furniture."

"Not anymore," she conceded, then drew up short, knowing he wasn't listening. He couldn't be, not when he was looking at her that way, smiling that way. Making her want to take his hand and follow him deeper into that tunnel, believing anything was possible if she just held on tight.

But from where she stood, she could still see some light, still make it home, which was where she belonged.

"You have to know I didn't mean for this happen," she said. "I fought it all the way."

"And then some," he said, so solemnly, so seriously, she had to smile. Which was, as always, her undoing.

"I do love you, Sam. And I'm damned if I can figure out what to do about it."

"Maybe I can help you with that," he said quietly, and a shiver moved through her as he came the rest of the way to meet her.

His hands were warm and strong, cupping her face as he bent to her, closing his eyes and touching his lips to hers softly; softer than any man had ever kissed her, making her feel as though she was a treasure, something precious to be cherished. When he lifted his head to look at her, brushing his thumbs across her lips, as though not quite believing she was there, that she was his, she pressed against him; forgetting they were in a parking lot as she pulled him down, kissing him back only deeper, harder. Showing him that she was real. And she wasn't going anywhere, for now.

He drew back then, his eyes dark, his breathing as shallow and ragged as her own. "You really want to listen to a concert?"

"Concert?"

"Me neither," he said, grabbing her hand as he

slammed the tailgate shut, Paris-to-go left behind as they raced to the door.

A door Max hadn't seen before, hidden as it was in the shadows on the far end of the building. And she felt herself smile as they went through, for secret doors and smiling moons and the crazy wonderful magic of love.

The staircase was dark and he hit a switch, turning on a light on the landing above. He led and she followed, up stairs that were narrow and steep. Old stairs in an old building that creaked with each footstep, and she wondered how many lovers had come this way; running as they were now, laughing and stumbling into a room bathed in shadows, with only one thought between them.

The bedroom was at the back of the building, large and well furnished, remnants of his life in Manhattan. Sheer curtains billowed at the window, carried into the room on a breeze that was laced with music and spices.

The rhythm of the pub was softer here, dampened by space and heavy wooden beams, and he led her to a bed covered in a plain white spread that seemed to float in the darkness. He turned to her and any hesitation melted, giving way to a fire that had smouldered for far too long.

His kiss was different again, bolder, deeper, more urgent than any yet. And Max rose up, meeting him thrust for thrust as she reached between them, wanting his shirt off and her hands on his skin. She fumbled with buttons, her need exceeding her skill, and they pulled apart, laughing and frustrated, working together to get rid of that shirt once and for all.

She ran her hands across his chest, feeling the beat of his heart, strong and fast against her palms as she leaned into him, pressing whisper-soft kisses to his throat, his chest, and nipples that were small and taut. And knowing she was doing something right when he gripped her shoulders and breathed her name against her hair.

She raised her head, her own breath catching as she

watched his eyes narrow and darken while one fingertip
followed the line of hair from the top of his chest, all
the way down his belly to where it disappeared into his
jeans.

With trembling hands, Sam drew her close, sliding his
hands down her back, taking hold of the hem of her dress
and lifting it slowly. Sliding that red silk up her thighs
and over her hips. Loving the way her eyes grew round
yet held his gaze as she raised her arms, letting him lift
the dress higher and higher, then over her head and off.

She stood before him in bra and panties so sheer and
scandalous, he wondered why she'd even bothered. And
he knew just by looking at her that they were as new as
the nightgown Peter had never seen either.

"So, did it work?" he asked, and smiled when she
looked confused. "The charm," he whispered.

Her smile was small and a little lopsided. "Never
doubt a gnome," she said as she reached for him.

And he let that be proof enough as he bent to her,
tossing doubt aside as she had the little red charm.

He brushed his lips across her neck, her shoulder, the
hollow of her delicate throat. Raising his head as he
worked the clasp loose, slipped the straps down and
watched her moisten her lips as that scandalous bra fell
to the floor.

He had held her naked in his arms once and was im-
patient now to hold her again, but also to take his time,
exploring every curve and line of that sleek, smooth
body. But she was having none of it. And he had never
been harder than when she laid her tiny hands against
his chest and pushed him back on the bed.

There was nothing shy or unsure about the way she
climbed on his lap, straddling his legs as she dealt with
his jeans, not efficiently but enthusiastically, making him
wonder when torture had ever been so sweet.

"I do love you," he whispered, needing her to hear it,

to know it was true as he reached for her, pulling her down and tucking her in beside him.

She wriggled in closer, a smile on her face that was smug and content, and he felt his heart swell with love for this woman who wasn't anything he'd planned but was all he'd ever need.

He rose up, covering her mouth with his as a hand moved over her breasts, feeling her arch against his palm as she threaded her fingers through his hair, holding him fast and kissing him back, taking what he gave and giving back in equal measure.

Sam prided himself on being a patient man, a Southern gentleman when it came to loving. He knew the pleasure in a long, hot night, and time spent letting that heat swirl and build. But that patience was sorely tried when he raised his head, meaning to kiss a slow path down the side of her throat, only to have her guide his mouth to her breast instead.

He was greedy now, his control finely stretched, not content with only the taste of her mouth, her breasts, her heated skin, and he moved lower, sliding her panties down and off.

She was on unfamiliar ground now, the boundaries blurring fast as he kissed her belly, her thighs; her legs falling open of their own accord as his fingers sought and found that tender, swollen spot where she ached for him. His touch was light, deft, taking her to the edge again and again but never taking her over.

She heard herself moan as her hips lifted, giving, taking, seeking more, seeking everything. Knowing she could find it here, with him. Then his mouth was there, right there, and she was lost, falling again yet this time with no fear, no limits, knowing he was there to catch her.

He could wait no more, not even for her to calm, to get her breath. He moved over her and she sensed his need, opening to him, rising to meet him and wrapping her legs tightly around him and taking him deep inside. They moved with a rhythm that was ageless yet new, unique to them, to this love they were making. Forming something from nothing in his room above the pub, and holding on tight as they were swept up and falling, going over the edge together and landing safely on the other side.

It was three in the morning when they finally left the bed, and only then because hunger drove them out in search of food. Sam stood at the window looking out at the parking lot, watching a raccoon in the back of his pickup, enjoying the last of Michael's galette.

He hadn't noticed when the party downstairs ended. Hadn't heard the last of the music or the starting of trucks. All he'd heard was her voice in his ear, whispering his name as she took him inside her, letting him love her all over again.

They'd slept, he knew that, for he woke to find her tucked close against him, fitting perfectly, as though it was her spot, her right, and she'd been there forever. Then he'd closed his eyes and drifted, wondering how long it would be before she left.

"Paris-to-go is out of the question," she said. "Which leaves what on the menu?"

He looked over to see her picking up her dress and giving it a critical once-over. She'd wrapped a sheet around her, modest now that they were out of bed, and he smiled as he crossed to his armoire and pulled out a shirt.

"The beauty of living above a restaurant," he told her, "is that the choices in takeout are limitless, as long as we don't turn on the grill." He held out the shirt and she exchanged it for the dress, leaving him holding it but not sure why. It was just one of the many mysteries of Max that he would be willing to spend a lifetime unraveling. But since he only had a short time, he carried the dress to the armoire and hung it up.

"What do you feel like?" he asked, tugging on his jeans while she shrugged on the shirt, surprised that it actually covered her knees and amazed at how many times a sleeve could be rolled.

"You're not ready to hear what I feel like," she said, her smile cocky and carefree as she threw an arm around his neck and kissed him. "But if you're asking what I want to eat, I don't care as long as it's ready fast."

They went down the stairs, pausing at the door, then dashing across the empty parking lot to the kitchen door. Sam had remembered his keys, which Max found very clever since she hadn't even remembered her underwear. And she promised to reward his intelligence later, in a profoundly unacademic fashion.

Spurred on by images he wouldn't put into words, Sam opened the fridge and smiled. Paris might have fallen, but chicken salad was forever.

"How about a sandwich?" he asked, and when there was no reply, turned to find himself alone. Since an executive decision was in order, he pulled out the chicken salad and a head of lettuce and closed the door.

She came back into the kitchen as he was dropping bread into the toaster. "Do you have a quarter?" she asked, shoving her hands into his pockets and taking her sweet time about finding the coins at the bottom.

He growled a warning that made her laugh and take even longer, and only confirmed what he already knew. They were good together. Easy and natural, as though they had been down this road before and were simply finding their way back. Fitting into a groove that was well-worn and comfortable, and meant to be followed all the way to the end. And it tore him apart to know that he'd have to let her go so soon, when it had taken so long to find her.

"You really ought to get some more records for that jukebox," she said, holding up a quarter as she strolled out to the pub.

"They're on order," he called after her, and made the sandwiches with the strains of "Blue Moon" in the background.

When she didn't come back, he placed sliced dill pickles on one side of the plates, colored nacho chips on the other, and carried them out to the pub.

The staff had done the usual, left the place clean and ready for the lunch hour, and Sam didn't feel at all guilty for having left them to do it alone. Setting the plates on a table by the jukebox, he went to the fridge by the bar for something cold, and glanced around, searching for Max while he poured two glasses.

The pub wasn't large and there were no corners for hiding, and he crossed over to where a plastic sheet hung in front of the future dining room, betting that was where he would find her.

She'd thrown back the shutters, and the hardwood floor was dotted with squares of pale, ghostly light. She was no more than a shadow in the far corner herself, walking slowly as though pacing off footages—placing furniture, perhaps. Or was that only in his own mind? A fantasy so compelling, so rich, he couldn't shake it, even when reason told him it would never be.

It was a selfish fantasy, he knew. One that allowed him everything he wanted, needed, in a place that was still haunted by ghosts and unfinished business for Max. Even now, knowing he loved her, knowing she loved him, there was no peace for her here. He saw that in the way she moved, not pacing off distances but simply pacing. Unable to sit still, to put the past to rest and let a new future unfold.

Yet for all that he knew she was stubborn and scared, hard to persuade, when she turned and smiled, he knew he couldn't give up on them yet.

"Dinner is served," he said. "It's not a romantic world tour, but it will get you through to breakfast."

She laughed and he swung an arm around her shoulder while she looped one around his waist, and they walked back together to their table in the pub.

"This is good," she said between bites, only just realizing how hungry she was. "Did Michael make it?"

Sam nodded and popped a chip into his mouth. "And he will blow up in the morning when he finds a hole in the middle of the bowl."

She smiled and pointed her pickle at him. "You were lucky to find him. He's talented."

"And moody, and temperamental."

"Most artists are. I know Peter was," she said, polishing off the first half and eyeing the second, knowing she wouldn't sleep if she ate it. She looked over at Sam, figured sleep wasn't going to be an issue anyway, and tucked into the rest of the sandwich, telling herself that she would need her strength.

"How will it be, do you think, to work with him now?"

She shrugged and scraped her chair back, too full to finish and needing to stand, to make sure she could move. "I can't see a problem. We've always been friends."

"So you have no cold-light-of-dawn regrets?"

"It's not dawn yet," she said and walked over to the window. "You'll have to ask me then."

The street was deserted, the shop windows dark. No music at the post office, no ice cream at Cy's, just a coyote loping by, on his way home from a night of hunting.

She glanced over at the yellow and white door across the road, the one with the bell on the other side that would jingle when you came in, letting Cy know you'd arrived for coffee, a sandwich, a bit of news.

She wondered briefly if the story of her broken engagement had already made it through. The whys and the wherefores providing enough grist to keep that mill running for the rest of the summer. And if not, could she get there first? Knock on the door when it was just the old man and a coffeemaker, and she could tell the story her way, make sure he got all the details straight before the morning crew arrived. And maybe find out the latest on Gwen.

She drew back, shocked as much at the idea as the fact that it appealed to her. That some part of her wanted to know, wanted to find out if Gwen was staying or going, was happy or miserable, and how the hell she had lived with herself for all these years.

"Quiet out there," Sam said as he came up behind her, startling her a little but bringing her back, taking her away from questions she didn't want to think about, and answers that didn't matter.

"Not for long," she said, leaning into him as he wrapped his arms around her waist, his lips finding the sensitive spot beneath her ear. Pressing tiny kisses to her earlobe, her throat, nudging the collar aside to find the tender flesh of her shoulder.

She sighed and tilted her head as a wave of deep contentment washed over her, through her, filling up all the dark and empty spaces she'd ignored for so long, she'd forgotten they were there. Until now, until Sam.

She closed her eyes, wishing she could stay forever, letting him hold her, kiss her; knowing he would do everything in his power to make her happy. Knowing too that in another time, another place, it wouldn't take much more than this.

"When will you leave?" he whispered, as though he

could read her very thoughts, understand her every mood.

She squeezed her eyes shut as tears, as unexpected as they were useless, burned hot behind her lashes. Why now? she wondered, when she'd thought herself so steeled, so ready, so damn well-prepared.

"Before the sun comes up," she whispered. "I have the photo shoot for Eva's ad, and the setup takes time—"

"I meant when will you leave for New York."

She heard the change in his tone, felt the shift in his stance and pulled away, suddenly wary. "Tomorrow, maybe Monday."

"What if I asked you to stay? To marry me and open that café you're still thinking about. What would you say?"

"Sam, we've been through this—"

He took hold of her shoulders, turned her to face him. "Then what if I tell you I'll leave? Put a 'For Sale' sign in the window and move back to New York. What would you say?"

"I'd say you're bluffing."

He shook his head. "I never bluff."

And she'd lost enough poker games to know it was true.

"I'll call a real estate agent in the morning," he continued. "My old brokerage house after that. You go work with Peter in the morning, come back here at night and we'll catch the first flight out on Sunday." He waited a beat, let her catch up. "What do you say now?"

He was looking straight at her, into her, and she met him squarely, refusing to be swayed. "I can't let you do that and you know it." She turned and walked back to the table. "You'd be miserable and I won't be held responsible. I won't have you resent me just because I can't stay here."

"Because of Gwen?"

"And Brian, and everything else." She turned back, anger replacing sadness. Glad to be leaving, to be free once and for all. "What are you trying to prove?"

He walked toward her, each step slow, measured. "Only that it's time we went and talked to Gwen. In fact, I think we should go right now, you and me. Drive up to the Connor place and knock on her door. She'll be home, I'm sure of it, and we'll find out what happened once and for all."

She folded her arms, planted her feet. "I'm not going anywhere, especially Gwen's. I told you before, I'm not interested in anything she has to say."

He stopped just back from her, his eyes softening along with his tone. "What are you so afraid of, Max?"

"Nothing, nothing at all. I just don't see the point in dredging it all up again."

"You'd rather just keep running away, is that it?"

"I am not running," she said. "I simply choose to move on."

"Away from Schomberg, away from me."

She lowered her head. "I told you before, Sam. Love is not enough."

He reached out suddenly and dragged her against him. But when he kissed her there was nothing but tenderness and a longing so strong, so real, she could taste it. Taste the love reaching deep inside her, wrapping itself around her heart, making it hard to breathe, to think.

And then he was letting her go, stepping back, and she knew when he turned away that she had finally lost him.

"Get dressed," he said as he headed for the kitchen. "I'll take you home now."

SIXTEEN

Eva was in the garden when Max came down the back steps.

Sam had dropped her off before first light, the ride in from town silent and tense. She'd sat huddled against the door, cursing herself for not having her own car and the town for not having a taxi. And pressing her lips tightly together to keep from calling his name as he drove away without once looking back.

She'd crept through the front door like a thief, both annoyed and grateful to find it unlocked, since she wasn't ready to face anyone yet.

Peter's car had been parked out front and she'd hurried past Delia's door, tempted to tap, to find out what had happened last night, and know if Peter was with her. Hoping he was, because the two of them at least had a chance. They lived in the same city, worked together, liked the same restaurants—just as she and Peter had, only better.

But she moved on, anxious to shower and change, to get ready for the day's photo shoot; planning to lose herself in her work, to forget about everything but making her mother's ad perfect. And when the day was over, she would hop on a plane and go home, and start learning to live without Sam.

In the kitchen, she'd started right in, making coffee,

helping herself to a muffin from the plate on the table and booking a ticket on a flight back to New York. She was searching for an apron and dragging bowls from the cupboard when she'd heard a voice outside. Eva, she realized, and took a second mug from the cupboard.

Her mother was down on the ground wearing a big floppy hat and knee pads, attacking weeds with a vigor that never failed to amaze Max. And it didn't seem at all odd to see wallabies sleeping in a playpen and a llama by the fence, eyeing her mother's daylilies as though they were breakfast.

"Do you ever sleep?" Max asked as she crossed the lawn.

"When I remember to pencil it in," Eva said, grinning as she reached for the mug. "You're a mind reader," she added and actually groaned when she took the first sip. Then she shucked off her knee pads and sat down cross-legged. "Are you all right?"

"You mean about Peter?" Max gave a brisk nod, knowing Delia would have told her what happened, and wandered over to take a closer look at the llama. "I'm fine," she said, surprised when the animal raised his head and looked at her, as if asking what she wanted. She reached out and ran a hand down the llama's neck, and he stepped forward, letting her know it was all right.

She patted him again and glanced back at her mother. "He was right, by the way, when he called the first time. The wedding was a bad idea."

Eva nodded. "And you and Sam?"

"Fine too," Max said, and the llama drew back, studying her almost as hard as Eva was.

Her mother was torn, Max knew that. Wanting to know more, to ask about Sam and where Max had been all night. But Max had spent so many years keeping her mother at arm's length that it was hard for her now to risk coming too close, when oddly enough it was just what Max wanted.

"Mom," she said, and finally looked over. "It's all right, you can ask." Which must have pleased the llama because he stepped a little closer still.

Max stroked the soft smooth wool, while Eva considered—years of conditioning falling away slowly. "Are you in love with him?" she said at last.

Max's hand stilled but she nodded.

"Is he in love with you?"

Max turned her face away and starting patting a little harder but nodded again.

"Then it's good you broke it off with Peter when you did. But if everything is fine, and you and Sam love each other, why are you home so early?"

"For the photo shoot," she said, and the llama turned and walked away. *What did he know, anyway?* she thought as she watched him go. Disappointed because she had only just started to discover that her mother's theory was right—it was hard to stay stressed when you pat a llama.

But she wasn't ready to apologize, or bare her soul, not yet. And she hadn't been lying, just avoiding. The photo shoot was real, and she would stick with it because it was easy. And easy was all she wanted right now. She didn't want to think, she simply wanted to act, to move, to work.

"Peter wants to get everything out of the way today," she said, strolling over to the table Eva had set yesterday. "The setup always takes a while, so I wanted to get an early start."

The netting was still in place, but everything else had been taken back into the house for the night. After coffee, she would start the cooking in earnest, Peter would set up his equipment and before the afternoon was out, her mother's ad would be well on its way to completion and she would be on her way home.

"Will Sam be coming by later?" Eva asked. "I could make dinner—"

"Saturdays are busy at the Tap Room. He won't have time."

"Sunday, then?"

"I'll be gone tonight."

"Gone?" Eva stared at her. "Tonight?"

"Lots of work to catch up on." She turned and saw the llama was back, watching her over the top of Eva's head. "Are you going to play prop girl again?"

Eva studied her a moment longer, then shook her head. "I think it would be safer if I stayed out of the way. You obviously know what you're doing."

"You're right," Max said, quietly. "I do."

She took a deep breath, trying to loosen Sam's hold on her heart. And not sure how to begin. So she wandered back to pat the llama, avoiding the animal's questioning eyes as she looked out across the lawn to the paddocks, the barn, the loafing shed in the distance. A few ponies were still there, sleeping late, but the rest were out grazing with the llamas and goats.

The ostriches were up too, and from where she stood, Squiggy looked a little red around the neck. He was also following Laverne, who seemed to want nothing to do with him, but every once in a while she'd glance back, making sure he was there.

"He's growing up," Eva said, on her feet now, clipping spent blooms from the roses. "And when that neck of his turns bright red, Laverne won't be able to run fast enough."

"She'll like that," Max said, as Laverne fluttered her wings, letting him know she was ready to make up.

Max smiled as she turned back to the llama. Funny

how things turned out some times. She glanced over at Eva. "What about you and Ben?"

Eva shrugged and kept her eyes on the roses. "I never found him. I went over to Cy's, down to the bridge, even hung around at the concert for a while, thinking he might turn up, but he didn't. I called his truck, left a message at his house—three if you want the truth—but I haven't heard from him." She stopped clipping and turned to Max. "And I don't think I will."

"Sure you will," Max said, taking the clippers and laying her mother's hand on the llama. "Ben loves you. You know that, don't you?"

"He's told me that," Eva said, patting the other side of the llama's neck as the animal looked from one to the other, quite reasonably confused. "I always laughed it off, of course. Told him it was just indigestion, that sort of thing. I figured we'd go on that way forever, friends, good, good friends. But yesterday he told me he wants more. He's tired of going home to an empty house, tired of spending his nights alone." Her hand stilled and she glanced down at the ground. "He asked me to marry him."

"And what did you say?"

She looked over at Max. "I said no." Her arm dropped to her side and she headed over to the porch, even llama therapy not enough for this. "How can I marry Ben when your father was the love of my life?"

"Because he's been gone a long time," Max said gently.

"What's that got to do with anything?" Eva dropped down on the bottom step of the porch, pulled her hat off and tossed it aside. "When I met your father I had nothing and no one. He was the sweetest man I'd ever met. Kind, gentle, not a mean bone in his body. I spent a year trying to get him to leave me alone, convinced that no one like him could want me, that he'd only break my heart. Then I let him bring me here one day, and that was it." She looked over at Max. "Your dad and this farm saved my life. He loved me in spite of myself. Taught me what it was to have hope again, and dreams." She gave her head a small shake, her eyes begging Max to understand. "How can I betray a love like that?"

"You're not betraying it, Mom, you're celebrating it. You said yourself, Dad taught you what it is to love. What makes you think he wouldn't want you to use that lesson again? With someone like Ben?"

Eva sighed and stared straight ahead. "That's just the problem. I do love Ben. I look forward to seeing him, to being with him. Little by little he's replacing your father in my mind and my heart." She looked over at Max, stricken. "I can't even remember the sound of his voice anymore. All I hear is Ben."

Max covered her mother's hand with hers. "And there's nothing wrong with that."

"Even if I wanted to believe you, I think Ben is finished with me. I have never seen him as angry as he was last night."

"He's hurt and probably frustrated right now. But I can't see him staying away forever."

"But he's so stubborn and ornery. . . ." She broke off with a quick shake of her head. "I don't know what difference it would make anyway, I still can't promise to marry him."

Max leaned close and whispered, "Then why don't you just start with a movie?"

"Isn't it a beautiful morning?" Delia said as she all but floated out the front door and perched on the stairs.

She wore no makeup and her hair was wet from the shower, yet she had a glow about her that made Max sigh. For some people, love was indeed grand.

"Have a good night, did you?" Eva said.

Delia plunked her chin on her hands, a satisfied smile

easing across her face. "The man is an animal." She glanced over at Max. "You should have warned me."

If she'd known she would have, but as it was, Max had all she could do to keep her jaw from dropping open.

"I'll have to call my sisters, of course." She grinned at Eva. "They are going to be so green."

Delia suddenly sat up straighter, her smile dimming as she turned back to Max. "Are you all right?"

"Of course."

"Then why are you here so early?"

"The shoot," she said, and glanced over her shoulder as Peter stepped out on the porch.

He was dressed and combed, ready for the day. The way Delia looked at him, Max figured that wouldn't have lasted long if there hadn't been an audience. And she felt herself sigh again and wished them well. Lord knew, someone deserved to be happy.

"Morning, all," he said, then stopped dead and looked straight at Max. "How come you're here so early?"

"The photo shoot." She smacked her hands on her knees as she got to her feet. "Am I the only one ready to work today?"

They all shook their heads and avoided her gaze as she walked up the steps, heading for the kitchen. "I don't know about you, but I'm ready to start."

She had an apron on and was setting out bowls and recipes, pans and serving dishes, when Delia came into the kitchen.

Max held up an apron. "You feel like playing stylist again?"

Delia nodded and caught the apron in midair. "If you want the truth, I really enjoyed myself. More than I ever have working with account books or files."

"I'll start the pancakes, you go to work on the biscuits." Max unfolded the menu and stuck it to the fridge with a magnet. "And it sounds like it's time for a career change to me."

"Could be." Delia reached under the kitchen table and pulled out Max's styling kit. "I'll talk to Peter about it later."

Max glanced over as she took flour and baking powder from the cupboard. "Other than the fact that he's an animal, how did it go last night?"

"Interesting," she said as she flipped open the locks on Max's kit. "After you left, everybody looked at me as though I was the other woman."

Max laughed. "I'll bet you loved that."

Delia gave a thoughtful nod. "For a while. The femme fatale has always been my role of choice. But then some guy named Cy came rushing in, bought Peter and me a drink, and we told him the truth."

"The truth," Max said. "Now there's an interesting concept for Cy." She measured flour into a bowl, thinking that it was just as well she hadn't waited around to tell her side. "The two of you are giving it a shot as a couple then, I take it."

"We talked a long time last night." She shot Max a grin. "He was a gentleman before he was an animal."

Now that sounded like Peter, but Max kept it to herself as Delia continued.

"We're going to take it slow though, let things progress as they will. But he did invite me up to meet his family next weekend. What do you think that means?"

Max saw it all in Delia's face. The hope, the wonder, everything she'd pushed away in Sam. "I think it means your sisters are going to be bridesmaids."

Delia laughed. "And you will be the maid of honor. But let's not count the chickens, as they say." She opened Max's kit and glanced back. "So it's pancakes and biscuits first."

Max watched her reach into the box and pull out a

hypodermic needle, hair spray, plastic squeeze bottles. "Hold on. Put that stuff away. I'll tell Peter we're switching to a table shot only, no close-ups. That way we don't need to touch the food with any of those things."

"What about extra baking powder in the pancakes?"

Max looked down at the bowl in front of her. "It will make Eva's day if we can eat them afterward. Mine too, since I love pancakes." She walked over to the fridge for eggs. "Do you know, this will be the first honest shoot I've ever done?"

"Honesty in advertising. Another unique concept." Delia laid the tools back in the bag and set it on the floor. "Speaking of honesty, why are you really back so early?" She glanced over as she straightened. "I should warn you, I have spent time with the llamas. I know truth."

Max had to smile. Delia had always known the truth. "Let's just say that you don't have to worry about throwing a shower for me any time soon."

Delia pulled a cookbook from the shelf and opened it to the marked page. "Are you seeing him at least?"

"It's not likely." Max cracked an egg into the bowl and went to the fridge for milk. "Not when I turned down every offer he made."

"What offers?"

"To marry him and open a café, or have him sell the Tap Room and move back to New York."

"He's willing to move?"

"Said he'd put the place up for sale today if I asked him." Max measured out a cup of milk and poured it into the bowl. "Of course he was pretty safe with that, since I would never ask him to do it."

"Do you believe that's why he offered, because he didn't think you'd take him up on it?"

"No, it was genuine." She sighed and reached for a whisk. "He has also spent time with the llama."

Delia snatched the flour from under Max's nose. "I

have to tell you, none of it makes sense to me. You cancel your wedding to Peter to go and find Sam; then you turn down every chance to be with him." She shook her head as she shook flour into a cup. "I must have missed something somewhere."

"It's complicated," Max admitted, then glanced out into the yard to see Eva and one of the Jenkins boys carrying the wallabies out to see their new bedroom in the barn. "And just part of life at Peacock Manor."

"From where I sit, it looks pretty straightforward. You're letting Gwen win again."

Max's hand froze on the way to the corn oil. "What is that supposed to mean?"

Delia smacked the flour bag down. "It means you've got it in your head somehow that if you'd only seen something in Gwen, some indication that she wasn't what everybody thought, then your brother would be alive today. But even if you'd picked up some kind of bad vibration from the girl, from what I've heard of Brian, he wouldn't have listened anyway, would he?"

Max sighed and abandoned the pancake batter to wander over to the window, seeing Brian in her mind: getting thrown by a horse, falling out of the tree and almost electrocuting himself with the giant's harp up on the barn roof, all because he liked to find things out for himself— the hard way.

Max closed her eyes and leaned her hands on the sill. "You're right. He was a stubborn cuss."

"And if you'd told him something was wrong with Gwen, he'd have turned on you the way he turned on Sam, and gone after her just the same."

"But at least we might have been able to make sense of what happened."

"Maybe you still could if someone would only talk to Gwen."

"I tried. Years ago," Max said, remembering. "But I could never find her. It was like she disappeared."

"Well, you know where she is now, don't you? Why don't you go up and ask?"

Max shook her head as she pulled back from the window. "I can't. I don't care—"

"I know Eva would love to march up there and give her a good shake, but she can't either. Won't, actually, because she won't risk ticking you off. It's like Gwen has this whole family in some kind of choke hold."

She turned on Delia. "I don't know what you're talking about."

"No? Then how come there's a man not ten miles from here who loves you, is willing to do whatever it takes to be with you, yet you'd rather go back to New York and live alone? You're willing to throw away the one thing that's the hardest to find, because you won't go and get what you need from Gwen." She gave her head a disgusted shake. "Which means she wins again. She destroyed Brian's happiness, your happiness and Sam's, without doing a thing. Three out of three. Not bad at all."

Max looked out the window at the barn, the paddock, the fields and mountains, all the places Gwen had been. And she saw her life stretching out between them, narrow and stunted, because she couldn't risk brushing up against the memories or the pain, or the guilt that had been with her for so long.

And then she saw Sam, the man she loved, reaching out to her from that long, dark tunnel. When she looked closer, she realized it wasn't so dark in there after all. There was a home at the end, and a life that was rich and full. But only if she made it past Gwen.

She untied the apron and lifted it over her head. "I'll be back in a while." She snatched up her purse and headed for the door. "I've got some bridges to burn."

* * *

Max didn't need to be reminded where Gwen was staying. She didn't need directions either. The Connors had
started renting out cabins to tourists around the same
time Max's family had opened the bed-and-breakfast—
everybody doing what needed to be done to hold on to
the family farm. As she pulled into the driveway, Max
didn't begrudge them Gwen's rent; she just wished she
could tell which cabin they'd given her.

Mrs. Connor appeared on the doorstep of her house
as Max's car drew closer, as though she was expecting
another guest. She had been one of the few women who
hadn't come to the shower, and when Max saw her face
fall, she figured she knew why. So she stuck her arm
out the window and waved. "Hello, Mrs. Connor," she
called. "How are you?"

Mrs. Connor gave her a small sheepish grin as she
came down to the gate. "Maxine, I'm sorry, but the girl
needed a place to stay, and it's been slow—"

Max smiled and held up a hand. "You don't have to
explain. It's business, it's fine."

"I'm glad you understand." She pointed to the row of
bunkies beyond the parking lot. "What you're looking
for is in cabin three." Then she lowered her voice and
put a hand to the side of her mouth. "I saved the newer
ones for the other guests."

Max laughed. "I appreciate that," she said and pulled
into the parking lot to the right of the driveway.

Swinging her purse over her shoulder, she smiled at
Mrs. Connor, told herself she could do this and marched
along the gravel path to cabin number three; coming to
a dead stop just back from the porch steps.

She'd thought herself prepared. Had even said her
speech out loud in the car on the way over, working herself into a good, hot anger before she pulled off the main

road. But as the woman on the porch of that tiny cabin rose and turned toward her, Max realized she wasn't ready at all.

Her hair was still that wonderful fiery red, her body slender and graceful. There were a few tiny lines at the corners of her eyes, but then, Gwen had always been one to laugh. And her gaze was as clear and direct as it had always been, as though she had nothing at all to hide.

They stared at each other across the railing, all the questions that had been waiting so long to be answered whirling inside Max's head. Yet Gwen was the first one to speak, and take a tentative step forward.

"I'm glad you came," she said, then motioned to the chairs on the porch. "Why don't you sit down? I've just made iced tea. And we've got a lot to talk about."

Max hung back, not wanting to sit or drink tea, or in any way imply that she was there to mend fences. "I only want one thing from you."

Gwen nodded, her shoulders slumping. "You want to know where I was the night Brian and I were supposed to run away and get married."

"That's a good place to start," Max said and folded her arms; her heart pounding so painfully hard it was difficult to breathe, to stand. But she would not sit down with Gwen.

Gwen looked at her, lips pressed tightly together as though she was fighting to hold back the words for some reason. "As hard as this will be for you to understand, I was sitting in my room back in Washington, crying my heart out because Brian didn't want me."

Max held up a hand. "That's ridiculous and you know it."

"Now I do, but back then . . ." She turned away with a shake of her head. "Back then I was young and stupid and my father could be very convincing."

Max remembered Gwen's father at the gas station, so

self-assured, so overpowering. Making everyone but Brian believe what he'd said about Gwen.

"I didn't know how he found out about our plans." Gwen gave a short, humorless laugh and looked down at her hands. "I suppose we thought we were covering our tracks so well, so carefully. But he knew everything. Where we were meeting, where we were heading, as though he'd been there when we made the plans. And when he asked me how I thought he could know all of these things, I didn't have an answer. Then he said it was because Brian had told him. Brian had come to him, laid out the whole thing and then told my father that he couldn't go through with it."

Max nodded, furious. "And you believed him?"

Gwen glanced at her. "He was my father. He'd never lied to me in my life. Why would I think he was lying to me then?"

"Because Brian loved you."

"And I loved him," Gwen shot back. "But he told my father it wasn't enough. He said I should go to school, be a lawyer, do all the things I had planned to do before we met." She groaned and walked a few steps from the railing. "It sounded so much like what Brian always said. He felt so guilty about taking those things away and sticking me on a farm with cows and sheep. As though I didn't love that farm as much as he did. And didn't know exactly what I wanted." She looked over at Max. "I believed my father because I knew Brian. I knew he would think he was doing the right thing, the honorable thing. But he just couldn't look me in the eye and tell me to go away." She closed her eyes and turned away. "So I left. I went home and packed for school. And I kept thinking Brian would call, or send me a note. I even dialed your house a hundred times but always hung up before it rang because I was hurt and proud, and it was up to Brian to call me first." She sighed and stared at the sky. "I didn't even know he was already dead."

Max blinked back sad, hot tears as she approached the porch. "Your father didn't tell you about the accident?"

"How could he?" Gwen asked, and Max could see that her loyalties were still torn after all these years. "If he told me what happened, I would have known he lied to me." She turned back to Max. "He didn't mean to kill Brian. He was just doing what he thought was best for me, because I was young and romantic." She hung her head. "He carried that guilt around for ten years. Long enough for me to become a lawyer, marry the wrong man and end up miserable, burned out and divorced."

Max put a foot on the bottom step, realizing there was no threat here, no demon. And when Gwen looked at her there was nothing false or cunning in her eyes, nothing to make Max doubt that what she said was true. There was only Gwen, with her red hair and her freckled nose. And Max remembered now why Brian had loved her.

"So now you're back," she said, taking the last steps up to the porch.

Gwen nodded and turned her head, her gaze drifting out over the mountains, the valleys. "Just for the summer. I had all these plans when I got here, things I had to do." She turned as Max came toward her. "Believe it or not, talking to you and Eva was at the top of the list, but I never even got that far." She gave Max a tiny smile. "You look good, by the way. I love your hair."

Max smiled. "Me too," she said, the tension between them slipping away as she sank into one of the chairs.

Gwen settled into the chair next to her and tipped her face up to the sun. "Have you been here all these years, then?"

Max shook her head, realizing that Gwen had been in the dark as much as anyone. Sam had said that people hadn't made it easy for her, and she could see that now. "I only came back a while ago myself."

Gwen nodded. "How long are you here for?"

Max glanced down at her hands. "I'm not sure. There are still a couple of things I have to do." She felt a smile tug at her lips as she looked over at Gwen. "You ever have beer with the spirits?"

SEVENTEEN

The sun was just starting to settle into the mountains for the night when Sam came through the front door of the Tap Room. Inside, the tables were full, the staff was hopping and people were asking what time he was going to roll out the dance floor.

If nothing else, Max's party had put him on the map. Word about the good time to be had at Sam's had spread almost as fast as the story of Max's breakup. He'd known from the curious glances when he walked into Cy's that everyone knew he'd been involved somewhere. And even though he wasn't fully clear on what had happened himself, there was no doubt in his mind that a version of the truth would get back to him someday. One that would be easier to accept than the fact that Max had been right all along. Sometimes, love wasn't enough.

He didn't need to close his eyes to see her, to feel her. She was right there in his mind, everything he wanted and nothing he could have. And when he got a free minute, he was going to try to wrap that haircloth coat around his heart again, and this time he was going to fasten it tight.

In the meantime, he had to figure out how to get some more staff into the pub, what it cost to have a decent sound system installed, and where he was going to squeeze in a permanent dance floor. It hadn't been in the original plan, but he was learning to be flexible these days.

He turned and was about to go back inside when he paused on the step. He didn't know what made him stop, look back. There'd been no noise, nothing seen from the corner of his eyes. Just a sense, a tug that drew him around in time to see a white sedan at the corner, by the hardware store. The car was ordinary by any standard, nothing that set it apart from any other that might pass through town. But as it turned right and headed the other way along Center Street, Sam knew it was Max. The only thing he didn't know was why she was still in town. And why the hell she was heading for the bridge.

"If you have nothing to do, I'll be pleased to find you something."

Sam turned to see Ben scowling at him from the front door. The scowl was nothing new. The old man had been wearing it since the morning. And when he finally wanted to talk about it, Sam was sure Eva would be the source of his misery.

But he had no time for talk or the Tap Room, and he held up a hand as he started off at a trot. "Sorry, Ben, but you'll have to hold the fort a little longer."

"Where you going in such a hurry?"

"The bridge," he called over his shoulder. And broke into a run when he saw that the traffic jam was already starting.

Cars were backed up almost to the top of the hill by the time he rounded the last curve. His heart was pounding as much from anticipation as exertion. But he drew up sharply when he realized that Max wasn't the cause. A black van had lost a rooftop carrier on the bridge, and a crowd was out there now, gathering up the sleeping bags and suitcases that had scattered all over the road.

He put his hands on his knees and tried to calm his breath as he looked past the van, wondering if she'd made it over, if she'd finally crossed the bridge after all these years. But then he spotted her car. Parked on the shoulder, and still on this side.

He straightened, wiped the back of his arm across his forehead, giving himself some time to decide what to do. If she'd wanted his help or him, she'd have come looking. But she hadn't, and if anyone had asked him what would be the smart thing to do right now he'd have said, leave it alone. Go back to the pub.

But then, he'd never been very good at following advice, especially his own. So he crossed the road, telling himself that he was only doing it because it was neighborly. And had nothing to do with the fact that he simply wanted to see her one more time.

He realized before he reached the driver's side door that she wasn't in the car at all. He stood on the shoulder, looking around, trying to figure out where she could be, when a kid with a fishing pole glanced over.

"If you're looking for the lady who owns that car, she went down there," he said and pointed under the bridge.

Sam thanked the boy, his heart beating fast all over again, even though he was only walking this time. Just strolling down the path at the side of the bridge, the one that would take him to the parkette and the picnic tables, and the rocks where Brian's car had landed.

In his heart, he didn't believe she'd be there. Thought the kid mistaken, that she'd really headed back up to the town, leaving her car there until the traffic jam was over and she could make a quiet U-turn and go home. So he wasn't prepared when he saw her sitting on the grass just looking out over the river, as though everything was right with the world.

He didn't call her name. Made no move toward her. Yet she turned and looked straight at him, as though she'd felt him there, watching her. And when she smiled, his heart all but stopped completely, because what he saw couldn't be any more real than the sight of her sitting there. And if she wasn't on her feet now, running toward him, then he would have to see someone in the morning. Because he was going to need some serious help after this.

She stopped running and walked the last few feet, her steps slowing as she drew closer and coming to a stop a little ways back from him, just out of reach. Then she tipped her head to the side, her eyes still on him as she put her hands behind her back, as though afraid of what they might do on their own.

"I know we missed breakfast," she said, "but I was sitting there thinking that maybe we could have dinner, or a sandwich. I'm partial to chicken salad. With pickles. And a beer." She stopped then, looked down at her shoes, then up at him, her eyes wide and a little too bright. "Or am I too late for last call?"

He shook his head. "You're right on time."

And she was suddenly right there in front of him, her arms reaching up, her hands pulling him down, and that warm, sweet mouth breathing life back into him as she kissed him there in the parkette, with the traffic jam above and the river flowing by, and the whole town watching if they wanted to.

He kissed her back, letting her know she was welcome for dinner or forever, or whatever was on her mind. But she pulled away, obviously needing to say something again. And he sank down on the grass and held out a hand to her, figuring they weren't going to be eating anytime soon.

She dropped her purse beside him and sat down. "I went to see Gwen."

He inclined his head. "And?"

"It was interesting. Seems her father managed to fool everybody that summer, including Gwen." She turned and looked out over the river. "It's a long story, and I'll tell you all about it later." She flashed him a smile. "At Cy's."

Sam nodded. "That will pretty much make his year."

"I was thinking the same thing." She brought her knees up then and wrapped her arms around them. "I was also thinking about what you said. About staying here, opening a café. Getting married."

He nodded, trying hard to remember he was a patient man. "And?"

"And if the offers still stand"—she turned her head, her smile small and a little lopsided—"I'd like to take you up on one or two."

"Which two?"

"One and three," she said, that smile widening to a grin as he tried to remember the order. "I want to stay," she said. "And I want to get married."

He reached for her, pressed her down on the grass. "You don't want a café?"

"Oh, I do," she said. And that smile turned decidedly wicked as she laced her fingers behind his neck and pulled him down with her. "Just not with you."

He drew his head back. "You don't want my dining room?"

"No," she said, then laughed and touched a quick kiss to his lips. "I told you before, no partners. I want a place of my own, overlooking the river. Besides, you're going to need that space for the pub. I have a feeling that dance floor is going to be a permanent fixture."

He bent to her, close enough to feel her breath on his lips. "You could be right about that."

"Besides, Michael and I could never share a kitchen. And who would Ben argue with if he left?"

"Another good point," he whispered, and was about to seal their deal when she pushed a hand against his chest, holding him off.

"I love you, Sam. You know that don't you?"

He had to smile at her earnest expression. "I think so."

"And I'm not doing any of this lightly, or because the moon smiled or any of those reasons."

He nodded, having no clue what she was talking about but figuring he'd find that out later too.

"I'm here because I can't imagine being anywhere else. And I can't imagine ever being happy without you."

"Neither can I," he said, and was just leaning down to put a stop to the talk once and for all, when a pair of boots appeared off to his left. Familiar boots. Ones that belonged in the Tap Room.

He glanced up to see Ben standing there, still scowling. And Sam only hoped it wasn't going to be permanent.

"Well, you two certainly look comfortable," he said, folding his arms as they got to their feet. Then he turned his scowl on Max. "You had me worried. Your mother too."

"You talked to Eva?"

"She called the pub. I answered the phone."

Max gave her head a shake. "She called the pub looking for me?"

"No, she called looking for me." He shuffled his feet, tipped his cap down a little lower. "And she got me."

Both Max and Sam leaned closer. "And?"

"And nothing. I told her you were down at the bridge and she started to cry. She said something about you going to Gwen's and she hoped you were all right—" He broke off and stared out at the river. "I hate it when she cries."

Max reached down and picked up her purse. "So what are you going to do about it?"

"Nothing," he snapped, then turned and looked from her to Sam. "What's going on here?"

"We're getting married," Sam said, drawing her close.

"Married?" Ben's scowl lightened. "Well, that's good."

He glanced at Max. "Your mother doesn't know yet, does she?"

She shook her head. "Not yet. I'll call her from the pub. And when she hears, she'll probably cry."

Ben nodded. "She shouldn't be alone then."

Sam smiled. "That would probably be best."

Max opened her purse and reached inside. "I could wait till you get there to place the call."

Ben stared at her. "Wouldn't take me more than twenty minutes. Fifteen if I hurry."

"I can wait that long," she said, and pulled the love charm from her purse. It was soft and warm, the golden threads glittering in the last rays of the sun. And Max knew that somewhere, the moon was smiling.

She lifted Ben's hand and placed the charm in his palm. "When you see Eva, give her that." She sighed as she pulled Sam close. "And tell her Iona sent you."

Put a Little Romance in Your Life With
Fern Michaels

__Dear Emily	0-8217-5676-1	$6.99US/$8.50CAN
__Sara's Song	0-8217-5856-X	$6.99US/$8.50CAN
__Wish List	0-8217-5228-6	$6.99US/$7.99CAN
__Vegas Rich	0-8217-5594-3	$6.99US/$8.50CAN
__Vegas Heat	0-8217-5758-X	$6.99US/$8.50CAN
__Vegas Sunrise	1-55817-5983-3	$6.99US/$8.50CAN
__Whitefire	0-8217-5638-9	$6.99US/$8.50CAN